GW00771603

MIRRORS OF NARCISSUS

First published 2000 by Millivres Ltd,
part of the Millivres Prowler Group,
Worldwide House, 116-134 Bayham St, London NW1 0BA

World Copyright © 2000 Guy Willard

Guy Willard has asserted his right to be identified as the author of this work in
accordance with the Copyright, Designs and Patents Act 1988

A CIP catalogue record for this book is available
from the British Library

ISBN 1 902852 07 9

Distributed in Europe by Central Books,
99 Wallis Rd, London E9 5LN

Distributed in North America by InBook/LPC Group,
1436 West Randolph, Chicago, IL 60607

Distributed in Australia by Bulldog Books,
P O Box 300, Beaconsfield, NSW 2014

Printed and bound in the EU by WS Bookwell, Finland 2000

Part One: Axis Mundi

1

They were out there again today. I could tell by the way their curtains twitched. I'd never seen their faces, but I knew there were two roommates in the women's dorm across the way who watched me regularly.

Without closing my own curtains, I put my books on the desk and stripped down to my t-shirt and briefs. Then I pulled the dumb-bells out from under the bed. Usually I worked out with them every day after my last class for about fifteen minutes before taking a shower.

I stood in front of the mirror atop the dresser and began curling the weights alternately to my shoulders in sets of fifteen. I'd always worked out in front of a mirror to better enjoy the results of my exercise: the blood rushing to the muscles engorged them, filling them out sexily and making me look brawnier than I was. But ever since I'd noticed my secret admirers across the way, I'd angled the mirror so I could see their window reflected in it. I didn't mind being watched at all.

Finishing up my sets of curls, I set the weights down for a moment. Under my t-shirt, I could feel my pectorals hard and tight. I switched my grip on the weights and commenced my next set of exercises. With both dumbbells resting on my shoulders, I lifted the left one straight up, then lowered it, simultaneously raising the right one. I continued pumping them in this fashion — left, right, left, right — my elbows pointing straight outward from my body.

I was breathing in through my nose, blowing out loudly through my mouth. In the mirror, the dark pink of my nipples was faintly visible beneath the white cotton of my t-shirt. I set the weights down again and wiped my hands on my shorts. Then I started in on some exercises designed to build up my triceps.

As I gazed at my reflection in the mirror and, beyond my reflected shoulder, at the girls' window, I imagined them kneeling down to spy on me from their posts behind the curtains. To know that I had an audience, however secret, added to the pleasure I got from working out. I even went to the trouble to give my voyeurs a little extra something for their pains.

The work-out had caused my t-shirt to become drenched with sweat. I tightened my abdominal muscles to make my chest look even bigger, stretching the fabric tighter against my skin. Then I gripped the bottom of the t-shirt with both hands and slowly pulled it up over my head. I wiped my face with it, then casually walked over to the window with my bare chest exposed, continuing my work-out with the dumb-bells there, pumping them until my muscles were so engorged with blood that the veins were popping out, and a sheen of sweat had covered the surface of my skin.

Sometimes I wondered if the girls knew I was performing for them. It would be dangerous to make it too obvious, for one boy in our dorm had been expelled from school for exposing himself from his window. I'd never pulled off my briefs with the curtains open, because I knew that the sight of me walking around in only my shorts was more than enough for my voyeurs. Anything more would be too much — for my purposes as well as theirs.

I whisked the curtains shut and stepped out of my shorts, then dumped them, along with the wet t-shirt, into the laundry hamper. Just as I stepped into the showers, I heard the door to the hallway open. In a moment, the shower door was opened, and Jonesy, my room-mate, popped his head in. "Hey, Guy," he said. "Didn't know you were in."

I could tell by his expression that he had a girl with him. "You're back early."

"You gonna be studying here?" he asked. This was our secret signal that he wanted to use the room for a while.

"No. I think I'll use the library this afternoon."

"Great. Because I've brought a guest in."

He shut the door and I began taking my shower, wondering what kind of girl he'd brought in this time. He went out drinking almost every night at Erewhon, a disco just off campus well-known as a good spot to pick up girls. I would sometimes kid him later about his taste in women, and he would confess to me with a grimace that they'd looked so much better the night before, when he was drunk. But he really didn't care how they looked, so long as they put out. He often said he would be content to put a bag over a girl's face, as long as she had what was necessary down below. I think he secretly enjoyed bringing home girls who were easy lays — it verified his low opinion of women in general.

When we'd first met, he'd made it clear that there had to be some system for bringing girls to the room. There wasn't much space for privacy. We shared a single room with a large closet to the left as you entered, and a shower room to the right. Against the far wall, beneath the one window, were our two beds, convertible to sofas during the day. We each had a dresser beside our beds, and a study desk next to that.

Theoretically, the left side of the room was my half, and the right side Jonesy's. A folding partition could be pulled out to separate the two sides for privacy, but we never used it — and neither did anyone else in the other rooms.

In my part of the room, I had a small refrigerator in which I kept soft drinks and food. Jonesy would sometimes borrow a beer or two from it. On top of the refrigerator was the coffee maker I'd brought from home.

Jonesy's side of the room was a perpetual mess, and though I was at pains to have him clean it up, he seemed constitutionally incapable of being neat. Despite my help, he was never able to bring any kind of order to the place. There were dried beer rings on the window sill, empty, crushed beer cans lying everywhere, and a rich, musty, masculine smell hovering over the whole place like a fine mist. His underwear and socks were everywhere underfoot. Beneath his bed were stacks of girly magazines, and tacked up on his wall were nude pin-ups cut out from them.

Jonesy was the life of every party, the one who was always getting things going... and had been ever since the very start, when we'd all just come here as strangers, a little disoriented and shy. He'd gathered us together that first evening and suggested that we all go out and get 'shit-faced drunk'. Which we proceeded to do. By the end of the evening we were all good friends.

He was almost a parody of tough, macho masculinity, and there was something innately vulgar about it, the way he walked about the floor in only his boxer shorts, a can of beer in one hand, scratching his balls, plunking himself down in the lounge to watch a football game... However, the heavy-lidded look to his eyes, and his firm jawline gave him an appealingly cocky quality.

When I stepped out of the shower, Jonesy and a thin, red-haired girl were sitting on his bed listening to music. She had brought a radio-cassette player.

"Hello," she said to me.

"Hi." I didn't recognize her. I proceeded to dress, then picked up some books from my desk. "Guess I'm off to the library."

"Don't rush off on my account," said Jonesy. The girl giggled.

"No, seriously," I said. "I have to catch up on some reading."

"Wish I had your study habits."

"There's a mid-term coming up, buddy."

"Aw, I'll hack it. No sweat." He didn't seem to have a care in the world about his grades, but somehow always managed to squeak through his classes. It was a wonder how he did it, with all the partying he did. He'd received several administrative warnings, and was even now on the Dean's warning list.

"Later, Guy." He winked at me

I nodded to the girl, then to him. "See you later, Jonesy." I stepped out into the hall.

Laughter erupted from down the hallway and I could hear music playing. As usual, there seemed to be a party going on in the lounge and, from the sound of the voices, a couple of girls from the dormitory across the way must have been invited. I intended to slip past the lounge without being seen, and duck down the stairs at the end of the hall, but my plan was thwarted.

"Hey Guy, where you headed? You're missing a good party." It was Frank, who'd apparently just stepped out to use the restroom.

"I'm going to the library. Which is what you guys should be doing, too, if you don't want to flunk out."

"Listen to you. As if you wasn't one of the biggest partyers here." He came over to me and lowered his voice. "Hey, listen. Can you spot me for a ten? I'm all out of rubbers." Frank was the "mooch" of the floor, always borrowing soap, razor blades, or toothpaste from the others. He never seemed to have anything of his own. As he was heavily bearded, there was a perpetual five-o'clock shadow on his jaws which I found quite sexy.

"Borrow some from Jonesy."

"Jonesy kicked you out of your room, huh?" He grinned and pulled me closer. "I seen that chick he was with. He's probably dogging her right now. She was all over him. A real nympho. I think I'm gonna try for her after Jonesy gets through with her."

"Just don't pick up the crabs again, huh?"

"Aw." He pulled me by force into the lounge, where I was greeted with a shout. There were four boys from our floor, and three girls I'd never seen before. I nodded my greetings to Billy, Corky, and Diego. Billy raised the can of beer he had in his hand and dug out another one from the pile on the table. "Hey, Guy, come join us."

"Naw, not this time."

"Party-pooper."

I glanced around. Our lounge was typical of all the ones in the dorm. There was a dilapidated sofa which no one used (sprawling on the floor was preferred,) a television set which worked intermittently (more often, the guys would gather at a private television in one of the boys' rooms,) and the paperback bookcase. The only other furniture was a small coffee table, which was now covered with beer cans and smoking ashtrays.

Corky was talking to one of the girls, a big grin on his face, his eyes unfocussed. To me, he seemed out of place in such an atmosphere. He would probably rather be having quieter fun, but he was trying hard to be the buddy Jonesy wanted us all to be — drinking, flirting, partying. And he paid for it the next morning, too, with his painful hangovers.

Diego came over and dug a knuckle into my ribs. "Don't give me this study crap. You're not going out to study."

I raised the books I was holding at my side. "What do you call this?"

He shook his head. "You're going to Christine's room. That's where you're going."

Christine was my girlfriend.

Corky looked over. "I wonder what he's gonna *study* there."

Billy laughed. "I wish I could study that particular subject."

Frank overheard us. "It ain't books he's gonna open up tonight. Hell, with a girlfriend like Christine, he don't need none of this, does he?"

"Come on, Guy, at least have a beer with us."

"No thanks. Maybe later."

"All right. But you'll live to regret it."

"I know... "

I stepped out of the lounge and turned down the hallway towards the stairs. Three flights down, on the first floor, was a foyer which we jokingly called the lobby. Against the wall by the front door was a bulletin board on which were pinned notices of concerts, rallies, or marches. On the opposite side was a row of mailboxes. I checked my own box before heading out.

"Hey, Guy, wait."

I turned around.

It was Kruk, the boy who lived next door to me and Jonesy. Kruk was the 'fat boy' of the floor, and Frank's room-mate. A quiet, studious type, he was generally hidden away in his room with a science fiction novel or a comic book. He wore oversized t-shirts with the name of our school on the front, which made him look even fatter than he was. His stomach hung out obscenely over his belt, and the slacks he wore looked like baggy balloons. I was put off by his unnerving habit of absent-mindedly crunching on sugar cubes. He kept boxes of them in his room, and would un-thinkingly scoop up a handful and pop one into his mouth, much as people munch on candy. He would stuff them into his pockets when he went out. Because of this habit, his teeth had practically rotted out, the two front ones curving like fangs with linings of black where cavities were eating away at the tooth enamel.

"Hi, Kruk. What's up?" Nobody ever used his first name. In fact, I think many of the boys didn't know it. I didn't.

He gazed at me through his thick glasses in an enigmatic way and peered about as if making sure we weren't being overheard.

"What's the matter, Kruk? You look like you're trying to hide from someone."

"Can we talk, Guy?" It was the first time I'd ever seen him with this furtive, cautious look.

"Sure. Have a seat." I sat down on a stair.

He took a step toward me but didn't sit down. "Guy, have you been missing anything recently?"

"What do you mean?"

"I think there's a thief in the dorm."

"What?"

"There's a thief in the dorm. I've had some things stolen from my room."

We'd been warned about theft when we first moved in. The dorm regulations made it imperative that we keep our valuables locked up at all times in the top drawers of our desks, the only one with a lock. No one had taken the warnings very seriously, though. In fact, because of the perpetual party atmosphere of the floor, most of the guys didn't even lock their doors, allowing anyone to go in and out of their rooms as they pleased.

"Did you report it to the housing office?"

He nodded. "Yes. And to the campus police, too. They say it's most likely someone in the dorm. It happens all the time, so I just wanted to warn you to be careful."

"Is there anyone you suspect?"

"No. But I'm pretty sure it's someone on our floor." He looked uneasy. "I've talked to some of the others. They're missing things, too."

I didn't have any valuables in my room, only my bank checkbook and some loose bills. I didn't want to believe that one of the guys could be a thief. I wanted it to be all in Kruk's imagination. Who could it be? The dorm supervisor had a master key, or duplicate keys, but he was a trustworthy person. The faces of all our dorm mates went through my mind.

Suddenly I felt as if I, too, might be under suspicion.

"All right. Thanks for the warning. I'll be on the lookout for anyone suspicious."

"You do that, Guy."

2

There were three libraries at our school, but the one I liked best was the oldest and least-used, all the way at the other end of the campus. The Spenser Undergraduate Library was built during the 1930s in a classical style, and exemplified everything I found charming about my university.

My route to the library took me on a bicycle path which meandered across the entire campus, first, alongside the stream which crossed the grounds from east to west, then over a small bridge and through some trees which grew thickly on the westernmost part of the campus. Many of the buildings here dated from the end of World War Two and had been used to house scientists doing wartime research at the school. I liked the dilapidated quality of the area. It had a romantic feeling of historical antiquity.

Yet all of this was slated to go some day. The school was planning to rebuild this section into a model housing/recreation area. Housing had always been a problem with the school, and was a high priority in the current restructuring program. Indeed, my own dorm was destined to be torn down as soon as more substantial funds were forthcoming. The building itself had been quickly built — a prefabricated, slapdash affair put together temporarily to ease the housing crunch caused by ever-increasing enrollments.

I felt a little sad at all the changes taking place. Though I'd only been in school for a few months, I'd already grown attached to the ambience of the old college town.

I stepped in through the main entrance of the library. The floors were all carpeted, and there was a heavy hush throughout the building. On the first floor, the innumerable study carrels and tables were filled with students busily taking notes. This entire floor was set aside for the reference books, bound periodicals, and texts which the instructors had put on reserve for their students to use. The upper two floors contained open book stacks through which we were free to wander, browsing if we chose.

I went up the stairs to the third floor.

There were fewer people on the upper floors, as most of the space was taken up by seemingly endless rows of bookshelves. The hush up here was inviting. I always felt as if I were stepping into a secret wood.

For me, reading had always been bound up with sexual discovery. I'd learned the facts of life through a sex education book for youths in my junior high school library. And when I made the wonderful discovery that there were books which dealt with homosexuality, some of them containing explicit description of homoerotic acts, I became an avid explorer of the public library stacks.

It had started in the main library of my hometown, where I accidentally discovered *Naked Lunch*. I was initially attracted by its bizarre title. Its dust jacket informed me that it was an underground classic. When I opened it at random, I found myself reading a description of two young boys on a river bank masturbating each other. With a sense of unreality, I read on, about two other young boys, naked, sucking each other off, then fucking each other in the ass. I couldn't believe how explicit the prose was. It was the first time I'd read sex scenes which reproduced all those fantasies which I'd thought I was the only one in the world to have, the things I'd daydreamed about in the privacy of my own mind, feeling that if

12

anyone else were to view them I'd be burned at the stake.

Not having the courage to check it out and take it home, I'd devoured it in the library during a couple of days in the summer before my last year of high school. Because most of my reading pleasure was focussed on the sex scenes in novels, the act of reading itself had acquired a sexual cast for me. Indeed it was a sexual act.

Since coming to college and discovering the Spenser Library, I'd been on the lookout for any more books dealing with homosexuality. I seemed to have a built-in radar for zeroing in on them. Something in a title would alert me, and I would pull the book out and scan the dust jacket. If the blurbs contained words like 'forbidden love', 'illicit passions', 'underground', 'secret', 'daring', 'previously banned', 'taboo subject', or 'unexpurgated', I knew I was on the right track.

There were so few other people using this section of the library that it felt like my own personal library. In the quiet, little-used stacks I could roam at my ease. In the evenings I would choose one of the many comfortable leather armchairs located in hidden nooks and crannies of the labyrinthine aisles. With a small table and reading lamp beside me, I devoured books whose titles — *The Immoralist, Confessions of a Mask, Our Lady of the Flowers, The City and the Pillar, Cities of the Night* — gave no idea of the inflammatory material contained within them. I would never have dared to check them out and read them back at the dorm, but it was enough for me to have this secret retreat.

My excitement at reading these books was only eclipsed by the thought that I knew there were others in school besides me who liked them. Unlike the other libraries on campus, which had computerized their check-out system, this library still used the old system. Anyone who wanted to borrow a book had to write his name and telephone number on an old-fashioned check-out card.

Whenever I discovered a gay book, I always scanned the list of people who'd checked it out, hoping to find someone I knew. One of the names which I frequently encountered was an 'H. Golden', who always seemed to be there before me. I wondered who he could be. It was obvious we shared the same interest, and I began to expect the bold letters of his name on the card whenever I opened a book which dealt with a gay theme. In fact, I took to verifying first to see if he'd checked out the book. If his clear, distinctive signature jumped out at me, I would feel as if I'd received his recommendation, his stamp of approval.

Over the months, I had build up my own picture of him. From the sound of his name I imagined a golden young boy, athletic and blond and beautiful, who agonized over the fact that he was all alone with his secrets, just as I was. I dreamed of meeting him.

I'd copied his telephone number from a check-out card and had been keeping it in my wallet with the half-formed intention of giving him a ring sometime. I had no idea what I wanted to say to him. All I knew was that he was probably gay, and the fact that I knew the name of at least one gay out there gave me a sense of security: I was not alone.

I located the copy of *The City and the Pillar* by Gore Vidal which I had been reading for the past several days, and sat down in my usual armchair. But for some reason I couldn't lose myself in the story. I kept thinking about what Kruk had told me earlier.

There was a thief in the dorm. I imagined him — whoever he was — sneaking into other boys' rooms stealthily opening drawers, pocketing valuables, brazenly assuming ownership of a friend's possession, touching, caressing his property. In a manner which I couldn't quite understand, there was something provocatively sexual about the thought. For me, anything secretive immediately assumed an erotic aspect. Perhaps it was because the nature of my own sexual desires having forced me to keep them secret from others, secrecy itself had become part of the landscape of my desire.

I shut the book and put it away, then headed for what was probably the least frequented part of the library, the section containing books on health and fitness. There was a particular book I was after, and I only hoped it hadn't been checked out. To my relief, I found it in its usual place on the top shelf, in a corner set aside for oversized books.

It was the autobiography of a Swedish body-builder whom I'd idolized as a boy. He had been the one who'd sparked my interest in training my body. In high school I'd bought several of his books on weight-lifting and had religiously followed the regimen he'd set down — the bench presses, snatches, and jerks with which he had developed his own body. Every day I'd drunk the 'stamina drink' he'd recommended — bananas, milk, and honey whipped up into a protein-filled milk-shake. To my delight, I'd watched my body fill out and harden with muscles, but it had never approached the ideal masculine form which he represented for me.

He was my god.

I began flipping through the book.

Sectioned among the pages of text were plates of the most exquisite photographs. He had the body of a classical Greek statue. Unlike many professional weight lifters, his muscles didn't bulge to unsightly proportions, nor did he wax and oil his skin till it gleamed like metal. And it wasn't overly tanned, as was the skin of most body-builders in muscle magazines. His skin had a completely natural tone, though he did depilate most of his body hair.

All his muscles — from his shoulders and chest, to his thighs and calves — were perfectly proportioned. And because he was tall enough, the large muscles didn't make him look too top-heavy, as often happened with shorter men.

In a skimpy black bikini, he flexed on a beach, the sea breeze ruffling his hair slightly, bits of sand clinging to his chest and belly. The clean curves of his pectorals made his chest look like the twin shields of a refined, flawless body armor, and the tight abdominal muscles below them were a firm, compact plate on which I spotted tiny hairs glinting in the sunlight. His shoulders were so fully muscled that the line from his neck to shoulder was a steep slope.

His face, with its classical Nordic lines — a steep brow, high cheekbones, a firm jawline, and full, sensuous lips — was the face of a warrior-hero, a marauding Viking sacking villages, leaving them in smoking ruins, spear in hand, his long, flowing, golden hair streaming behind him, his blue eyes glinting without the slightest trace of mercy, his lips curled back in disdainful superiority.

I wondered how many other boys had stood here flipping through this book. It looked well-thumbed. And I doubted if all those who gazed at the pictures were gay, either. But surely these pictures would be enough to turn a straight boy queer.

I looked around again, and listened. For all I knew, I was the only person on the entire floor. The ripping sound could barely be heard as I excised the page from the book. Folding it once, I slipped it into the pages of a book I was carrying.

The men's room was located at the far corner near the elevator. The restrooms in this library were quite spacious and well-ventilated. Inside, there were three stalls enclosed within wooden partitions painted a dark green, with a six- or eight-inch gap between their lower end and the floor. A quick glance assured me that none of the stalls was occupied.

I selected the one farthest from the door, entered, shut the door behind me.

I lowered the seat and sat down on it, then opened the book on my lap, pulled out the purloined page and unfolded it. Holding it out before me, I gazed at it with a greedy hunger I would never have dared reveal out there.

It was my favorite picture. He was standing in front of some gym equipment flexing his biceps which bulged sexily, rivetting my attention by their sheer magnitude. He was wearing a skimpy sleeveless runner's shirt which was stretched so tightly over his expanded chest that I could easily see his nipples under them, well-defined, round as quarters, and a healthy pink in color. Tiny wisps of underarm hair peeped out from under his armpit.

I felt a tremor run through me.

With my free hand I undid my jeans and, lifting my hips slightly, hooked my thumbs under the elastic waistband of my undershorts and pulled down, until my jeans were down to my knees. As my penis was freed, it flipped up and slapped solidly against my belly, pungent with the sexy aroma of semen.

The glans was so swollen that it was purplish, and gave off a slight glow, as if lit up from within like a dark bulb. Its moistness made it look like some kind of ripe fruit, a juicy plum ready to burst from its skin. The solid brown shaft supporting it was enwrapped with pulsing veins, throbbing to the beat of my excitement.

Normally, I didn't like to masturbate in my dorm. It wasn't that I didn't have the privacy there — I could easily do it in bed at night, or in the shower, as I knew the others did. But somehow, I felt more comfortable doing it in here where I was an anonymous student.

And I wasn't the only one who availed himself of the privacy afforded by the stall. There was evidence all around me that others were attracted to the same purpose. Crude drawings of naked women showing their genitals covered the walls (which were regularly painted over by the maintenance staff.) Sometimes I would find, tucked away behind the toilet paper dispenser, a folded-up page from a men's magazine displaying a picture of a naked woman with her legs spread magnanimously open.

Such evidence of universal lust gave me a sense of camaraderie with those other boys. As I pictured them sitting on this very same toilet seat, stroking themselves for all they were worth, one ear cocked for the sound of anyone coming in, I felt my own excitement augmented. It was as if I'd joined them, was one of their company, and doing it in rhythm with them.

I concentrated upon the picture. I felt like a humble worshipper offering my devotions to a god who didn't deign to look upon me, who exacted the most humiliating postures and abasement for the supreme privilege of looking upon him. Here in this toilet stall, my shrine dedicated to him, I was figuratively upon my knees, prostrated before him — and he merely smiled blandly, as if it were all his due... I was his most worshipful servant.

My slow, elaborate caresses gradually became intensely focussed upon their goal, and the rhythm accelerated into the steady, familiar beat of the final sprint. There was a slight slapping sound as the heel of my hand hit repeatedly against my groin, but the restroom was empty and I didn't worry.

I never let my eyes leave the face and body of my idol by as much as a fraction.

And then I heard the door to the men's room open.

In no time at all, I'd folded up the picture into a tiny square and stuffed it behind the toilet paper dispenser. With my heart pounding, and my breath held, I waited to discover what the other was doing. He seemed to be standing before the sink. I heard the water being turned on, running for a while, then turned off. There was a silence, during which I could only assume that he was standing before the mirror looking at himself.

A minute passed. A long minute passed. And then he was gone, out the door.

For a while I just sat there trying to regain my calm.

I didn't feel like continuing. My mood had been shattered. Leaving the picture where it was, I pulled my pants up and hurriedly left the stall. Perhaps another lonely gay student might find it there and be able to make use of it.

I made my way down the stairs to the first floor, and outside the library, to fresh air. Beside the shrubs which circled the building, I stood for a while, still a little shaken. I didn't feel like heading back to the dorm.

I thought about the photo I'd left in the stall and wondered if it would be there again when I went back. I doubted it. Now that I realized I might never see it again, I regretted my hasty decision.

Still, it would have been unsafe to have it on me. What were the chances that another gay student would come across it? Most likely a straight boy would pull it out, and in his disappointment, flush it down the toilet. I almost started to go back up and retrieve it, but the risk was too great.

I wondered how many others there were like me, lonely, unhappy, scared, having to resort to hasty, hidden pleasures for their only real satisfaction? I thought again of the 'H. Golden' who liked to check out gay books.

About twenty feet away from me, tucked away among the shrubs which surrounded the library, was a little-used telephone booth. The hedge surrounding the library had been allowed to grow around it, making it almost invisible from the footpath. I decided on the spur of the moment to try calling 'H. Golden' from here. There was no one about; I would have all the privacy I wanted.

From my wallet I pulled out the little slip of paper with his number on it and dialled.

"Hello?" The voice which answered the phone sounded much deeper and richer than I'd expected. My image of him modulated into that of an older man. I checked my impulse to hang up and managed to ask:

"Is this H. Golden?"

"Yes. Who is calling?"

"My name is Tim Glade," I said, ready with a false name.

"I don't recognize the name. Have we met?"

"No, never."

"Are you a student?"

"Yeah."

I'd called him half expecting him to hang up when he realized it was only a prank call, but he didn't seem upset by my unsolicited intrusion. He even sounded a little worried for me. His straightforward questions disarmed me, and I found myself replying openly.

"How long have you been in school?" he asked.

"I'm a freshman."

"Why are you calling me, Tim?"

I hesitated. In fact, I didn't know myself exactly why I'd suddenly decided to call him. Could he understand that I only felt a deep-rooted desire to connect to someone, anyone, anywhere? Or did that sound too far-fetched?

There was a long pause during which I was sure he would hang up, but he remained on the line, listening intently, at the other end. Finally I managed to ask:

"Are you gay?"

There was the slightest pause before he answered. "Yes. Are you?"

"I'm not sure," I said.

"Do you want to talk about it?"

"I'm not sure."

"You're being very evasive. How did you get my number?"

"A friend."

"Can you tell me his name?"

There was someone coming up the footpath. "Look, I'll call you again, okay?"

"Sure. Maybe you can give me your number?"

"I'm not so sure about that. Bye, now."

I stepped out of the booth just as a girl turned off the footpath. She was coming my way, and smiled as she recognized me.

"They told me I'd find you here," she said. It was Christine, my girlfriend.

3

Christine lived in an apartment just off campus, in a picturesque, tree-shaded neighborhood of Victorian style homes with bay windows out front and terraces in the back. It was the sort of place which usually appeared in movies about college life. I was never very comfortable there, and infinitely preferred the messy disorder of my dorm. Christine couldn't understand my preference.

We were in her room which she shared with a friend named Nancy. All during our walk here, she'd been dying to tell me something, and only now allowed herself to open up about it. Nancy was out and we had the place to ourselves.

"You won't believe what happened to me today," she said. She was carefully pouring hot water from the tea kettle into a tea strainer placed over a cup; in her latest fad, she was experimenting with various exotic teas which she ordered from a specialty shop in San Francisco.

"What happened?" I said. "You seem a little upset."

"I am." She went on to tell me how her English professor had drawn her aside after class and whispered: "If you dress like that again for next class, I'll give you an A on the mid-term." Christine wasn't wearing a bra today, and the low neckline of her blouse had apparently, when she was bent down taking notes at her desk, allowed the professor a generous glimpse of her breasts. She always sat in the first row quite close to the lectern.

"Damn," I said. "That was pretty cheeky of him."

"I think it's disgusting, is what I think." Yet her indignation could barely conceal the pleasure she got from reporting it. "I couldn't believe it. This school has such high academic standards, too. He doesn't have the least interest in my academic abilities. All I am for him is a pair of tits. And I'm not even well-endowed in that department, either."

"So, are you going to do it?" I asked.

"Are you crazy? You're suggesting I should take him up on it?"

"Sure."

She looked at me, trying to judge how serious I was. As I imagined the professor peering surreptitiously down her blouse, getting excited by a mere glimpse of her breasts, I said: "If he finds you sexually attractive, why not give him a little pleasure? It costs you nothing. And you get an A out of it."

"You're serious, aren't you?"

"Of course I am. If you know you have a sure A in English, you can spend that much more time studying for your other tests. If it were me, I know I'd do it."

"I thought you'd be jealous. I mean, another man seeing my breasts."

"I am jealous."

In fact, the thought that other men found her attractive only excited me. Whenever we entered a room together, all the men's eyes would be on her. I would secretly enjoy the way they stared at her, and the way their eyes travelled up and down her body.

Far from being upset by these attentions, I made efforts to encourage them. Though Christine would have preferred to wear sloppy t-shirts and jeans, it was I who constantly urged her to wear more provocative clothes: scanty short-shorts, tank tops, miniskirts, and low-cut camisoles. It was as if she were my doll and I was dressing her up to please the guys. And my pleasure in it was ignited by a process of reflection: the other boys' excitement excited me. I imagined that all the male attention she drew to her stuck to the surface of her skin, so that when I caressed her, I was caressing those male glances.

For her part, she thought it was my jealousy which stimulated me, so she made efforts to fan that jealousy. She never missed a chance to report being stared at by boys, or being propositioned by them. She knew these tales only excited me by letting me know just how attractive she was to other guys. Perhaps she secretly sensed that if she didn't have the power to attract them, I wouldn't have been as drawn to her as I was.

She had the androgynous kind of beauty which I've found most attractive in women. Her body was lithe, long-limbed, and athletic-looking, and she walked with a slightly over-exuberant bounce which made her hair swing from side to side. At my request, she'd cut her hair short; her thick blond hair came straight down to her eyebrows, and was cut short all around, making it look as if she were wearing a shiny helmet. Her eyes were green with glints of gold in them, and were slightly slanted. This, combined with her high cheekbones, made her look quite exotic.

When Jonesy first saw her, he'd said jokingly: "Thank you, Atilla the Hun." Christine had a Polish background, and I suppose Jonesy was imagining the distant past when Mongol armies had swept into Poland, pillaging, plundering, and raping, leaving behind them those genetic traits which, when blended with the local Polish ones, had bequeathed this exotic look to Christine.

"I refuse to use sex as a weapon," she was saying. When she pouted, the way her lips pushed together gave her a winsomely stubborn look.

I laughed. "Come on, Chrissie, I was only joking. But I guess I've learned why all the good-looking girls seem to get such good grades around here. Did you ever notice that?"

She nodded, suddenly turning serious. "You know, it's true. The better looking you are, the more likely you'll do well in school. But there's a deeper reason for that."

"Uh-oh. I think the psychologist in you is about to emerge."

Unlike myself — who still couldn't decide what my major would be — Christine had always known she wanted to major in psychology. She was constantly reading up on various psychological experiments, and whenever she launched into her explanation of one of them, her face became most animated.

"No, seriously," she said. "I was just reading up on something dealing with that. Physical attractiveness has been shown to be a very important factor in the way we're perceived by others — much more so than most people would think. There was a psychological experiment conducted on some kindergarten and elementary school teachers." She paused, looking at me questioningly. "Are you interested in hearing this, or am I boring you?"

"No, go on. I wanna hear about it."

"All right. Well, the teachers weren't told the nature of the test they were undergoing though they knew they were being tested for something. They were shown a series of photographs of children and asked to rate them on an attractiveness scale, from one to ten."

"That sounds like the guys in my dorm judging girls. Go on."

"Anyway, these same photographs were then given to another group of teachers who were asked to study the photos and determine — just from first impressions — what they believed the personality of the child to be like. These results were then tallied against the results of the attractiveness test."

"I can imagine the results. Probably the same thing that we all learned in junior high and high school — that attractive kids are more popular."

"Exactly. The children who'd been rated low in attractiveness by the first group were almost invariably described as potential troublemakers, unsociable, unintelligent, or withdrawn. The attractive children, on the other hand, were judged to be more outgoing, friendly, intelligent, and creative. Mind you, all this was about children the teachers had never even met."

"So what does all that prove? I could have told you that without an experiment."

She became serious, a tiny wrinkle appearing between her eyebrows. "Well, the result seems to show that a teacher's initial impression of a child will determine how he will act toward the child — whether he will give him encouragement, or ignore the child's true potentials. Naturally, children who receive more attention and love will respond in ways which stimulate their intellectual and social growth — in other words, succeed in the ways by which society measures accomplishment. So from a very young age, the dice are loaded against unattractive children."

"It's not only teachers. We all judge people by their looks. Subconsciously and otherwise."

"True. I have to admit that's what first drew me to you, Guy."

"Bingo."

Christine was the first girl who'd ever been open about her sexual attraction towards me. Perhaps it was all the psychology she'd studied, but she had never been shy about expressing her erotic feelings. And she liked to enunciate clearly what it was about me, physically, that she liked. It was that which excited me most: I could see myself through her eyes, and become aroused by the image of myself I saw there.

For her, sexuality was the key to a person's character. She was completely open about her own sexuality. We had long talks about our sexual awakenings, and (on my part, guardedly) about our love affairs in the past. I'd told her about the many girlfriends I'd had, but not about the thoughts that went through my head as I was making love with them, or what I had to do to excite myself. I hadn't quite opened up with her to the point where I could confess that all the girls had merely been for decoration, to hide my true inclinations. And that in my mind I'd had to change many of them into boys before I could become sexually interested in them.

Christine, for her part, kept nothing back from me. That was how I knew I was the fourth boy she'd made love to. I knew all about my predecessors, Craig, David, Brian, and Julian. She knew I was curious about the boys in her past and didn't try to hide anything. I wasn't exactly the jealous type. I'd fantasized about being able to enter her body and watch out of her eyes as she made love with other boys.

Because of her open attitude toward sex, people felt relaxed in her presence, and would confess things they wouldn't have dreamed of revealing to other people. I'd even told her about my one homosexual experience in high school. My ability to confess this to her — and I felt able to, perhaps because she was a woman — was another bond between us.

She felt that all people were basically bisexual — a belief which I shared — and that we all had a sort of gauge within us, one side indicating heterosexuality, the other, homosexuality. With most people, the needle pointed closer to heterosexual, with varying degrees of distance from it. Nobody was completely hetero, or for that matter, homo. She felt that we all had urges both ways, which fluctuated with time and circumstances.

In junior high school, she had had a crush on an older girl in school, even to the point of writing secret love letters. So she could understand homosexuality. I told her that my adolescence was also a confusing period of transition, though I stopped short of telling her that my most satisfying sexual experience had been with that one boy, and that my most vivid and erotic sexual fantasies were those involving men.

She wanted no secrets between us, so it was a torture for me not to be able to tell her everything. I longed to do away with this great secret which I carried, but I knew that this very secret was the bond which linked us so tightly together. And though she was the only person to whom I was ready to confess everything, that very confession would have destroyed what we had together. Her love would never be able to withstand that revelation. And I didn't want to hurt her. I wanted to protect her for my own reasons: because I needed her love. My relationship with her had been the most fulfilling relationship of my life. So I had to keep up the pretense that I was what I seemed to be on the outside — just another heterosexual boy.

But I'd come very close to revealing myself. She knew I was excited by the way other men were attracted to her. And she knew I fantasized about other men making love to her... and that I was hungry for details about the other boys in her life.

About clumsy Craig, her first boyfriend, in the eighth grade. He would come over to see her as she babysat for a neighbor. After the kids had gone to sleep, they would sit on the sofa watching TV and kissing, for hours, until she became frantic with desire. Craig would eventually slip his hand into her blouse, so eagerly, yet so awkwardly, that she wished she could take his hand and guide him.

In her sophomore year of high school she'd gone steady with David, who was not much better. He was a redhead, a hotshot tennis player and a boy scout. Christine practically had to seduce him, but she finally lost her virginity to him one night in a girlfriend's bedroom.

Then there was the brief flirtation with Brian in her junior year. Christine lost her interest in him when she discovered that, despite his outward braggadocio, he suffered from premature ejaculation. Their lovemaking never got to the point of insertion.

The boy who changed it all was Julian, the bad boy in school. He was the one who first gave Christine the feeling that sex was not just a naughty prize to give away to a boy, to spite the grown-up world, or to prove your adulthood. Before she ever met him, she'd been fascinated by his reputation: since junior high school he'd been linked with the pregnancies of several girls. In high school there was talk that he'd slept with a student teacher from college. He exuded a confident virility, and it was this which excited Christine... and me.

"Was he that good looking?" I asked her.

"No, not really. He was tall and pale, with dark, curly hair and searching eyes. He wasn't conventionally handsome. But there was something about him which the girls in my school found endlessly fascinating."

"Did he have a good body?"

"Oh yes. Firmly muscled, slim hips..."

Of course Christine thought she was stoking my jealousy as a preliminary to our lovemaking. But for me, hearing about Julian enhanced our lovemaking, was a vital part of it. This was the only way I could get close to a boy — to see his nudity, to know how he kissed and caressed, the way he smelled, the way he made love.

"Did he have a big dick?"

"About average, I guess."

"But he sure knew how to use it, huh?"

"Oh, yes. But not nearly as good as you. You're the best ever."

"Oh?"

"And you're the best looking guy I've ever been with."

"What is it about me you like?"

"Your butt, for one. I love your butt."

"Girls usually tell me that." Her hands were on my buttocks, caressing them. "What else?"

"Your chest." She pulled off my shirt. "I love your chest, and your shoulders. You worked out today, didn't you?"

"Oh yes."

She felt the hardness of my muscles with the palms of both hands. Seeing the desire in her eyes as she looked at my body excited me. I could see myself reflected in her pupils. There was a lascivious hunger in them. Her lips were slightly parted and I saw her tongue flicker inside. Even in the darkness her eyes glowed greedily when I slipped off my briefs. Feeling her lust, I became aroused. It was her desire for a boy's body that pierced me now. She made no effort to hide it or disguise it. I could feel it so keenly that my head swam. Maybe this was the nearest I would ever come to making love with another boy. Only Christine had been able to do this to me. And she would do anything for me, to stretch her erotic boundaries in an almost reckless fashion. Only with her had I not had to resort to my imagination. My excitement was what I might have felt if I were naked on a bed together with another boy.

Her slender, boyish figure, and the androgynous, classical beauty of her face easily enhanced the illusion. When her hair was brushed straight back, as it was now, the exquisite shape of her head and the perfection of her ears make her seem like the beautiful young prince of childhood fairy tales.

I reached up and gathered her hair in a bunch behind her head. "Now you look like a boy."

"Meaning you wish I had bigger tits."

"No way. I love you just the way you are."

I lay on my back and she sat atop me straddling my thighs, the better to stroke my erection. From the way she was sitting it looked as if my upthrusting penis were hers, completing the illusion that she was a boy.

"You look like a young kid beating off," I said.

"Oh?" She smiled naughtily, immediately sensing what I wanted. Without hesitation, she began stroking my dick with smooth, practiced motions of the wrist, parting her lips and running her tongue over them. Then she opened her mouth slightly and let out a soft moan. It was a beautiful performance.

"Is this how you do it?" she asked.

"Oh yes. You do it so well."

Looking at the expression on her face, it was difficult to believe she wasn't feeling exactly what I was feeling. Yes, of course she'd seen a boy's pleasure at firsthand. I thought of her masturbating her boyfriends by hand. I was now looking at Julian's face...

She refined the illusion by peering around furtively as she stroked, like a boy in his bedroom fearful of being caught at it. I thought of myself earlier in the library restroom.

"Oh yes..."

She closed her eyes and began sighing, moaning, grimacing, a little exaggeratedly at first, but then more and more realistically. A strange and wonderful boy-girl had been created before my eyes, and I could feel each nuance of his pleasure as he masturbated himself, for he and I were one, stroking and being stroked, boy on boy.

The illusion was perfect.

"Come on, baby..." She had gripped her shaft and was giving herself up to a straight pumping action, jerking it up and down in a rhythmic motion which made the glans bob drunkenly. Her hair had come loose and now flopped rhythmically against her cheekbones to the beat of the creaking of the bed beneath us. The heel of her hand made a slight slapping sound as it hit repeatedly against her groin.

She glanced at me wickedly. She knew I liked what I saw.

And my excitement in turn ignited hers. She became lost in her performance, excited by it, exploring the perverse corners of her own soul. As she sensed the onset of my pleasure, she really seemed to forget for a moment that she was a girl. Suddenly she threw her head back and her thighs gripped me tighter and her lips made a tight O as she shot her warm semen all over my chest.

I was in heaven...

4

Peter Cockle lived north of the campus among the hills overlooking the city. I'd spoken with him over the phone and had taken him for just another art student. But after I'd learned more about him from Christine, I began to feel a little nervous about meeting him. Apparently he was already something of a campus celebrity, being one of the most talented artists in school. There were those who called him a genius. The art professors treated him a little deferentially, and there was a lot of envy among the other art students.

It was Christine who had introduced me to modelling. She'd started to model herself under the work-study program offered by the school, which gave students part-time employment around campus. These jobs barely paid minimum wages, but were convenient and easy. The fine arts department was looking for models for the art students, and the pay was reasonable; Christine had applied and immediately been accepted.

I used to watch her sometimes as she sat for the students, wishing she could be posing in the nude. School regulations prohibited nude modelling during class periods ever since some student's mother had complained about it, but students or groups of students could make private arrangements with a model for extracurricular sessions, even using the art room after school hours. Christine herself refused such offers, but when I told her I would be willing, she recommended them to me. She had told me it was easy work and, knowing I could use the money, urged me to try it, too. I'd never modelled before so I agreed initially out of curiosity. Since then, I'd posed privately on a number of occasions, almost always in the nude.

Peter Cockle had apparently seen me posing for someone else, and had contacted me over the phone. He wondered if I would be willing to model privately for him. I'd agreed, then gone to Christine to find out more about him. What she told me made me curious to meet him, especially as he was apparently widely rumored to be gay.

When he came to the door in answer to my ring, he was wiping his glasses.

"I'm so glad you could come, Guy," he said, extending a thin white hand. I shook it — it was limp, and a little damp. "Come on in."

He was a pale, intense aesthete, the stereotypical artist. Thick lenses magnified his eyes, which had a stark, questioning look. His hair was thin and wispy, already going bald. He wore a black turtle neck sweater under a pair of faded workman's overalls. He was barefoot.

He was obviously the type who became so absorbed in his painting that he forgot to eat. If it weren't for his careless way of dressing, and the complete lack of interest he took in his grooming, he could have passed for a business ed major — a future bank manager or advertising executive.

His apartment was cramped and smelled of oil paints and turpentine. Canvases filled every room, most with their faces turned to the wall. Their backs, wooden-framed, looked naked, and were covered with titles scribbled in pencil. Rows of them leaned out from the wall into the middle of the room, and we had to maneuver carefully past them to get to the workroom.

Peter apparently did all his painting in this small, well-lighted space with a paint-spattered workbench in the middle. Pinned to the walls everywhere in kaleidoscopic disarray were newspaper clippings, photos torn out of magazines, comic strips, and Polaroid shots of street scenes. There was a camera on a tripod beside the bathroom door. The floor was littered with cans, bottles, and various knick-knacks obviously picked up at antique stores and junkyards. Amid all the clutter was a strange wooden contraption which looked like a tiny replica of the Wright brothers' first airplane. Propped inside it was a small mirror, angled so that the viewer's eye stared back at him. Next to it was a book checked out from the library turned face down, a collection of African art.

"Sit down," he said. "I'll get you something to drink before we get started."

It was difficult to find a place to sit among the jumble of things scattered haphazardly all over the place. I sat down in a low slung canvas director's chair.

He opened a portable refrigerator under the workbench — I caught a glimpse of rows of paints and camera film inside — and pulled out a can of Coke. Picking up a glass from a small table, he blew the dust off it and handed it to me with the drink.

"I can't pay you very much," he said. "But I'll do the best I can." He named a price and I nodded; it was well over what I usually got.

"What kind of work are you doing now?" I asked.

"Believe it or not, a series of illustrations dealing with themes from Greek mythology. Look."

He picked out one of the canvasses leaning against the wall and turned it around so I could see. It was a painting of a boy half-undressed, in a secluded grove peering through some bushes at a bathing woman — a goddess, presumably.

"No one does this sort of thing nowadays," he said, "though it used to be the standard practice for artists. But that's exactly why I want to do it. For one thing, I like the challenge of painting naturalistically. Everyone thinks that all I can paint are those abstracts which the professors are making such a fuss over. I want to prove to them that I can do other things — that I have mastered the traditional techniques. Just when they think they have me pegged, blam, I turn around and do something completely unexpected."

I was barely listening to him, so mesmerized was I by the painting. I remembered looking at pictures very much like this in

29

my mother's art books back home when I was a boy, but this was somehow different. Though its theme was just as traditional, there was something very modern about the way it had been done.

The whole scene glowed with life, emanated a sense of reality, almost a super-reality, which rivetted my attention. I'd never seen such minuteness, such painstaking attention to detail before. No photograph could ever be this realistic. It was as if Peter had actually gone back into a mythological time and had been there to record the moment. I was astonished. This painting transcended realism — gloriously. It lived, breathed.

I was especially struck by the beauty of the boy's face, and the attention Peter had paid to the delineation of his muscles, and wondered who the model was. Just the way the boy's arm angled back to expose the tiny wisp of underarm hair made me ache with longing. I felt a hollow hurt in the depths of my chest.

"Am I gonna look like that?"

"Something very similar," he said. "You're going to be my model for Narcissus. You know who he is, don't you?"

"Isn't that where the word narcissist comes from?" When speaking with highly intelligent people, I sometimes found myself almost unconsciously acting less intelligent than I was, as if adopting a pose of simple-mindedness.

"Exactly. Narcissus was a beautiful young man who fell in love with his own image — and got turned into a flower for it." He pointed to a flower in a wine bottle amid the clutter on the floor. "That's Narcissus today, a lovely but somewhat over-refined flower."

"Why did you pick me?"

"You fit my image of him perfectly. There's something about you which makes you just right for what I wanted — something in your eyes, maybe. You seem so deep within yourself — as if you were gazing into a deep pool. And there's also something about you which makes me feel that you've never been in love with anyone — that you might be incapable of loving as others love."

"Oh?"

"Please don't be offended," he added quickly, blushing hard. "I don't mean it to sound insulting. It's just that that detached quality was exactly what I had in mind for my Narcissus."

"Well, I really don't know what you're talking about. As a matter of fact, I have been in love. Several times, in fact."

"Me and my big mouth. Please ignore what I just said. Sometimes I don't know what I'm saying. I guess I got so carried away with planning my work that I'm still lost in it."

"I understand." But in my heart I felt he'd touched on a truth inside me. I did have a secret fear that I could never love anyone in the manner he mentioned — the normal way all people fell in love and lived happy, fulfilled lives. I could only have crushes on people I could never have. Unrequited love suited me, and had been all I ever experienced. Perhaps it had been too easy for me to possess any girl I desired, for I seemed to lose all my desire the moment I possessed her. But the boys I got crushes on stayed in my heart for that very reason — because I could never have them, they remained unattainable dream ideals whose reality never intruded upon my immaculate images of them.

"I like to play jazz records as I paint. I hope you don't mind. It helps me concentrate."

"No problem."

He went over to the record player and picked out an album from a pile of them on the bench, put it on. Then, as he spread a rather thick rug on the floor before the window, he mumbled something I couldn't catch.

"What's that?" I asked.

He cleared his throat. "You don't mind modelling in the nude, do you?"

"No, of course not." I felt a prickling along the back of my neck. Thinking of the rumors about his sexual inclinations, I tried to repress the thrill which surged through me.

"Would you be willing to pose fully nude?"

"Of course. I suppose when you're dealing with ancient Greek myths, it comes with the territory."

"Sometime in the future I might ask you to. But for today, all I need is the shirt off."

"All right." As I pulled off my t-shirt I felt relief and disappointment in equal measure. It would have been nice to savor the heady danger involved in being watched by a gay man. But at the same time I was relieved of my worry that I might let my own excitement show. In any case, this painting of Narcissus might not require full nudity; perhaps the lower half of my body would be covered by a piece of cloth. "Shall I take my jeans off?"

"Please." He turned his back and began fussing with the palette and some tubes of paint. His eyes avoided mine as he set up the easel. He was trying hard to act nonchalant, but I could see his Adam's apple bob up and down each time he swallowed.

I pulled off my jeans and put them on the stool on top of my t-shirt. I was down to my white cotton briefs. In a way, it was even sexier to be in briefs rather than fully nude. "Do you paint many nudes?"

"Some."

"Mostly male or female?"

"Both." He pushed his glasses back up onto the bridge of his nose. "Well, shall we get started?"

"Sure."

He glanced at me and came over. "Please kneel down on the rug." Guiding me with his hands, he had me sit gazing slightly downward at the bare floor, adjusting me slightly every few minutes until he had the pose he wanted. Then he began doing a rough pencil sketch of me directly onto the canvas.

The room was a little cool. I felt a tiny tension in my nipples and along the surface of my skin. The idea that Peter might make a pass at me was at the root of the tension I felt, even though he seemed so otherworldly, as if sex were, for him, secondary to painting. I imagined his glances at my body as tiny caresses, brushing feather-like here and there, occasionally rasping roughly as if a finger were rubbing an unshaven cheek. I was praying that I wouldn't get aroused. But I needn't have worried. As soon as he began painting, he was lost in his work, and I began losing my own self-consciousness.

He dove into his work with a voracious appetite, animated by a hidden power which seemed to have taken over his conscious self. I could tell he was in another time and place. His unblinking gaze went up to me then back to the canvas, communicating some message from eye to brain to hand. His face had no expression at all; I felt he was seeing right through me, at something which wasn't of this world, and I was a little frightened by it.

For him I was nothing more than a problem in lines, colors, shades. I had been reduced to the reflection of lights on the surface of my skin. For all he cared, I might have been a desk, an apple, a sunset.

But I was used to this by now. Modelling hadn't been as easy as I'd thought it would be at first. Standing still for thirty minutes at a time, sometimes in an uncomfortable pose, knowing I was being closely scrutinized, mentally stripped down to the bare lines and planes of my physical existence — all of this was sometimes quite unsettling. During a posing session, every inch of me was public property; I was merely a life-sized doll to be analyzed for the angles of my bones, the shade of light against my skin.

And sitting so still before a classroom full of students was often a test of endurance, almost a zen-like discipline. I thought of it as a Spartan training to achieve mental detachment. Indeed, the way I concentrated on my breathing, the sensations on the surface of my skin, the play of light in the air — all this was a sort of meditation. At such times, I was not the usual me but another, more abstract being. My mind went blank and I thought of nothing, only occasionally brought back to reality by the tiny sounds made by hatching pencils, rubbed erasers, dropped paintbrushes.

Still, the ferocity with which Peter was attacking the canvas could very well be seen as a sublimation of his sexual desire for me. His intense, bug-eyed expression and the sweat popping out on his forehead only added to the bizarre illusion.

I wondered if he found me sexually attractive. The most satisfying thing about being a model, of course, was the sheer joy of just being looked at. I'd always been self-conscious of my looks, perhaps too much so, for I'd known from an early age that I was attractive, and this knowledge carried with it a burden as well as joy. Whenever I walked down the street, I always secretly counted the number of heads I'd turned, the number of people who'd stared at me. And if no one or almost no one looked in admiration, I began to worry if my looks were going. By modelling for artists, I knew I was being looked at by people who knew and cared about how beautiful my body was. It was a way of reassuring myself that I was desirable.

"Can I see what you've done so far?" I asked. I was curious to see what I'd inspired, in the same way everyone wants to know how his photo came out.

"Sorry. I'd rather you didn't see it just yet. You'll have to wait until it's done, okay?"

"When will that be?"

"Don't know." When he saw my reaction, his expression softened. "I'm sorry if I seem rude. But that's just the way I am. I hate for someone to look at a work in progress. It's a superstition

I have. I don't know if I can explain it."

"That's all right. I guess with your talent, you're entitled to be a little eccentric."

"Talent? What is this talent that everyone talks about? I hate to be singled out like some kind of freak. Everyone has some kind of talent."

"Not me."

He stared at me. "You do have a talent. Your beauty."

"Beauty is a talent?"

"Of course it is. Beauty is a God-given talent. That sounds strange, I know. But believe me, I've given it a lot of thought. Beautiful people are that way by an act of will. They seem to radiate something from within, some sort of power which is the source of their attraction. I say this because I've seen many people who have all the attributes of physical beauty — the proper proportions of face and body, and so forth — but who don't attract us. And on the other hand, there are others who might not have the natural material of a beautiful person, but who have this strange ability to draw our eyes. I'm not talking about charisma, either, or 'personality.' I'm talking about the true source of beauty, the magical talent for clothing oneself in physical desirability."

"I think you're making too much of all this."

With a trembling hand, he took off his glasses and began polishing them with a handkerchief. Evidently excited by the topic, he continued on, stammering occasionally in his rush to elaborate. "Physical beauty is something we all want — if we don't have it ourselves, we seek it in others. We want to possess it. And if we can't possess it, we make it. I've always been fascinated by attractive people. Not being attractive myself, maybe I was jealous. I wanted to think that they were unable to be touched — that their surface beauty came between them and any sort of human contact. An unattractive person who is used to pining away for someone wants to feel that the burning desire he feels for his beloved is something which the beloved can never feel."

He put on his glasses again and looked at me but I couldn't see the expression on his face because the setting sun outside had lit the sky up in an orange glow and was reflected on the surface of his lenses. All I saw was a twin pair of orange ovals. I said nothing and he went on:

"Our society categorizes people by their looks. We pretend

it isn't so, but it's true. Supposedly we are all created equal — we all have an equal chance to succeed. That's all bullshit. In everything, whether it's sports, business, or academics, the odds are stacked heavily in favor of those with good looks. Look at all the successful people, and nine times out of ten, except for geniuses, the successful ones are those who look good.

"In a society which prides itself on egalitarianism, desire for beauty is supposedly an unhealthy trait. But we are slaves to our instincts. It's ingrained in us for survival. When we lived by the laws of the jungle, the best chance of surviving, and having offspring survive, was for the female to seek a strong male. A male with a strong, muscular body could fight off enemies. That is the very type we identify as sexually attractive. The weaker males also gathered around him for protection against worse dangers. Even today, leaders — whether in sports, business, or politics — tend to be attractive. We feel we can rely on them to keep the wolves at bay. When we see athletes on a playing field, we feel an atavistic longing within us. Deep within our genetic memory is the shared experience of relying on such rough brutes for protection."

He paused and I shivered. I was struck by the incongruity of sitting almost nude listening to his spontaneous discourse, but couldn't help but be strangely moved by his stumbling, stammering speech. He went on:

"Maybe that's why I try to compensate by my art. If I wasn't so unattractive, I might not paint at all. But the fact is, given a choice, I'd rather be an untalented but beautiful person than an unattractive genius. I think all artists feel the same way. Deep down, we all want to be desired and loved by those whom we love. We try to capture the beauty which we lack, which we want. I use my talent in revenge against a world which gives all its adoration to the beautiful people."

As he said all this, there was no trace of bitterness; he was merely stating facts drily, even a little tiredly.

"I don't think you're unattractive, Peter," I said, awkwardly. "In fact, when you — "

He put his brush down and picked up a piece of paint-stained cloth. "I think we've had enough of a break. Let's get back to work, shall we?"

"All right."

I resumed my pose and heard him begin to mix paints again.

I posed for Peter three more times in the following week, after which he said he had enough to go on. At the last session he asked me rather diffidently if I would take off my briefs, which I did without any qualms. By then I had been longing for it to happen, and was somewhat disappointed at his seeming indifference to my finally becoming completely nude.

The next day, I decided to go to the library to find out more about Narcissus. I vaguely remembered reading something about him back in high school, but now I felt a need to learn all I could about my mythical alter-ego.

For me, there had always been something excitingly illicit about the Greek myths. I remembered my high school English teacher, Mr. Brown, telling us that many of the gods, including Zeus, were bisexual, with male lovers as well as female. In fact, the ancient Greeks — to the amazement of my classmates — seemed to have accepted sex between men as a normal activity. I wondered now if the story of Narcissus might not hold a secret waiting to be unlocked by me.

I found what I wanted in the classic literature section of the Spenser Library: an illustrated reference book which contained capsule histories of all the major gods and heroes.

Apparently Narcissus was a demi-god, whose father was the river god Cephisus and his mother a water nymph named Liriope. He was a beautiful youth; by the age of sixteen he was adored by both boys and girls. Almost everyone who saw him fell in love with him, but he himself seemed incapable of feeling a similar passion for anyone. Knowing nothing of the pain of love, he saw it as a weakness, a form of derangement which made people do ridiculous things. He mocked those whose hearts were broken by him.

One of the boys who had been spurned by him prayed to the gods in anger that Narcissus would suffer as so many others had for his sake — that he would fall in love with someone and never have it requited. The gods heard his prayer and answered it.

One day Narcissus became lost in a forest where no man or beast had ever ventured. In his wanderings, he came upon a hidden pool surrounded by tall grass and trees. To quench his thirst, he knelt down to take a drink, and as he did so, saw his own reflection for the first time in his life.

As he gazed upon the face of the most beautiful boy he'd ever seen, he experienced something he'd never known before. At first, he was happy just to gaze upon the other boy's face, but before long, he desired more. He knew the other wanted the same. But though they stretched their arms out to each other, they could never touch. And when they tried to kiss, their frustrated passion dissolved into shimmering ripples.

Two lovers pining away for each other, from different worlds, so close yet so far, separated by the thinnest of curtains — that separating reality and illusion, whose dichotomy generates the most desperate and powerful of all loves.

Obsessed by his twin, Narcissus lost all desire for food or sleep. His physical strength began to ebb away, his will to live sapped by his sorrow. Either because the gods were moved by his sorrow or by his beauty, they turned him into a flower forever peering down at its own reflection in the water, the flower which bears his name today, the flower I'd seen in the wine bottle at Peter's studio.

This story had a strange appeal for me. Like Narcissus, I had always known that I was attractive, and been proud of the fact, even using my looks as a weapon to get certain things I wanted. But there was always a kind of guilt attached to my pride. I was made to feel that it was vulgar — especially for a boy — to flaunt his looks. The word 'narcissism' invariably had a negative connotation. And because it was considered something like bad manners to feel that I was more attractive than the average boy, my self-love had to be hidden away in my deepest, most secret place. If someone should suddenly walk in when I was admiring myself in the mirror, I felt as if I'd been discovered in a shameful act.

All my life, I'd spent an inordinate amount of time in front of mirrors, though I tried to hide it from others. I would lose all sense of time as I examined my reflection, until my face had lost all its familiarity and became a stranger's. Like the feeling you have when you look at a word for a long time and eventually the word becomes unfamiliar and loses all meaning. In the mirror, the other boy's beauty had somehow faded. I felt an almost obsessive need to find the tiniest little flaws that might detract from his looks, and to exaggerate them. I was happy to find tiny lines, the beginnings of wrinkles, veins in my eyes, a dark mole on my chest. I ended up feeling that I was ugly, and went into a depression. But this was only temporary, for I had a confident — even arrogant — faith in my own beauty.

Also like Narcissus, I seemed unable to feel true passion for anyone. What I felt for Christine wasn't love, but something closer to friendship. When Peter had hinted that I seemed incapable of loving another, he'd unwittingly touched upon one of my deepest fears.

I'd always wanted an ideal soul-mate — someone who was exactly like me, and could understand everything I thought and felt. It was almost as if I pined after a twin brother I'd never had. I toyed with the thought that I might have been separated from him at birth, or perhaps he'd died at birth, and his grave was somewhere unknown to me.

I had a fantasy that each time I peered into a mirror, I was searching for him. The boy I saw trapped in the mirror was my long lost twin brother, and the only place we could meet was at that thin glass border which separated my side — reality — from his side — fantasy. Narcissism might be the search for the long-lost mirror twin we all once had.

Perhaps that was why I was unable to love anyone else.

The illustration accompanying the legend of Narcissus showed a young boy kneeling beside the fateful pool. He looked a little too effeminate for my taste; I certainly wouldn't have fallen in love with him.

I wondered how Peter would depict me. It excited me to think that for him, I was the present day Narcissus. I tried to imagine his feelings as he'd looked at my body. Perhaps for him, I was like that image in the water — so close yet so out of reach.

From his spontaneous confession about his adoration of beautiful people, I knew that he probably desired me sexually. His having me sit before him naked, obeying his every command, had been a sort of possession of me. In fact, I suspected that painting was, for him, a way to possess the boys he craved. If that was true, then the satisfaction he'd experienced had been mutual. For, as I'd posed for him, I'd felt that his will had conquered me in the fullest sense. I'd been made submissive before a burning, omnipotent gaze which laid bare my most secret needs. The way his all-seeing eyes had travelled over every inch of my body, leaving nowhere untouched, had been like being caressed by him in the most intimate way possible — with the eyes only, without a single touch. He probably knew that posing for him had satisfied something within me which could be satisfied in no other way.

I looked around at the other students in the library. After my heady meditation, they suddenly seemed so prosaic, busily occupied as they were in their tedious academic studies. It was about four o'clock in the afternoon, the time of day when the library was most crowded.

I caught a quick movement out of the corner of my eye and turned to look. A boy was hastily looking down at his book. Undoubtedly, he'd been staring at me. I didn't recognize him. Perhaps he'd mistaken me for someone else. Anyway, this wasn't the first time an unknown boy had stared at me.

I got up to return the book to the shelf, then headed to the restroom. I usually checked myself in the mirror after being stared at by someone, because sometimes I had the nagging feeling that I hadn't looked my best.

I stood in front of the first sink, eying my reflection carefully, leaning in to check on the progress of a nascent pimple near the corner of my mouth. It was a barely noticeable swelling below the skin, but it bothered me. I thought of those disgusting boys back in high school who popped their pimples right in class, leaving bright red splotches of blood on their faces.

Giving my face a final inspection, I took my comb out of my back pocket and ran it through my hair. My eyes never left the mirror. The restroom mirror: modern-day descendant of Narcissus's pool in the woods.

I walked over to a urinal and unzipped.

The door creaked open as someone entered the restroom. Staring straight at the wall in front of me, I noted out of the corner of my eye that it was the boy I'd caught earlier staring at me. For a second, I thought he might have followed me in here, but immediately dismissed it. I was always trying to find hidden motives for the least coincidence.

He placed his books on the shelf above the first sink and began examining the mirror. I knew from experience that it was possible to angle your gaze from there to spy on the boy standing at the first urinal... but I didn't dare look up to confirm it. After a moment he came over to the urinals and took the one to my immediate left. This in itself was a little strange, as most boys would have taken the one on the far left, leaving one empty between us for modesty's sake. I became too tense to urinate.

Pretending to be done, I gave my dick a loose shake to signal I was done, and out of the corner of my eye saw him turn his head toward me. When I turned to look, our eyes met and locked. He was looking straight at me, and I immediately recognized the look. There was no mistaking it, though it usually came from an older man, not from someone my own age.

In answer to my questioning glance, he boldly shifted his gaze down to my dick, then brought his eyes up to meet mine again. Unable to meet his look, I lowered my eyes, only to find myself examining his dick. Without even the pretense of urinating, he was merely holding himself. As I watched, his dick began swelling out with no coaxing on his part. It gave a heavy dip before slowly rearing up; the fingers gripped it more tightly and encouraged it with a few slow strokes.

As I gazed at its steady rise, I felt the rude shock of cold porcelain. My own dick had gotten erect so fast I didn't have time to think of stepping back from the urinal. And still I couldn't pull my eyes away from his dick. There was a dream-like sense of unreality to the whole thing. A moment ago I had been sitting in the library; now I was displaying myself to a complete stranger.

Who was he? I couldn't remember seeing him before. It was possible I'd passed him in the hallway any number of times without paying the least attention. He had the looks one might see anywhere: sandy blond hair, pale blue eyes, light, colorless lashes, freckles. He was an anonymous student, unremarkable in every way, just another face in the crowd. Yet in this brief interval, I already had the impression that I'd known him from some period in my life far, far back.

Time was standing perilously still. I felt as if we were having a silent conversation; he wanted me to make a move but I didn't want to. I was playing a game whose rules I didn't know. I'd heard that this sort of thing happened sometimes, but had only half believed in it, never thinking it would happen to me.

I was afraid of continuing this dangerous game, yet at the same time didn't want it to end.

I listened intently for sounds from outside, but all was quiet. Without looking away from my eyes, he reached for my dick and gripped it. Instinctively I reached down to cover his hand with my own. I felt myself being stroked, and found myself stroking along with him.

Though this was like something out of one of my sexual fantasies, in fact there was a mechanical, lifeless air to the whole thing which was far from erotic. Perhaps it was my tenseness, but all I could feel was a baffled amazement at the incongruity of its happening to me right now, right here in school.

His manner seemed so assured that I was certain he'd done this often before. How many others had there been? And how had he known I might not be averse to being approached? Did I have a look which gave me away — was there a certain something in my face or eyes which singled me out?

Suddenly a door slammed somewhere and we both froze — but it was far off, and after listening intently for a moment he resumed his movements.

I felt a strange calmness come over me, even the luxury of giving myself up to enjoyment. My hand dropped away from his; I let him have complete control. With his fingers he lightly stroked my balls, and the ball of his thumb gently teased the underside of my glans, the part where it felt best. My dick gave several involuntary twitches.

I was beginning to lose my resistance... my mask was slowly melting...

And then the restroom door opened. Instantly he was standing at the far urinal with all the appearance of just zipping up. I, too, after the initial shock, found myself feigning the same. But the sound we'd heard had come from the women's room next door, magnified by our hair-trigger alertness and the intense silence of our activity. In any case, a large wooden blind just within the entrance shielded the inner room from immediate view. I felt weak with relief.

But almost immediately after, the door swung open, this time the men's room for sure. Just as someone walked in past the blind, my partner melted away, grabbing his books and slipping outside. We hadn't once looked at each other since the first scare. Shocked back into strangers, we'd reverted to our former aloofness. Already the brief encounter seemed like a dream, fading away like a half-forgotten vision.

The boy who'd entered looked lost and confused, bustling around trying to find a dry place to put his books. When he found one, he proceeded to noisily wash his hands at the sink and dry them off with a paper towel.

Standing at the next sink combing my hair, I watched him in the mirror until he locked himself in the far stall. Then I filled the sink with cold water and splashed some onto my face.

I could hear people outside in the library, but for a long time was afraid to step out there again. I didn't want to meet the boy with whom I'd had my encounter.

The toilet in the far stall flushed, and as if in delayed reaction, my hands began to tremble. From there the trembling spread throughout my body, until I was shaking like a leaf. I imagined shimmering ripples radiating outward from me, passing through the restroom walls, spreading out across the campus, to the far ends of the universe.

6

Even after I'd gotten back to the safety of my dorm room, I still felt shaken by the encounter. Now that a little time had passed, it seemed more like a dream than ever, like something I'd imagined.

I decided to work out with the dumbbells for a little while to clear my mind. Just as I'd taken them out from under my bed, a sudden knocking on the door almost made my heart stop.

"Who is it?" I called out.

A voice I didn't recognize answered. For an insane moment, I imagined it was the boy from the restroom, who'd followed me here.

In dread, I opened the door. It was a boy I'd never seen before.

"Can I help you?" I said.

"Is this where Jonesy lives?"

"Yeah. But he's not in right now."

He thrust a handful of photographs at me. "These are his. Could you give them to him?"

I took them. "Where'd you get them?"

"He sold me his camera last week. But he must have forgot there was still half a roll of film left in it. So I shot the rest of the roll and developed his pics for him."

"I'll make sure he gets them," I said.

"He owes me about 50 cents, but I'll let it slide. He sold me the camera pretty cheap."

After he left, I looked at the photographs. Strangely, there wasn't a single picture of Jonesy, though there were many of Kruk, and some people who looked like Kruk's parents.

I walked down the hall and knocked on Kruk's door. He came to the door right away, almost as if he'd been waiting for my knock.

"Oh, hi, Guy. What's up?"

"Do these look familiar?" I handed him a few photos.

He glanced at one, then peered at it more closely. He flipped through the rest, then grabbed the entire batch out of my hand.

"Where'd you get them?" he asked.

"From a guy who bought a camera off Jonesy."

"These are from my stolen camera."

"What?"

We stared at each other for a sickening moment and then Kruk whispered: "Jonesy is the thief." His voice was shaking.

My first thought was: Impossible. But the more I thought about it, the more likely it became. So that was where Jonesy had gotten all his partying money. As it sank in, I felt the blood drain from my face, and then a wretched feeling settled in the pit of my stomach. I felt a little sick.

"He didn't even bother to take the film out," said Kruk. "I can't believe it. He left the friggin' film inside."

Kruk and I continued to look at each other blankly.

"We'd better tell the other guys," I said.

"I'm going to the campus police," he said.

I went back to my room and made a quick inspection of my effects. As far as I could tell, there was nothing missing, but the thought of Jonesy going through my things looking for something gave me a creepy feeling.

Ever since Kruk had first told me about a possible thief, more things had been disappearing from our floor — watches, rings, money. An air of suspicion had fallen over the dorm. Reports were made to the campus police each time a new theft occurred, and they filed the reports and made lists of the missing objects, but we knew nothing more would come of it. Such cases were quite common, they said, and it was almost impossible to catch the culprits.

Now it would be different. Kruk had firsthand evidence.

I looked over at Jonesy's side of the room. It looked the same as ever. Nothing was different, yet there was a strange feeling of change in the room's atmosphere.

Now that I'd discovered another, hidden aspect of Jonesy, suddenly the boy I'd known all along seemed false. And strangely, it was I who felt ashamed and embarrassed about it. A hidden part of his personality had been exposed, and it was like glimpsing a part of him which shouldn't have been seen, as if I'd accidentally stumbled into the bathroom while he was defecating.

I wasn't angry; he'd stolen nothing of mine. But the fact that he'd stolen things from the other guys on the floor meant that I could no longer talk with him. He was no longer one of us.

But even as I fought to master my disgust, this new, sinister Jonesy began to exert a strange attractiveness for me. His outcast status evoked a tenderness in me toward him. Mingled with my repugnance was a queer feeling of kinship with him.

I felt restless sitting in my room. If Jonesy were to come back I wouldn't know what to say to him, or how to act toward him. A sudden dread filled me. I realized I was afraid of facing him. I didn't want to be here when he came back tonight.

I put away my dumbbells and slipped on my windbreaker. I knew Christine would be in her room studying, and she wouldn't mind if I stayed over.

As I suspected, she was at her books when I got there.

"Guy, what's the matter? You look like you've seen a ghost."

"Christine, it was Jonesy. Jonesy was the thief."

"Oh, no." Her face blanched. "So that was where he got all his money for partying."

"I guess so."

"He *has* been acting strangely recently. His drinking's been getting out of hand. And remember what I told you that time?"

She was referring to her suspicions that Jonesy had been making a play for her, disguising it as friendship. He had called her apartment a few times when he knew I wouldn't be there. We both knew he'd had an infatuation for her ever since I first introduced them; he hadn't made a secret of it. In fact, it was a joke between us: if I didn't watch out, he'd steal her away from me.

I let out my breath. "He had his bad points, I guess. But we did have a lot of fun together, especially in the early days. You wouldn't believe some of the stunts he pulled."

"You talk of him in the past tense already."

"Now that he's known as a thief, it's impossible for him to stay in the dorm. There's no telling how someone might retaliate. He's finished."

"Sounds like the wild west or something. The world of macho codes."

"It's hard to believe I only met him three months ago. The dorm will sure be different without him."

"Why don't you move out?"

"What?"

"Nobody says you have to live there." She began fingering her hair searching for split ends. "When you live in a dorm, you have to live with all the risks which come with communal living."

"What are you getting at?" But I knew already what she was leading up to. She had the tired look on her face which she always got whenever she brought up a topic she knew I wanted to avoid. "You mean about us living together," I said, dumbly.

"Mm-hm."

It was a topic which was coming up between us with greater and greater frequency, especially since Christine's room-mate, Nancy, was considering moving in with *her* boyfriend.

There had been a time when it was I who was pushing for the idea of living together. When we were first going out, I'd fondly dreamed of a domestic arrangement — probably out of homesickness more than anything else. In addition, there had been the desire to impress the guys in the dorm: it was considered the ultimate sign of manhood to live with a girl. But now I realized that such an arrangement would never work for me. I'd grown much too fond of living in the dorm. And I needed my freedom.

"I don't know, Christine. I'm worried that if we lived together, I might not be able to concentrate on my studies."

"That's an excuse and you know it. If you can study in that dorm, you'd be able to study anywhere. This quiet apartment is much more suited to study, if that's what's worrying you."

She was right, of course. But I disliked it when she tried to force her way with me. Our relationship as it was satisfied me, and I couldn't understand why she wanted more. Meeting two or three times a week was fine with me. I couldn't imagine seeing her every day, no matter how much she meant to me. It would be like we were married, and that was something I didn't want.

"Will you give me time to think about it, Chrissie?"

"That's what you always say. I don't see what there is to think about. Either you want to live together or not. It seems pretty straight-forward to me."

There was an almost desperate look on her face which I'd rarely seen, and it frightened me. I knew she was only voicing her feelings out of love, yet I detected a spitefulness coming from her, even a desire to hurt me. I hated her when she was like this; she was ugly.

"It isn't like I'm asking you to marry me," she said. "If it doesn't work out, we can always go back to the way things were. What are you afraid of, Guy? You make it seem like imprisonment or something."

"I don't know. Maybe I'm a little afraid it *won't* work out. Maybe I'm afraid it'll be what breaks us up."

"Don't you want to grow up? I mean, look at the guys in the dorm. They're just kids, a bunch of childish babies. You're so much more mature than them."

Was she jealous of the dorm? I laughed. "We're only nine-teen, after all, Chrissie. I want to have fun, too. Living with the guys has its good moments."

"I'm sure it does."

"Why do you feel so insecure, Christine? You make it sound like you're worried about my feelings for you. You know I love you. Our living together isn't going to change that."

"I know," she said, and a worried look crossed her face. She herself had confessed that she was a little dismayed at the strength of her own desire for domesticity. She'd never before wanted to live with a guy until she met me. I, on the other hand, was growing more resistant to being tied down — I wanted endless possibilities in life. To settle down with a woman was to concede that those possibilities were limited, restricted.

"Look, I wish you hadn't brought this up just now, Christine. I just found out my room-mate is a thief, and here you are already making arrangements for my future. Hell, if I move out now, the guys might think I'm the thief. They'll mix it up in their minds when they think back over it."

She laughed. "I'm sorry, Guy. I get like this sometimes. It must be hell going with me."

"No it isn't. Not at all." I grinned. "Listen, Chrissie, after having refused your offer to move in with you, this might seem cheeky, but I have a little favor to ask."

"Sure. What is it?"

"Can I spend the night over tonight? I don't know if I can face Jonesy, knowing what I do about him."

She raised her fist and made as if to strike me, but she was only joking. She sighed. "Sure. I understand. But I'm gonna be up half the night studying for my midterm."

"That's all right. I'll probably sack out while you hit the books."

I was glad to be able to be alone with my thoughts, not only about Jonesy, but about my encounter in the restroom with the unknown boy. Too many things were happening at once. Christine's room was a sanctuary from it all.

I took up a book and lay down on the bed to read, but Christine seemed unable to concentrate at her desk. As if she'd been thinking it over for a while, she asked me without turning around:

"Guy, am I being a bitch?"

I sat up, concerned by the undertone of seriousness in her question. "No, you're not being a bitch. Why do you say such a thing?"

"Well, one wants to know these things." She shrugged.

Her pretended unconcern touched me. "Look at me, Christine." She turned around. "We've always said we wanted openness in our relationship, right? And you were only voicing your true wishes. And I was voicing my own." And then I became a little bolder. "And anyway, does it look to you like I think you're a bitch?" I lay there on my side and saw her glance flicker down to my lap. Now that all the excitement of the day had wound down and I was relaxed, an unasked-for erection had blossomed during our talk.

She smiled. "I don't know. Let me get a better look."

"What about your mid-terms?"

"That can wait." She pushed her book aside.

"And Nancy?"

"She's spending the night with David."

As she came over to the bed, I undid my jeans and pulled them down, then unbuttoned my shirt and took it off.

She lay down alongside me and put her arms around me. As

always, the contrast between her fully-clothed body and my complete nudity intensified my arousal. Unlike with Peter, I could allow my excitement to blossom unchecked. I felt her clothes against my skin as she pressed herself against me and then the moist warmth of her mouth sought mine.

Some of the girls I'd been with had claimed that kissing gave them more pleasure than the sexual act itself. Often I'd kissed girls for — seemingly — hours on end, until their lips grew hot and their bodies trembled. I'd been told by them that most boys can't kiss a girl for very long, for they become so aroused that they want to get to 'the real thing' as quickly as possible. Unlike those straight boys, however, I could control my emotions long enough for the girl to get as much pleasure as she liked from kissing.

I helped Christine out of her clothes, and soon we were locked in our familiar embrace, with me sitting cross-legged and her on my lap, my dick deep inside her. I usually started out by not moving at all, just kissing her and caressing her all over with my hands. In Christine's case, because she was so self-conscious about the smallness of her breasts, I concentrated most of my caresses on them, rhythmically kneading them and gently pinching their nipples, leaning down to kiss and suck at them. Only after she made it clear that she couldn't stand it anymore did I push her back onto the bed and begin pumping into her with long, slow thrusts.

In high school, after my initial dismay at encountering a girl's body, I gradually forced myself to learn to like it, as I was resigned to the possibility that it would be all I could ever have. And perhaps a part of me was hoping that after enough times, I could 'cure' myself of my more powerful homosexual inclination. And still another factor was that I wanted to prove to the straight world — who would have crucified me for my true inclinations — that I was every bit as good as the straights, that I could compete with them at their game, even better them at it. If I couldn't have what I really wanted, I might as well put up with what I could, and make the most of it. At any rate, I accepted the fact that I would have to at least be able to pretend heterosexuality. My first few times were clumsy, but I gradually learned the geography of a girl's body.

My lack of true passion gave me a certain clinical detachment in my explorations, and this in turn allowed me the objectivity that most boys were denied. Most of them, no doubt, became so overwhelmed by the feel of her naked skin against theirs, the taste of her lips, that they couldn't keep back the rising tide of orgasm, which erupted much too soon, just when she was becoming aroused. Unlike those boys, however, I was able to last much longer, my secret sobriety allowing me to concentrate on *her* pleasure. It usually takes women so much longer to achieve gratification — even after a long session of kissing and fondling — that I really can't blame those men who are unable to hold out that long.

So I got a reputation among certain girls as the experienced one, the mature one. Little did they realize that I was only using the whole thing as a cover-up: going out with girl after girl and almost mechanically going through the motions, playing the numbers game, ranking the girls according to my own system of values, judging them by physical beauty, degree of sexual passion, the extent of their emotional involvement with me. Above all, I loved the irony of the fact that I, who had no true passion for girls, probably had the reputation in my school as the most mature and skillful lover.

Boys would sometimes confide to me that they didn't know if their girlfriends had orgasms or not. They were either afraid to ask or worried that they would be lied to if they did. For some reason I had much more open communication with my girls, and I'd learned that most of them really weren't as much concerned about orgasm as the boys thought. What they cared more about was being held by a boy they loved, and giving him pleasure.

Christine, always the eager explorer, had discovered orgasm when she was 16, through clitoral masturbation. She'd excitedly told her friends about this but most of them, to her surprise, were loathe to try the experiment, either through prudery or fear. She herself found nothing wrong with masturbation; sometimes during our lovemaking, she would openly caress herself. Or I would caress her clitoris for her. I knew just the right touch she liked — it was different for every girl.

Tonight, though, she seemed happy with standard coitus. Her lips had drawn back and I could see her teeth clenched together hard. The muscles in her neck were corded and she was emitting short, powerful gasps. Usually, the sight of a girl's sexual excitement left me cold, even blunted my own. Christine had been the first with whom I normally didn't have to resort to mental substitutes for the final effort, but tonight my mind was too stimulated to do otherwise.

I pulled her legs up behind my hips, then pushed myself up off my knees, balancing all my weight upon my toes for a more steeply angled pivot. As her loosely crossed ankles came to rest on my buttocks, I began thrusting into her, harder, deeper, and faster. My motions caused her heels to rub rhythmically against my buttocks in a caressing manner.

I thought about Jonesy, and how he'd crept into other boys' rooms and fondled their valuables. This vision was somehow linked with the boy I'd encountered in the restroom today, whose naked erection had been so brazenly exposed to my view. The two images merged in my mind, and I had a vivid picture of Jonesy mischievously pumping his dick at me. It was going to be good. It was going to be very good.

Christine had given up any attempt at suppressing her cries. I listened to them absently for a moment before giving myself up completely to the pictures in my mind.

The next morning I had to go back to my dorm to get my books for class. As I was about to unlock the door to my room and step inside, I heard sounds coming from within. It had to be Jonesy, packing his things to leave.

He seemed to be in the shower room taking out his toothbrush, soap, shaving gear.

I listened intently, dreading the prospect of meeting him. Would he say good-bye? Or should I? Didn't I at least owe him that? Yet I was afraid of what the others would think. It would be like a betrayal, when he'd hurt so many of them. Leaving my post at the door, I quietly made my way down to the lounge. For about fifteen minutes I pretended to watch television, imagining I could hear the sounds of his packing. And then I heard a door opening, then shutting. Footsteps came down the hallway. I felt my eyeballs get hot.

But he didn't come to the lounge.

After a decent interval had passed, I stepped out into the hallway and went down to Kruk's room and knocked on his door. When he came to answer it, he looked drawn.

"What's up?" I asked.

"Jonesy just left."

"Yeah, I know. I heard him from out in the hall. But I didn't say anything to him. Did you see him?"

"Yeah. I cracked open my door so I could get a look. And he

saw me, too."

"Was he alone?"

"Yeah. He was lugging a suitcase and a box. There was a taxi waiting for him outside."

"Did he say anything? Any last words?"

"Nothing."

"No contrition, no excuses, no anger? He just left?"

"That's right. He couldn't even look me in the face."

I felt a sense of letdown, of having been cheated. Perhaps I had wanted drama — some indication of the impact he'd made on our lives. After all, he had been the virtual leader of the floor, the one who organized things, got things going, the life of every party. He'd been here since the beginning, was the first guy I'd met when I came here. And now he was gone from our lives. It was hard to believe, or accept.

I left Kruk and went to my own room. Except for Jonesy's bed, the night table, and the study desk, everything had been cleared away. His side of the room still looked dirty. There were tiny holes in the wall, left by the thumb tacks where pin-ups had hung; beer rings had hardened on the window ledge. He'd left behind a huge stack of men's magazines in the closet. I picked one up at random and idly flipped through it, then tossed it down.

I had to get to English class.

Part Two: Terra Incognita

1

I found out who 'H. Golden' was, the mysterious person who liked to check out gay books. I was looking for courses to take in the coming winter term when I came across his name in the course catalog; he was a professor at the college.

Apparently Harold Golden taught Western Art History, among other subjects. I knew instinctively that he had to be the one, and felt a little let down. I had wanted to keep him in my imagination as a young, attractive athlete.

I checked the Underground Guide to find out what kind of instructor he was. Written by past students of the school, this mimeographed publication put out by the student union rated all the instructors on campus, telling how difficult they were, whether they were interesting lecturers, how tough they were at grading, and how to pass their classes.

Professor Golden was apparently well thought of by former students. As a lecturer he was rated 'excellent', and his courses were in high demand. His Western Art History class was especially popular among students majoring in non-art fields, such as Engineering, P-Chem, and pre-med. For them, the course was interesting and, at the same time, satisfied the art requirement they needed for graduation. Athletes also favored the course; for them, it was highly recommended.

I decided to drop in on one of his lectures to see how 'H. Golden' looked.

My first sight of him was a disappointment. Perhaps I'd built him up too much in my imagination, but the middle-aged professor wearing old-fashioned glasses wasn't quite what I'd come to expect. Unlike some of the younger instructors, whose hairstyles and clothes made them virtually indistinguishable from their students, Professor Golden was immaculately groomed and dressed. There was an air of old-world culture about him, even though apparently he was from someplace in Indiana. With his gold-rimmed glasses and goatee, he seemed quite cosmopolitan, a little out of place in this university.

In any case, the lecture hall was packed. Unlike most of my other courses, in which by the end of fall term half of the students had dropped out, his class showed no signs that attendance had diminished at all.

It was easy to see why: his lecture was fascinating. Quite apart from what he was discussing — in this case the art of the Weimar Period, with music from the era softly accompanying his slide presentation — his voice was mesmerizing. It was deep, soothing, and authoritative, somewhat like a doctor's, and I wished it would go on and on. And his absorption in the topic was so infectious that I noticed students sitting on the edges of their chairs — students who probably normally wouldn't have been interested in art at all. The hour that I spent listening to him was like a wonderful time trip into a glamorous past.

When the class was over, even after most of the students had left, there was still a small crowd around him, eager to ask more questions. He was apparently something like a sage for these hangers-on. Perhaps it was the distance they felt from him which gave him this special aura, and I could understand their feeling, for he seemed so different from anyone I'd ever met before.

I wondered how many of his students knew he was gay. This secret knowledge had colored some of the things he'd said; a brief mention he'd made of the beauty of Michelangelo's David was for me tinged by the knowledge that he undoubtedly found the statue as sexually exciting as I did.

However, as I listened in on his talk with the students, I discovered that he made no secret of his gayness. I caught the word 'homosexual' just as I joined the circle gathered around his lectern. One of the boys was asking him about a book called *Maurice*, by E. M. Forster.

"I've read some of his other books," said the boy, "but they didn't interest me at all. I thought they were kind of boring. Flatulent. I've never understood why the critics regard him so highly."

Golden had been putting his notes into order, and now he put them aside and looked animatedly at the students around him. "A thing about literary criticism you have to understand is that there are certain academics who seem to feel that the more boring and obscure a book is, the deeper it is. Apart from Forster's other books, with which I feel you're being a little too harsh, what did you feel about *Maurice?*"

"It seemed a bit corny to me."

"Well, you have to understand the times in which it was written. Remember, when Forster was a young man, homosexuality was actually a prisonable offense. So you can easily understand why he remained a closet homosexual all his life, and why he didn't dare publish *Maurice* in his lifetime — which is a pity, because I think it's quite a good novel. He did leave instructions for it to be published after his death, though. But by that time his treatment of the subject had become rather passé. When he first wrote it, it was no doubt a daringly straightforward and honest portrayal of a homosexual love affair, but by today's standards, it's almost quaint. After all, by the time of his death, in 1970, we had seen the publication of writers like Burroughs, Vidal, Rechy, and Genet, who are much more explicit in their depictions of sexuality."

"Who's Genet?" asked one boy.

"A French writer who's still alive, though he hasn't written anything for quite some time now. He wrote in the 1940s, and his work was translated into English in the 1960s."

"What sort of stuff did he write?"

"He wrote five novels, dense with a rich, poetic prose, about his life in prison, about his — "

"He was in prison?"

"Yes, in fact, he wrote most of his books in prison. The rules of the prison forbade any form of creative writing, so he had to write his works on paper bags which he tore into page-sized sheets. Several times these works were discovered by prison officials and destroyed. But enough survived — and was published on the outside — to make his name well-known among the reading public. Finally, thanks to the efforts of some of France's leading literary figures — who rated his work quite highly — the government gave him a pardon."

"What did he go to prison for?"

"Well, theft. Before he went to prison, though, he spent much of his youth in and out of homes for juvenile delinquents. As an orphan he never knew who his real parents were. He grew up in foster homes, but didn't seem to be able to live the straight life. He grew up in the streets, learning to fight and steal in order to survive. As a young boy, he spent a lot of time in a succession of reform schools, and from them he just sort of graduated into adult prisons."

"And he wrote about all this?"

"Yes. But not in straightforward prose. His novels are a mixture of dreams, fantasies, sexual longings, as well as hard reality. He describes some of his criminal activities in *Confessions of a Thief*. But it's in his writing about his homosexuality that he reaches his greatest heights. He'd always been gay, but the special atmosphere of prison, which fosters ritualized homosexual relationships, appealed to his needs. His first book, *Our Lady of the Flowers*, gives wonderfully poetic, almost mystical descriptions of his sexual activities and fantasies. You can easily imagine how confinement in prison had enriched and deepened his fantasy life. It was his one method of escape from the grim realities around him."

"But he's out of prison now, right?"

"Yes. Maybe that's the reason why he seems to have fallen silent. But though he has become a free man, Genet always seems to wear the aura of an outlaw, someone who lives outside all normal bounds. That is his special appeal. His being homosexual, and suffering society's ostracism for it, only gave more impetus to the distrust and contempt he feels toward straight society. And by 'straight,' I mean straight in the jargon of both homosexuals and criminals."

"Which book of his do you recommend?"

"They're all good — *Our Lady of the Flowers, Confessions of a Thief, Miracle of the Rose, Querelle of Brest* — but I like *Funeral Rites* best."

I saw several students scribble these titles in their notebooks.

"Who were those other writers you mentioned?" asked a girl.

"Well, another interesting character is William S. Burroughs, who, though he never went to prison, was fascinated by the underworld. Perhaps as a result of his fascination, he began experimenting with drugs, almost willingly becoming a heroin addict in the process. Remember, as a young man, he lived in a time when drugs were almost exclusively linked with the shady underworld and jazz musicians. His experience as an addict gave him the materials for a series of books which form a searing indictment of American society. The world of Burroughs is the world of horror comics and bizarre science fiction — of paranoia, government conspiracies and erotic perversion. His style is a surrealistic blend of the most advanced literary experiments with popular genre fiction such as science fiction, hard-boiled detective novels, westerns, pornography. The result is a grotesque mirror world of our own society. His satire is keen and biting, though some of his descriptive passages are pure poetry. At one point, he was involved with literary experiments which he called cut-up. By actually cutting up a page of his writing and piecing it together in random patterns designed to give insights into a deeper reality, he was trying to produce the equivalent of cubism in literature. But he failed, and those are his least readable works. I still think the homoerotic parts of his books are some of the most erotic writing I've ever read. He presents a tough, masculine homosexuality which I hadn't come across until I'd read *Junky, Naked Lunch*, and other works by him."

I felt a shiver go through me. He was echoing exactly my own feelings about the 'good parts' in Burroughs's books. How many of the others here had read those passages? By now, our number had dwindled until only five of us remained. His eyes had lingered on mine a number of times during his talk, and though he spoke to all of us, I felt that his words were directed at me alone. It was like listening to a private lesson arranged for my benefit. Yet the other four students seemed just as fascinated as I.

Golden's student assistant had long ago put away the slide projector and tape recorder used for the lecture, and had left. But the professor himself seemed in no mood to halt his flow of talk. "Another interesting homosexual was the Japanese author Yukio Mishima."

"Isn't he the guy who committed hara-kiri? I didn't know he was gay."

"He wrote two books which deal with homosexuality: *Confessions of a Mask* and *Forbidden Colors*. Though I find Mishima's prose rather too baroque and ornate for my taste, the straightforward way he deals with homosexual themes was rather refreshing when I first read him as a boy. He was more into the sado-masochistic aspects of sex, obsessed with pain, mutilation, and death."

"Ugh."

Golden grinned. He seemed to take a boyish delight in seeing the students' shocked faces. Though they pretended to be mature and open-minded about his matter-of-fact acceptance of homosexuality, I knew most of them probably felt as I did, that we were flirting dangerously with the dark specters of our own demons.

"Well, he experienced his first orgasm while looking at a reproduction of Guido Reni's painting of St. Sebastian, showing the young martyr's death scene where he's bound half-naked to a tree and shot full of arrows. In a sense, that picture became the motif of Mishima's whole life: eroticism became bound up in a violent and beautiful death. Maybe because he was such a romantic, he never really outgrew his boyish dreams. He idealized manliness to an almost parodistic degree, and took up body-building because he was ashamed of his weak, intellectual's body. By the time he was in his thirties, he was so proud of his muscles that he posed for a series of nude and semi-nude photographs. In his forties he became an extreme Japanese nationalist, but I think what excited him about the Japanese past was its tough, samurai idealism, a manly, stoic philosophy which honors endurance of pain and discomfort. I don't think he was deeply into the political aspects of Emperor worship. Be that as it may, he started a private para-military group, the Society of Shields, dedicated to the glory of the Emperor. He designed its uniforms himself, and was successful in recruiting a group of young men, mostly right-wing college students, to wear them. All of this was his preparation for the climax of his life — his own glorious death. And it had to be both violent and beautiful if it was to be the work of art he wanted it to be."

"When was this?" asked a boy.

"In 1970, coincidentally, the same year E. M. Forster died. What a world of difference between the two writers, though. The only thing linking them is their homosexuality and their dedication to literature."

"How did Mishima die?" asked another boy impatiently.

Golden smiled. "He attempted to stage a *coup d'état* at a Japanese Self-Defense Force base with a group of his followers. His idea was to incite the Self Defense Forces into action on behalf of the Emperor. He probably knew it was doomed to failure. But it gave him the excuse he needed; he took responsibility for his failure in the age-old Japanese way — he committed ritual suicide, disemboweling himself with a short sword. Immediately after, one of his followers, said by some to be his lover, chopped off his head with a longer sword. Mishima had always said that he didn't want to grow old — he wanted to die while still in the prime of his manhood, while he still had a beautiful body. He was forty-five years old when he staged his suicide. That morning, he had turned in to his publisher the last pages of the novel many consider his masterpiece. I think his suicide was, in the end, the culmination of his belief that death is the ultimate orgasm. With that dramatic climax, he'd turned his own life into his greatest novel. The moment of his death witnessed the apotheosis of his political, literary, *and* sexual philosophies."

We were all silent for a time after this; then a bookish-looking boy said:

"My literature classes are never this fun. Why don't they teach us about writers like this in school, instead of making us read boring classics?"

"There's nothing boring about the classics. And anyway, quite a few of them were written by gay men. Didn't your teachers ever make you read *Moby Dick*?"

"Of course. It's probably the greatest American novel. But are you saying Herman Melville was gay?"

"Oh yes. I recommend you read a book of his called *Pierre*. You'll find it quite revealing."

At this point the boy standing to my right made his first contribution. "It gives a whole other aspect to a writer's work, to know he's gay. I mean, none of the teachers in high school, or in college for that matter, really gets into that aspect of it. But it seems to me that a writer's sexual orientation would have a tremendous lot to do with how he perceives the world."

"Exactly," smiled Golden, obviously pleased. "When I was young, such things were hushed up. In the case of heterosexual writers and poets, there was no problem telling about their passionate love affairs with women, even married women. In fact, it somehow added spice to their legends. But in the case of gay writers, whose romances were just as passionate, love affairs were hushed up or re-labelled. Perhaps he had 'a very close friendship', or 'a lifelong devotion to a friend'. Or he was 'a confirmed bachelor not known to have had any passionate attachments'. In fact, these loves were often secret out of necessity, due to society's attitudes at the time. However, later scholars often continued the deception, covering up what they felt was a shameful secret which would only besmirch their subject's honor. It's only recently that scholars feel free to tell about a gay writer's sexual life. Take Walt Whitman, for instance."

"What? The Good Gray Poet?"

"None other. In many of his poems he's quite open about his love for men and the beauty of their bodies. And the physical nature of this love is not left in doubt." He raised his head slightly as he recited:

> "But just possibly with you on a high hill, first watching
> lest any person for miles around approach unawares
> "Or possibly with you sailing at sea, or on the beach of
> the sea or some quiet island
> "Here to put your lips upon mine I permit you
> "With the comrade's long-dwelling kiss or the new
> husband's kiss
> "For I am the new husband and I am the comrade."

He looked around at all of us, and his eyes met mine, and briefly held. I felt my heart beat faster. I had made no contribution to the discussion, though I felt on the verge of doing so several times. I was a little afraid that he would discover I wasn't registered in his class, not even auditing it. Or perhaps I had the irrational fear that he would recognize my voice from the time I'd called him anonymously from the phone booth outside the library. Or maybe it was just that I didn't want to reveal how fascinated I was by all this talk about gay writers.

He was still talking about Whitman. "Maybe he was able to 'get away with it' for such a long time because his love seemed to reach out beyond men and embrace everything: women, children, animals, the sky, the sea, the rolling plains, the mountains, the stars. I guess people thought his love of the male body was just a part of that vast cosmic love. He lived in a time which was more naive — perhaps more pure. For example, he would kiss his men friends on the mouth in greeting. This was thought to be a sign of his affectionate nature, his warm-lovingness — that he made no distinctions between men and women. Arm in arm with his comrades and all that. But in fact, his primary sexual orientation was gay. Though he was born in Brooklyn, he built up an image of himself as a 'rough-hewn son of the frontier,' and wore workmen's clothes, didn't shave, and was bluff and hearty in manner. He loved working class men above all. He would cruise them on the streetcar, downtown, or by the docks. Strictly speaking, he was not gay in the sense we mean today, but if you read some of his poems, you can see that he accepted his homosexuality and was proud of it in an open, honest way. His collection of poems, *Leaves of Grass*, is his masterpiece, and he often said his favorite part of that work was the section called 'Calamus.' This was where some of his most sexual poems were gathered. The calamus — or flag iris, as it is sometimes called — was his favorite flower. Look."

He went to the blackboard and, picking up a piece of chalk, sketched a flower. Its petals were flat and pointed, but a long, cylindrical stamen jutted up from its middle in the unmistakable shape of an erect penis.

"What does that remind you of?"

We laughed nervously.

He smiled at our discomfort briefly before erasing the picture he'd drawn. "I guess you can see why he'd have a special fondness for this flower."

He glanced at his watch and began putting his notes away into his briefcase. Then he looked up.

"Say, if any of you are interested, I'm planning to start an independent study group on gay studies. There are no credits involved, though eventually I'd like to introduce it into the school's curriculum. We'll probably meet at my house and I'll give a little talk, and afterwards we'll have a discussion session, over dinner or wine."

He looked right at me.

"Don't feel intimidated. You don't have to be gay to attend. Straight people, both men and women, are free to attend."

He smiled and, snapping his briefcase shut, gave us a little wave before walking away. I felt as if in that brief moment, he had seen deep into my heart, and that the invitation was meant for me alone.

2

On the way back to the dorm, I kept wondering why Golden had singled me out for the invitation. When coupled with my experience with the boy in the restroom, it was beginning to seem that there might be something about me which sent out a secret signal to other gays.

Was I being paranoid? I looked around at the other students walking about on campus, seemingly without any cares in the world.

I'd never again seen that boy who'd fondled me in the restroom, though I was still on the lookout for him. The truth was, I was afraid of running into him. After seeing the heedlessness he'd exhibited, I knew there was a good chance he already had some sort of reputation in the school.

There had been an unmistakable air of desperation about his act, as if he were an incurable addict giving in to a sinful craving. But no matter how desperate he might be, surely he wouldn't be completely indiscriminate about whom he chose to approach. After all, he was taking the risk of getting beaten up by any boy who wasn't sympathetic. To be safe, he would have to be certain that the proposed partner was, if not a gay, at least a potential one, or someone who would keep his mouth shut.

I had fit the bill perfectly. And even though it had been he who had instigated the encounter, I had, after my initial hesitation, actively participated. Even now, I often relived the experience in my mind, centering in on the little details I had missed while it was happening. I embroidered new fantasies upon what had happened. It now seemed much more erotic than it had actually been. Would it ever happen again? If so, where? When?

It was getting harder to deny that I was secretly hoping for another such encounter. In fact, in the past week or two, I'd begun visiting the men's rooms throughout the campus, dropping in even when I didn't feel the need. I had studied the campus map in order to learn where they were all located, and tried to visit each one on the chance that I might meet a similar experience.

I noticed a lot of gay graffiti in many of the toilet stalls — crude drawings of exaggeratedly enlarged penises, or of two boys embracing in the sixty-nine position. These graffiti were like codewords inviting the initiated to complete a vast, complicated but invisible puzzle. They were evidence of lonely, frustrated boys full of pent-up lusts, masturbating for quick thrills as I had done many a time.

There was one toilet stall in the recreation building which even had an explicit invitation on the wall: *Like boys? Meet me here Friday nite at 11:30. Knock 3 times.* I wondered what would happen if I 'accidentally' passed through one evening just to see if anything actually happened there at that time. But I feared some queer-hating jock who'd read the message might be waiting to ambush someone. It might even be a false message, a bait to lure some poor guy to a beating.

But the graffiti were secret hints of the extent of the invisible gay population in school. Like an archeologist seeking clues to the existence of a long-lost civilization, I tracked down these tantalizing tidbits, no matter how unlikely the spot. And when I found anything at all, I was reassured by the evidence that there were so many others like me out there.

When I got back to the dorm, I noticed my door was open. For a wild moment I thought Jonesy had come back, though he was officially expelled from school. He'd just dropped out of our lives, seemingly forever. For me, the discovery that he was a thief had added mysterious depths to his character that I would now never be able to explore. When Professor Golden was talking about the French writer Jean Genet, I'd been thinking about my former room-mate.

There was a new boy standing at Jonesy's desk putting his books in order. An open suitcase lay on the bed. The bed looked neater than I'd ever seen it; through the open window the afternoon sun shone on it in a refreshingly new way. Somehow I'd always thought of Jonesy's side of the room as being dark.

"Hi," I said.

He turned around and in the instant our eyes met, I felt as if I'd known him from a long, long time ago, in some far-off land.

He came toward me a little shyly, extending his hand. Though he seemed a quiet type, his eyes looked straight into mine as he firmly grasped my hand and shook it.

"My name's Scott."

He was about my height — six feet tall — with curly black hair and light blue eyes. The eyes were what held my attention. They were large and soulful, and hinted of artistic sensibilities. As if to confirm this, his skin was very fair, a shade too delicate for a boy, though it didn't make him seem effeminate in any way. He was of medium build and carried himself lightly, as long-distance runners do. He was very attractive.

"My name's Guy Willard." I sat down on his bed. "Do you need any help moving in?"

"No thanks. I've already unpacked everything I need."

"When did you get in?"

"Just an hour ago. With a suitcase and a box of books; I travel light." He smiled, looking around the room as if he still couldn't believe he were here.

"So what do you think of your new room?" I asked.

"It's great. You should have seen the place I was living in till now. One of those rundown apartments down by Parkside Theater. The location wasn't so bad, but the rent was just a little too high for what I was getting."

"I'll bet. The landlords will charge exorbitant rates if they know you're a student. You should have reported him to the rent council. They have pretty good organizations here for renters."

"I know. But I didn't want to get into any hassles. Besides, I was looking for a way to get out of there as soon as I could."

"How did you end up here?"

"I put my name on the waiting list for dorms at the housing office, though they told me I didn't have much hope of getting one. It's so hard to get a dorm these days. But last night I got a call from them, and here I am. Lucky me."

"Yeah... " I felt a happy glow within me, a premonition of wonderful times in store for both of us. "Have you met any of the other guys?"

"Not yet."

"Come on, I'll introduce you to them."

As I led him down the hall toward the lounge, I noticed he had a unique walk; the long strides he took made his head bob a little, and he trod very carefully — as if a careless misstep would send him bounding helplessly up into the sky.

In the lounge, we found only Kruk and Billy watching a cop show on TV. They nodded their greetings as I introduced them to Scott, and he went over to shake their hands. As I sat down on the sofa, I noticed Scott head straight to the bookshelves.

"See anything you like?" I asked, after he'd scanned the books a while.

"Couple of good ones here."

"If there's anything you wanna read, go ahead and take it. If you don't, the bookshelves will likely overflow. People just dump all their old books there."

"Where are you from, Scott?" said Kruk.

"Well, I grew up overseas," he said. "My dad is in the Air Force, so I never really had a hometown like you guys. I've lived in California, Germany, Montana, Turkey, and other places, but none of them is home for me."

"How long did you live in those places?" I asked.

"Only three years each. That's the usual tour of duty at any overseas post. After that your dad gets transferred to another base. Military families get re-assigned to other posts on a regular basis, so you're constantly moving around. Because of that, all my friend-ships were necessarily brief. If you make a friend, he's likely to move before the school year ends. Nothings lasts..."

"You don't seem so military to me," said Kruk.

"I'm not. I hate the military. My dad likes it well enough — he seems to thrive on order and routine. But not me. The sameness of it all — same uniforms, same thinking — all make me want to rebel."

"But think of all those exotic places you've been," I said. "I wish I could have grown up overseas like that. What was it like?"

"Not as exciting as you probably think," he said. "In the for-eign countries, all I really saw was the insides of military bases, and they all look the same."

"Say, I'm hungry," I said. "How about if we all go down to the student union cafeteria and grab a bite to eat?"

"Sure," said Scott.

The other two said they'd already eaten.

"Well, it looks like just me and you, Scott."

"Let me just drop these books off in the room and I'll be right back." He grabbed a couple of books from the shelves and left.

"What do you think of our new dorm-mate?" I asked the others.

"He looks really straight," said Kruk. "A big change from Jonesy."

"That's for sure," said Billy. "He doesn't seem like he'll be as much fun as Jonesy was, though."

"At least he's not a thief," I said.

Scott came back and we headed out.

"I like those guys," he said as we went down the stairs. "When I lived in the apartment, I really didn't get to know the other resi-dents. But here, on my very first day in the dorm, I already feel like I'm part of the group. All you guys seem to have good rela-tionships with one another. I hope you can accept me as one of you."

"Oh, don't worry. You'll fit right in. There's some weird

ones among them, but basically I think they're all right."

"Is there very much partying going on?"

"Partying is not the word for it. Some Sunday mornings, it looks like a hurricane's been through the lounge." For some reason I found myself making life in the dorm sound so much funner than it actually was. "You don't seem the type to go in for parties, though."

"You're right. To tell you the truth, I've been a little lonely ever since coming to this school. It can be a little intimidating here if you don't have any friends."

"I know what you mean."

Our school was known to be highly competitive, and coming straight from high school, I'd experienced something of a culture shock. Though I'd been in the upper ten percent academically in my high school, I hadn't been prepared for the high level of instruction given here. With its distinguished academic reputation, it had attracted the top students from all over the state, as well as from out of state. And there were many foreign students here as well, on government scholarships. The professors came from all over the world, and some of them had won Nobel Prizes. For kids just out of high school like Scott and me, it was like stepping into another world. I'd been amazed at the high intellectual level of some of my classmates, and for a long time had been afraid to open my mouth in class. Scott apparently felt the same way. Like me, he had come here expecting to carry on in the same way as high school. Used to getting straight A's, we had to learn to be content with B's, even C's.

"It's tough," I agreed. "I've never studied so hard in my life, or worked so hard for my grades."

"Yeah, me, too. But it's worth it."

"What's your major, Scott?"

At this question, he seemed a little embarrassed. "Well," he began, "One of the reasons I chose this school was because it's one of the few which has a creative writing program."

"So you want to be a writer."

"I guess so. I've always liked to write. Ever since fifth grade, I was the one whose essays and stories the teacher read out loud to the class. My classmates probably thought I was weird because I liked to read books and write, but I was never interested in the things they liked: football, cars, school dances, et cetera. Oh, I wasn't a pariah or anything like that, but I always did feel I was the different one, the one who didn't fit in with the others."

I looked at him, wondering if he was flashing a tiny secret message at me.

"What's your major, Guy?" he asked.

"I haven't decided yet. And I'm not exactly in a hurry to file for one, either. At this point, I still don't know what I want to do with my life. My father keeps dropping hints about the usefulness of getting a business degree or an engineering degree. I know he wants what's best for me and all that, but I just have no desire to follow his advice. And I feel a little guilty about it because he's paying for most of my education here. Oh, I'll pay him back, of course. But I hate the idea of being in debt to him."

"I see."

"The studies which might lead to a good job once I'm out of here don't interest me in the least. There's so much I want to learn about the world. That's why I came to college — to learn things. I didn't come here to enter some job training program."

"I know what you mean. What's your father's job?"

"He's an engineer for this company that makes instruments for airplane navigation. I think they're also involved somehow in the space program. I don't know."

"Wow. Sounds real high-tech."

"Yeah. I think I was a disappointment to him because I never cared for repairing car motors, or taking watches apart and putting them back together, that sort of thing. I happen to be completely unmechanical."

"I'm not very mechanically inclined, either. In a way, your dad seems a lot like mine. I haven't even told my dad yet that I'm majoring in creative writing. He would probably have a fit if he heard."

"But you're gonna have to tell him someday."

"I know. And I don't look forward to it, either."

"I can understand that."

We were silent for a while. As I'd guessed, Scott seemed to be the serious, scholarly type, though not the kind who concentrated on studies to the exclusion of everything else. He was highly intelligent, and his vocabulary was much larger than that of most of the others in the dorm. He was someone I could learn a lot from.

But there was something defenseless about him. I didn't know if it was because he'd led a sort of sheltered existence, but I felt that the ugly realities of the world would someday hurt him. Already, I found myself entertaining a protective feeling towards him. I wanted him to be as little hurt as possible.

Suddenly I asked: "Do you have a girlfriend, Scott?"

"Yeah. Though I don't know whether you'd call her a girl-friend or not. We write to each other at least once a week, but it isn't what you'd call 'serious'." He shrugged and didn't seem too concerned. "How about you?" he asked.

"Yeah. Girl named Christine."

"What's she like?"

"She's different. You have to meet her — she's not like any girl you'll ever meet. And I think she's one of the most intelligent people I know. She's here on a scholarship or something. But she isn't a grind — she likes to have fun. And there's a mystical side to her, too. She believes in the occult — you know, astrology, tarot cards, the whole works."

"She sounds interesting."

We'd arrived at the student union. The cafeteria was crowded and there was a long line.

"Looks like it might take a while," I said.

"I don't mind waiting. If you don't."

"No. Not at all." A secret wish had gradually been blossoming within me as we'd walked side by side. I was hoping with all my heart that he was gay. I envisioned a friendship between us, exclusive and inviolable, based upon mutual sexual attraction. Not with me secretly pining for an unattainable other, wallowing masochistically in the hopelessness of my desire, but an open, reciprocal relationship of two boys loving each other.

It was the first time I'd felt that way about any of my friends.

3

Before introducing them to each other, I first wanted to tell Christine about my new room-mate. We were having lunch at a burger restaurant east of the campus. The weather was pleasant so we were sitting at an outside table just beside the sidewalk.

"So what's he like, this new room-mate of yours?" she asked. She bit into her cheeseburger.

My excitement at meeting Scott was still very much with me. "He's nothing like Jonesy," I said, "At least I won't have to clean up after him or anything like that. It'll be a great change not having a slob for a room-mate."

"That's nice." She didn't seem to share my enthusiasm at all. I knew she'd just had a fight with her own room-mate, and I was praying she wouldn't bring up the subject of my moving in with her.

"And don't worry, Chrissie: he won't be making passes at you, either. He seems to be a gentleman, a very shy type. I think you'll get along great with him. He wants to be a writer."

"A writer type, huh? That sounds interesting."

"I suppose you want to analyze him and everything."

"Well naturally. Someone who wants to become a writer must suffer from all sorts of complexes. What a gold mine for study!"

"He doesn't exactly seem to be a neurotic type, to tell you the truth. If you ask me, he seems to be better adjusted than almost anyone else I know. Present company excepted, of course."

"Hmm. By the way, Guy, do you know that man over there? He's been staring at us for the past five minutes."

"Probably looking at your legs." She was wearing short-shorts, and her legs were crossed up high as she ate. I turned around and for a moment didn't recognize the man sitting two tables away. But just as he smiled, I realized it was Professor Golden.

"I'm sorry to disturb you," he said. "I was trying to recall if you were in one of my classes."

"Uh, no. My name is Guy Willard, and I dropped in on your Art History lecture the other day."

"Oh yes. I remember you now. I invited you to my independent studies group."

"This my girlfriend," I said rather hurriedly, "Christine."

"Hello, Christine."

"Hi. What sort of independent studies group is it?"

"About gay studies. I plan to discuss the history of the gay movement and its broader impact upon American society. You're both welcome to attend if you're interested."

"Even though we're not gay?" she said.

"Of course. Straight people needn't be afraid. I won't bite you."

We all laughed, but I got the impression he was smiling at

my nervousness.

"Actually, it sounds very interesting," said Christine. "I'm a psychology major, and homosexuality is one of the things which fascinates me." I knew she was telling the truth. Christine's attitude towards homosexuality was rather enlightened; she was as intrigued by it as she was by most things sexual.

"I don't wish to be pedantic," said Golden, "but there is a difference between 'gay' and 'homosexual'."

"Oh?"

"Why don't you join me here at my table. That way I won't have to raise my voice."

"Sure." Christine and I picked up our things and shifted over to Golden's table.

"What is the difference between 'gay' and 'homosexual'?" asked Christine as soon as we were settled.

Golden seemed pleased by her interest. I sensed that the teacher in him responded instinctively to an appreciative audience. "Well, homosexuality is an activity — two people of the same sex having, well, sex. You don't have to be gay to indulge in a homosexual act. A straight man or woman who has sex with a person of the same gender falls into this category. 'Gay', on the other hand, is a lifestyle, a philosophy, even a world view. Naturally, gay people indulge in homosexual acts of various kinds — they prefer it. But even they don't always limit their sex to homosexual couplings."

"I'm a little confused," said Christine.

"Let me explain. Homosexuality has always been around; it has existed since the beginning of documented history. And we have all kinds of other evidence that it was around in one form or another in almost every culture known to scholars. So we have to assume that homosexuality is a universal phenomenon. Anywhere you have a sizeable population of people, there will be men (a minority, to be sure) who are sexually attracted to other men. And depending on the society, there are various degrees of acceptability."

"All right. I'm with you so far. I know that it's simplistic to pigeon-hole people as gay or straight when there are so many people who have indulged in some sort of homosexual activity even if it's not their primary inclination. And there are so many people who are not even sure of their own primary sexual orientation."

"What you say is true. Now, a gay man is one who gets his greatest sexual pleasure from sex with another man. He might not always know that he is gay; after all, if he's never experienced sex with a man, how can he tell? Such people sometimes sublimate their desire for men by fantasizing about it while never actually consummating it. But even among those who do get their greatest pleasures through sex with other men, there are many who hide their true nature by keeping it secret, or disguising it, out of a need for self-protection or camouflage. In a way you can't blame these men because of the nature of our society. But all these men I've mentioned are homosexuals but not gays."

"What's the difference? Or should I say, how does a homosexual man become gay?"

"Good point. A gay man is one who lives his life as his inner personality dictates — not as society does. He may be confused or uncertain about his nature, or he may be proud, even militant about his gayness. But he is open about his homosexuality and makes no effort to hide it. Today we are witnessing a true gay revolution all around the world, but most especially here in the United States. We see gay men dressing, talking, acting in ways which express pride in their sexual orientation."

Here I made my first contribution. "So a man who enjoys sex with another man, but who isn't open about it, is not a true gay."

"Not by my definition. But you mustn't limit gayness to just the sex. We gay men are not just men who happen to prefer members of our own gender. We have a completely different way of looking at the world. We share an ambience, and have tastes in fashion and aesthetics which are purely our own. Yes, there *is* a gay sensibility — we see things differently, experience things differently. And not only because our sexual partners are not women. We are a different species, almost a different race, with our own culture, language, and history. Even our relationships are different. There are many people who think that two men in love are no different from a man and woman in love, except for their sexes. But a gay relationship is a completely different thing from hetero love — closely related but uniquely different."

Christine was thoughtful. "So by your definition, 'gay' as a phenomenon, or a social existence, is a very recent development."

"True. As I mentioned, though homosexuality has always

been around, the gay lifestyle is something new, a fairly recent phenomenon in history. As far as I'm concerned, the first truly gay man was Oscar Wilde." He picked up the book he'd been reading and showed us the frontispiece. "This is Oscar Wilde."

We saw a handsome man with long, straight hair parted in the middle. He was wearing a full-length fur coat and was clasping a pair of white gloves in his left hand.

"He was the first gay in the modern sense of the word. Oh, there were homosexual men before him, of course. But Wilde was the first to openly flaunt his gayness. He loved to camp it up, dressing outrageously for the sole purpose of outraging the world, becoming a rare bird of plumage in the gray monotonous world of Victorian England. People made fun of his mannerisms, the way he sniffed at violets, the way he fluttered his hands as he talked. And finally they crucified him — socially — for living as he did. For me, he is the patron saint of gay men, martyred for no other reason than for being gay."

"What about bisexuality?" I asked. "Someone who prefers both sexes equally."

"In my experience, the truly bisexual man is a very rare bird indeed. In a sense, we're all bisexual; it's the degree to which we desire men or women which characterizes us. In most cases, we stick to our main preference, but you'd be surprised at the number of basically straight men who dabble with other men. And at the number of gay men who have serious relationships with women."

"Is it possible?"

"Oh, yes. Especially if the man hasn't come to terms with his gayness. I know — I can speak from my own experience."

"You? But you seem so certain of yourself. I can't imagine you ever being hesitant or reluctant about expressing yourself."

He laughed. "You may think so. But when I was young, there didn't seem to be any other way. I was born twenty years too soon. Back in those days, there was no such thing as a homosexual — at least he didn't have a human shape. He was a monster, sordid and beastly... lurking in closets ready to jump out and get you. Convert you. So you can imagine how I felt when I discovered — gradually, to be sure — what my true inclinations were. I lied to myself. I told myself it couldn't be possible. I couldn't be one of *them*, one of *those*. Not me. I denied my true feelings all down the line. Was I falling in love with Gary? No, it was just friendship, just what one pal would feel for another, right?"

I could tell Christine was fascinated by this recital. She had forgotten all about her burger and was leaning forward toward Golden, trying to catch every word, mesmerized, like a small rodent by a snake. I found myself a little irritated at the hold he had over her, but I couldn't deny my own fascination.

Golden, at any rate, was used to this kind of attention on the part of his listeners. He seemed to be in his element. "Young people today don't have to worry about all the lies we were fed. I think that's probably why I'm so eager to educate people about gayness. I don't want others to waste their lives as I did. I really didn't begin to live until I was in my thirties. When I was your age, I was still living in a hypocritical world of lies, largely created by myself. Because of it, I... There was a boy in my class who made certain overtures... but I repelled them. I was indignant, disgusted. And I felt so righteous about it afterwards. Thanks to the stupid, idiotic conventions by which I was brainwashed, I let my whole youth slip away without once making the slightest 'mistake'. Pure? Oh, I was pure, all right."

This was beginning to sound uncomfortably like my own experience. I thought of my friend Mark Warren back in high school. I, too, had rebuffed his advances. Perhaps things hadn't changed very much after all. I found myself listening to Golden's recital with renewed attention.

"By the time I was sixteen, I couldn't lie to myself anymore. My dreams didn't lie. My own body didn't lie. As I look back on those days now, I see that I was living with a constant feeling of unrelieved dread. I felt the world would crucify me if it could see what went on inside my head. That dread was like a companion, a lifelong friend, the only true one I ever had. It was with me always, until it got to the point where I would have felt lost without him — naked."

The warm, burry tone of his voice had a soothing, hypnotic sound. As I listened to his talk flow on and on, I found myself willingly drifting downstream with it, heedless of where it might take me. It was wonderful.

"I wanted so badly to be normal, to be like all the others. Where most people want to be different, to stand out from the crowd, it was my fondest wish to blend in. To wake up one morning to find myself a regular boy, and that all the rest had been just a bad dream. I tried everything in my power to make it happen. It couldn't happen, of course, but no one would have been able to convince me of it back then. So, like everyone else, I got myself a girlfriend. When we'd been together the requisite amount of time, we got married. Just like everyone else — as if I was normal."

He gave a bitter laugh. "The marriage was a mistake on both our parts for a number of reasons, not the least of which was the fact that I was living a lie. All my life was one long lie until I finally opened up with myself and made the first tentative steps to accept the truth which I'd tried so long to hide, to deny. That was about five or six years after we'd been married."

His face creased into a bitter smile and his gaze seemed to wander into the past. "We had a so-called trial separation. I guess it was a feeble effort to save what was a disaster from start to finish — which was my fault because I was using her to 'cure myself'. Cure something for which there is no cure but one. Of course she didn't know the real reason why it wasn't working, and I made no effort to enlighten her. We got back together after a while when I couldn't stand being alone anymore. But it was a mere partnership, and a shaky one at that."

"Did you ever tell her you're gay?" asked Christine.

"Eventually, yes. I finally worked up the courage to tell her the truth. She couldn't stand it, of course. She took it as an insult, a judgement upon her as a woman. Which it wasn't, of course. For a while, she even tried to help me conquer my 'problem'... to no avail. It was pitiful. A mess. In the end, the divorce was her idea."

He looked at me as he said this. I could find no words to say. It was obvious that the relationship with his wife had been the major tragedy of his life, but I was made a little uncomfortable at the way he'd spread it all out before us, as if it were an exhibit of some kind. For once, Christine seemed to be at a loss for a sympathetic phrase.

"It was the times, I guess," I ventured. "Maybe there were a lot of people in the same situation."

"True."

For a moment there seemed to be a lull in the conversation. Then, abruptly, Golden gathered his books together and picked up his tray. He'd already finished his food.

"If you'll excuse me, I have to get back to earning a living. Sorry to have bothered you at your lunch."

"Oh, not at all," said Christine. "I found your talk quite fascinating."

He smiled at her. "As I said, if you and Guy feel like dropping by for the gay studies group, you're always welcome." He looked at me and nodded to us both, then walked away. Christine and I watched him deposit his tray on the counter, say a few words to the boy at the grill, and head out the door.

"What a character," she said, shaking her head slightly. "I can see why you find him so interesting."

"You seemed rather drawn to him yourself."

"Oh, I was. In fact, if I were a boy, I might even be making a play for him."

"Even if you were straight?"

"Especially if I were. After what he'd just said, I might want to try to stretch my horizons, so to speak."

"Well, he might be interested in girls who want to 'stretch their horizons'."

She looked at me mischievously, and the thought of her in Golden's arms, for some reason, gave me a sudden, powerful erection. I crossed my legs under the table. "Looks like I'm too late, though." She nodded up the street in the direction Golden had taken.

I looked and saw that he had stopped to chat with a boy. I thought I recognized him from the group of students who had gathered around Golden's lectern at the end of class that day. After a few words, they began walking off together up the street. I felt strangely envious of the picture they presented.

4

Unlike most of the other boys on the floor, Scott wasn't a party animal. There was a certain innocence about him which set him apart, for he seemed fundamentally different from the others. He dutifully went along when he was invited out to drinking parties, but it was easy to see his heart wasn't in it. He seemed most comfortable with a single friend — me — in serious conversation. He told me he was perfectly content as long as he had a good book to keep him company, but sometimes I felt a little guilty when I went out to see Christine, knowing he was going to be all alone in his room. So I tried as much as possible to invite him along when I went.

Christine didn't mind. The two of them had taken to each other from the moment I'd introduced them — something which would have been unthinkable with Jonesy — for they shared the same tastes in music and movies. Sometimes the three of us would go out together for the evening.

One of the reasons Scott didn't quite fit in with the others in the dorm was that he had the late arrival's complex — he was the new kid on the block. Even after he'd been my room-mate for a while, he still felt like a newcomer. The guys were always talking about Jonesy, he said, and he felt uncomfortable whenever he heard them recollecting yet another 'typical Jonesy stunt'... as if he'd been responsible for the eviction of a more popular tenant. (After Jonesy was expelled, most of us only brought up the fun times we'd had with him, and refrained, as if from a tacit understanding, from mentioning the terrible truth we'd learned about him.) Scott had never met Jonesy, yet the former's shadow always hung over him, a ghost which lingered.

So he seemed very comfortable when it was just the three of us in Christine's room. Sometimes Christine's room-mate would join us to make a foursome, but lately there was some bad blood between the girls, and Nancy had hinted more than once that she was ready to move out.

It was on an evening just after the mid-terms and the three of us were relaxing in Christine's room, drinking beers. The talk had turned to occult matters, and Christine seemed especially animated tonight as she began explaining a theory that dreams were sometimes like a 'reverse memory'.

Even I had never heard of this one from her before. "Reverse memory? What the hell is that?"

"Didn't you guys ever have dreams that predicted future events?" She turned to Scott.

"No, I can't say that I have," he said. He didn't share Christine's interest in the exotic byways of parapsychology but was willing to go along with her, for his intellectual curiosity made him open to many things which he really didn't believe in. As if he felt that if *someone* believed in them, they must have some validity.

Christine put her beer down and shook her hair out of her eyes. "Well I have — many times. I've seen things clearly in my dreams: places I've never been, people I've never seen. Yet I meet them, five, ten years later. It's the strangest thing, yet apparently quite a common phenomenon."

"That would mean the future is already decided, instead of being merely a blank possibility."

"That's one way of putting it. Though I don't think of myself as being a fatalist."

"Do you believe in fortune-tellers?" he asked.

"Oh yes. Not all of them, because I'm sure there's plenty of fakes out there. But there must be some who've managed to tap into the essence of time and be able to see future events."

"By reading palms and things like that?"

"Palm-reading is a very ancient art which has a lot of validity. I think it's very possible that a lot about ourselves is revealed in outward physical manifestations. After all, you know that DNA molecules contain the information which help to form our personalities. Well, those same DNA also contain the blueprint for the individual lines and creases found on our palms. There might be a connection there, you know, which the ancients might have accidentally discovered in the course of their studies. Have you ever had your palm read?"

"No."

"Will you let me? I'll bet I can tell a lot about you just by reading it."

"Sure. What do I do?"

"Nothing. Just let me look."

Christine had never manifested an interest in palm-reading before, so I knew she was probably just kidding around. She took his palm into her hand and bent over it, seemingly concentrating upon the whorls and lines there. With her index finger she lightly traced a pattern on his open palm and closely examined the minuscule ridges at the base of his thumb before announcing:

"You're creative... sensitive... and romantic. But your leadership line is very weak. You prefer to follow where led."

I was a little disappointed by the mundane nature of her analysis, but Scott seemed intrigued by her pronouncement.

"What else?"

"Am I right?" she asked, quickly looking up.

"Well... yeah. I guess I never was much of a leader in things. And I was always a loner... preferred to do things on my own."

"What were you like as a boy, Scott?" I asked.

"Very quiet. Not very adventurous, I'm afraid."

"Quite the opposite of Guy here," said Christine.

"Adventure?" I said, putting on a mock-worldly air. "Let me tell you, I've done it all; I've tried everything — sex, drugs, you name it. Maybe I was crazy, but I don't regret it."

Scott looked at me seriously, and a little sadly. "You know, Guy, I was thinking that if we'd met in high school, you'd probably have thought I was pretty dull."

"Why?"

"Oh, I don't know. I just never hung out with the kids that did the wild things."

I laughed. "I was exaggerating, Scott. Heck, probably the wildest things me and my friends did was hyperventilate."

"Hyperventilate? What's that?"

"It's a weird thing we used to do at parties, or even during school. Come here, I'll show you."

A little reluctantly, he came over to where I was. I turned him around to face Christine and stood right behind him, slipping my arms in front of him, clasping him so that both my forearms rested on his abdomen. I explained:

"You take about ten very deep breaths, as deeply as possible. Then, when you take your tenth breath, you hold it in while I squeeze your abdomen as hard as possible."

"What happens?"

"You pass out. I think it cuts off the oxygen supply to the brain or something. But you're out for only a few seconds."

"What if I fall down and hit my head on something?"

"Don't worry, I'm right behind you the whole time to catch you and lower you onto the sofa."

"So what's the point of it?"

"When you come to again, you experience the most fantastic feeling. It can't be described; you have to experience it. It's like an orgasm in a way, a sort of high — maybe caused by the rush of oxygen to the brain to bring consciousness back."

"It sounds a little dangerous to me."

"Well, the teachers and parents always discouraged it, but of course that only made us want to do it more. You wanna try it?"

"I'm not sure."

"Come on."

"I'll try it," said Christine quickly. She'd been listening all this time with a growing sense of excitement. I knew it was just the sort of thing to perk her interest.

"Watch this," I said to Scott, seeing the sudden interest in his eyes as Christine got ready to try it.

I positioned her so that we were standing just in front of the sofa. I put both my arms around her from behind, in a hold just below her ribcage. She began taking very deep breaths as Scott counted them off. Just as she finished taking her tenth, I gave an abrupt squeeze to her belly and felt her go suddenly limp in my arms. Gently, I lowered her onto the sofa and sat back on the floor to watch her return to consciousness. In a matter of seconds she came to with a wondering look on her face which made Scott and me laugh.

"What was it like?" asked Scott eagerly.

"It's... like bliss." She was smiling, with a slightly silly expression. "I really can't put it into words. It's more like a drug high than an orgasm."

"Come on, Scott, now it's your turn." I knew he was still a little reluctant to try it, yet I felt a perverse urge to push him to it. The thought of bringing him that quasi-sexual pleasure made me excited. In a way, it was also a test to see how much he would trust me. "You won't feel any pain, I promise you."

I pulled him over to me and steered him toward the sofa.

"Now breathe, very, very deeply." In my arms he became quite submissive. I felt his back expanding against my chest with every breath he took. Christine was looking on with delight, anticipating what he would be going through. After the tenth breath I squeezed. He slumped heavily in my arms and I let him down onto the sofa, then sat next to him, supporting him against me. He was out for about five seconds before coming to, blinking his eyes and looking around the room as if seeing it for the first time.

"Well?" I asked. "How was it?"

He didn't say a word, just sat there with a beatific expression on his face.

"Weird, isn't it?" said Christine.

"Yeah." He still wasn't sure what had happened. "What a rush."

As Christine and I laughed at his wonder, I felt that Scott and I had shared something a little illicit; something elusive and precious had passed between us. In my heart I whispered my gratitude.

Now Christine looked at me. "Your turn, Guy. Scott, you do the squeezing."

He got behind me and I began taking deep breaths, feeling his arms pressed against my belly. Just being like this, with his body so close to mine, was enough to make me happy. I lost count of the breaths as I felt my head getting light. Somewhere off in the corner of my vision was Christine, smiling, looking benevolently on. I thought, momentarily, that I still had something important left to say — and then I was gone.

In no time at all I was coming to from somewhere; I felt as if I were stepping into a brand new morning, the air fresh and pure. It was heavenly; I wanted it to last forever. This was a memory from out of my dreams, the glorious childhood feeling of endless possibilities.

The echo of a song was on the edge of my consciousness, a song I'd learned in the fifth grade, so pure and beautiful that I always imagined it sung by an angels' choir of boy sopranos. It was about the delights of wandering the mountain trails with a knapsack on my back... the trails of a fabulous land to which I wanted to return... always.

I looked in wonder at Christine and Scott, feeling as if I'd been away a long, long time. A hollow ache in my chest told me that a part of me was still wandering those mountain trails.

They were giggling at my look of baffled loss, but the whisper of a truth, desperately suppressed from the very start, now emerged within me, blossoming forth like a tropical flower in fastmotion: I was in love with Scott.

5

In my explorations of the secret homosexual underground on campus, I had come upon what looked like the most frequented spot: the cement bunker-like outdoor restroom by the football field, near the changing rooms. The graffiti in there was the most explicit I'd yet seen.

I recalled many times, late at night, going back to the dorm from the library and seeing dark shadows slinking in and out of it, and the orange cigarette glows hovering like lurid fireflies in the heavy gloom beyond. Now as I realized the true significance of those shadows, I became intrigued. In the daytime, the place was innocuous enough, but surely it must assume another aspect after dark.

I decided to go there and see at firsthand just what went on.

It was past eleven o'clock when I stepped out of the dorm and turned toward the football field. The autumn night was cool, and the stars were pinpoints of cold fire. Just beside the football field was a grassy hillock where music students during the day could often be seen practicing on their instruments. But at this hour it was empty. Here and there, like lonely beacons amid the trees behind the bleachers, were the dimly-lit yellow rape prevention phone boxes. There was a ghostly air to the whole scene and I began to wonder if I should continue.

I followed the paved bicycle path which I often took during the day to go to my classes. It looked deserted and forbidding. The campus now wore a completely different guise from the one I always saw in the daytime.

I was nearing the football field, but my destination was on the opposite side, and I didn't dare cross the vast expanse of the brightly-lit playing field. An oblique approach suited me better. Just past the football field, the path took a sharp bend to the left, curving down towards the arts building. Here, a tiny wooden bridge spanned the stream which meandered across the campus. A slight breeze made the trees beside it stir, and I listened for a moment to the rustling murmur they made.

Then I crossed the bridge, peering among the trees to the left under the eave of the arts building. There seemed to be no one about. I stepped off the path into the shade of the trees, suddenly plunging into greater darkness. Crickets fell silent at my approach. There were the usual sounds of night — a far-off siren downtown and the wind soughing in the trees.

Pressing myself among the shrubs lining the stream, I proceeded back toward the football field, approaching it from the rear. Some instinct within me was alerted to invisible emanations coming from among the trees, and I could feel a skin-tingling prickle of other presences unseen in the dark, hidden and watchful.

And then my heart almost stopped as I spotted a figure ahead of me, standing off to one side of the bicycle path, peering intently into the night. After a long moment of immobility, it stepped away from the shadows to reveal itself to me, then stepped back. The orange glow of a cigarette, man high, brightened and faded, then spun like a roman candle, scattering sparks along the ground.

I had an eerie dreamlike feeling of familiarity, as if I'd been here before.

Cautiously, I moved away from the bicycle path, farther into the cloaking shade of the bushes. I felt safer taking this more circuitous route to the football field. My immediate goal was a slight rise which gave me a vantage point from which I could observe the restroom and the area around it without being seen. As I approached it I knelt beside a bush and peered all around. Only after I'd reassured myself that no one else was about did I proceed. I made my way up the slope and found a suitably hidden hollow, bounded on one side by a huge rock. There was a clear view of the restroom below. I took up my post and waited.

For a while, nothing happened, and I began to wonder if I'd been imagining things earlier. And then I saw two men suddenly come out of the darkness, slipping past the shrubbery into the shadow of the trees beyond the restroom.

I was wondering whether I should follow them when I heard a faint noise coming from under the trees to my right, behind the bleachers. As my eyes adjusted to the dark, I could see in their shadows a man standing flush against a tree trunk. He appeared to be gazing in the direction of the restroom, but I could see no one down there.

All around me was silence. I could hear shouts from far off — a dorm party or people returning from the late movie at the Parkside. The man seemed to be waiting for something to happen. What?

And then I heard a rustling. About fifty feet away, down among the bushes to the left was a furtive movement. I strained my eyes and made out the man I'd seen earlier standing next to the bicycle path. He was walking up the shallow slope toward the bleachers beyond the rise. He stopped a moment and seemed to be looking around, then continued on.

Crossing a treeless open space, he walked straight to where the other man was. I couldn't see if they were talking, but they were constantly looking around. Then they both slipped away. It was all so silent, like the elaborate choreography of a strange, music-less ballet. There was something inhuman and cold about it all.

Mustering my courage, I began stealthily moving down the slope in their direction, keeping to the cover of the shrubs. I couldn't see where they'd gone, but sensed they'd withdrawn a little further into the shadows under the bleachers. My heart was racing; this felt like the combat games I used to play as a boy. I hadn't done this in a long time.

As I approached the bleachers from the rear, I suddenly saw them again. One of them was leaning with his back against a bleacher support and the other was standing right next to him. Both of them were peering about so busily that, for several seconds, I didn't realize what was going on. When I looked carefully, I saw that the second man had his hand down at the other's crotch and was openly fondling the erect penis.

A queasiness gripped my stomach and I felt sweat break out all over my body. Here in the open, in the middle of the campus! How long had all this been going on? And virtually under my very nose! I'd often ridden my bike through here during the day without the faintest idea of what went on at night! I strained my eyes to see more, my mouth dry with excitement.

And then — I don't know if it was a noise I made (for my blood was pounding in my ears too loudly for me to tell) — they looked up in my direction, and the one who was leaning back zipped up and began walking away. They parted swiftly, going separate ways. I ducked down farther into the bushes, my heart hammering so hard I felt a dull ache in my chest.

It took a long time for my excitement to die down. What if the two men hadn't spotted me? Despite the danger I felt, I knew I had to find out more about this strange nightworld. A whole hidden world was out here, an invisible world which overlapped and intersected all parts of the daytime world, but which only a chosen few could see. It was a different country, not on any map, a perverse wonderland of the dark corrupt instincts.

I didn't feel like returning to the dorm just yet. Until I could learn more about this new world, I knew I would feel incomplete, unsatisfied.

I decided it was time to go back and explore the restroom itself. It seemed to be the hub around which all the silent action in the dark revolved, their black heart. Indeed, the combination of the cool night air and my growing excitement necessitated a trip to the toilet.

I made my way back to the restroom by skirting the fence around this side of the football field. All about me was the sound of crickets and the far-off traffic of University Avenue. The darkness along the fence was even greater in contrast to the lights of the playing field which were always turned on at night, presumably for safety purposes. They had the effect of throwing the surrounding woods into complete shadow. It was here that the darkest shadows lurked.

The open area in front of the restroom appeared to be empty. I made my move. Stepping out into the open, I crossed the short distance and was just about to enter the restroom when I noticed someone sitting on a bench beyond it. I hadn't seen him at first because the lights of the playing field had momentarily blinded me. By the time I spotted him, he must have been watching me for some time. Feeling a little foolish I stepped into the restroom.

It was well-lit. I entered a stall and closed the door behind me. The graffiti on the walls was the same I'd seen earlier in my explorations, but now they had assumed an immediacy which they'd lacked before. I knew now that they described real actions, not just the lust-inspired fantasies of a dreamer. I waited a few minutes for my tension to die down enough for me to urinate.

When I stepped out of the stall, a boy was standing at the sink washing his hands. Was he the same boy who'd been sitting at the bench? His eyes in the mirror were looking right at me but I ignored him and quickly washed my hands and stepped out into the night again.

Just as I exited the restroom, another boy came walking up to the doorway — where had he come from? I could have sworn the surrounding area had been empty. He peered searchingly into my face, but, scared, I proceeded onward. Things were happening much too quickly for me.

I walked back toward the bicycle path as if I were on my way to the dorm. When I'd gotten far enough away from the restroom, I plunged back into the shrubbery and doubled back to a point beyond the bleachers, at the north end of the football field where the changing room was. From there I intended to make my way down through another wooded area, approaching the restroom from the other side.

As I neared the changing room, I could see a boy standing in the doorway. He was leaning against the wall as if standing guard there. I knew the building was locked up at night. Before he could see me I hid myself behind a shrub from where I could watch him.

Presently, an older man came out of the shadows behind the building and approached the front, giving the boy in the doorway a long look as he passed by. They looked hard at each other, the older man stopping to give his look added emphasis before continuing on. But the boy didn't move.

After a period of time, the boy stepped out from the doorway and began walking up the slope toward the football field. When he got to a slight ridge, he stopped and stood still, his hands on his hips as if posing. Under the illumination of starlight, I could see that he was a well-built boy wearing tight jeans and a long-sleeved t-shirt. The statue of a young prince of the night, arrogantly surveying his realm.

I wanted to get a better look at him. Cautiously, I got up from my crouch behind the shrub. But before I could make a move toward him, a middle-aged man — not the one who'd approached him earlier — crept out of the dense shrubbery and drew near the boy. The boy, seeing him, suddenly turned and walked back down the slope.

The man, undeterred, followed about ten paces behind. I followed them both like a stealthy animal of prey, nimble, silent, alert. But at the foot of the slope I lost sight of them in the dark shadows there. I continued walking in the same direction until I caught sight of the boy moving past a low hedge. Before the hedge was a line of benches. A young man sitting on the first one muttered something to the boy but the boy ignored him and walked straight on.

He walked firmly, erect, head up, glancing neither left nor right. The middle-aged man continued to follow him, always about ten paces behind. And, unknown to either, I trailed them both.

At the end of the path, the boy cut up through the shrubs again, with the man right behind him. The latter made no secret of the fact that he was doggedly following. The whole silent pantomime was like a grotesque farce. There was the beautiful young boy; and there was the unattractive middle-aged man. This man had eyes only for the boy — who was obviously disgusted by the other's attention. There was no subtlety in their actions. The man's posture, his rounded back, the slightly obsequious way he moved, revealed his utter infatuation with the boy. And the boy's disdain and loathing were evident in his haughty strides. Still, the man doggedly followed him. And I secretly following them both, was amused, yet fascinated by the entertainment. It was like watching the mating habits of animals who — unlike humans — make no secret of their desires and needs. Perhaps the older man felt that his persistence would pay off, that the boy would eventually give in out of sheer exhaustion, weary of trying to evade his attentions.

As we made our way past the bleachers to the south end of the football field, I heard the sounds of gravel steadily crunching. I looked right and saw that the road which looped down behind the main stand was filled with parked cars. Now I knew how all these men had gotten here. One car started up and turned on its headlights. As it swung around to back up, its headlights arced like a searchlight. The sweep of its glare washed over the boy who suddenly froze looking in the direction of the car. His face, caught momentarily in the light, was beautiful.

When the car had gone and all was dark, the boy turned his steps back toward the main campus. We were now walking up the sidewalk leading back to the arts building. It was lined on one side with statues. Here, the boy picked up his pace, and the older man was hard put to keep up with it.

Not taking my eyes off them, I'd become clumsy, knocking against a wire trash can in my haste. Before I knew it, I was nearly right up against them, not two paces behind, and almost ran into the man when he suddenly halted, turned around and hissed at me: "Stop following me, will you!"

I turned and fled into the night, feeling naked, and didn't stop running till I was back at the dorm.

6

The ringing of the campanile bells woke me. I counted them off as the hours sounded: eight... nine... ten o'clock. My mind was still so full of what I'd seen last night that it took a while for the time to register. And the day: today was Wednesday. I was late for my chemistry lecture. In a sudden panic, I jumped out of bed realizing I'd never make it in time.

What was I to do? And then I relaxed. As if I'd suddenly

remembered something from far back, the solution hit me: I would simply drop the course. Why not? I hated it anyway, it was the most boring class I took. Feeling as if a great load had been lifted off my shoulders, I lay back in bed. The decision to quit had come to me in an inspired flash, but I knew it had probably been building up in me for weeks.

From the very first lecture in that course, I'd felt lost, completely lost. With a sense of baffled amazement, I'd listened to the professor speaking in the most amazingly technical terms, and not a word of it had made any sense. It was as if he'd been speaking in a foreign language. Helplessly I'd taken notes but when I looked at them afterwards, they looked like they were written in code. I was beginning to wonder if college was the right place for me. Back in high school, the chem teacher had given me a B+; here, that grade didn't mean a thing.

I yawned and stretched. At this hour, almost all the other guys in the dorm were in class; the whole place was quiet. For all I knew, I had the whole dorm to myself. It was a luxury.

I got up from bed and went into the bathroom. After urinating, I came out and sat down on Scott's bed. It was neatly made and everything was in order. No doubt he'd tried to wake me this morning, and being unable to, had gone on to breakfast without me.

I liked to go over to his part of the room when he was out. We had each other's permission to use or borrow anything without asking; only the locked top drawers of our desks were completely private. Being alone in his side of the room, surrounded by his belongings, I felt I was absorbing his essence in a way otherwise denied to me. Sometimes when I saw his things without him, I felt even closer to him than when we were actually together.

His wall was hung with reproductions of famous paintings and his bookshelf was crammed to overflowing with books — textbooks, paperbacks, library books. He was a voracious reader. We shared a love of books but I was always surprised at the wide range of his reading. He explored areas of literature which I found boring: the novels of Walter Scott, Nathaniel Hawthorne, and Henry James. But he also read popular books, mysteries, science fiction, and spy novels.

We had begun lending each other the books which had moved us. It was an intimate exchange, I felt, because when a book touches you in some way, and you recommend it, you pass on a part of yourself. I read his personality in the books he liked, and in the passages he'd underlined. I, too, underlined the parts which I liked so that when I returned the book, he would see what had moved me. And we liked to write notes to each other in the margins, airing our comments about the writer's views or style. Later we would discuss each other's opinions.

Our tastes grew together, though I couldn't say whose influence on the other was stronger. It was mutual in the best sense. I felt we were growing together toward a sensibility which was uniquely ours. (I didn't dare tell him about the gay books I read, however.)

Often we would sit at our beds chatting half the night away, and I'd wish our meandering talk could go on forever. But he would yawn, glance at the clock, ruffle his hair and mention tomorrow's classes. And I would pull up my covers and turn to the wall, my heart a mixture of yearning and regret.

I was in love with Scott — helplessly, hopelessly, endlessly in love with him. Every morning when I woke up, I felt unaccountably happy — and it only took a few moments to realize that the cause of my happiness was the fact that I knew Scott was sleeping in a bed just across the room from me. And I knew we would go to breakfast together where, over cups of coffee, I could stare to my heart's content at his sleepy face.

In classes I found it hard to concentrate. My mind kept wandering to the last time I'd been with him, the words we'd said to each other. What color shirt was he wearing today? And later, we might meet sometime during the day, depending on our schedules. After classes, we would study together, then go out to eat dinner, often with Christine, her presence being a convenient cover-up for my almost unbridled joy at being with Scott. I felt so light-hearted when I was with him, and so let down when we couldn't be together. The talks we had were usually nothing special, but I cherished them.

This feeling of happiness was something which simply inundated me, which colored my whole life from morning to night, changed the way I looked at the world. Now I loved the world, loved life. And my life was Scott. The sky looked so much bluer than it had ever been, the air tasted sweeter, everything was more vivid, alive with the intrinsic rapture of being. I smiled at strangers and they smiled back. I saw couples in love and knew I was of their number, though secretly. I felt lucky to be alive at the same time as Scott. Cruel fate could have had us born in different times, in different countries. But here we were, both miraculously in the same country, in the same state, on the same campus, and — most incredible of all — in the very same dorm, sharing the same room! Why was I so blessed? Did I deserve such luck?

This was a new experience for me. I'd never been in love — truly in love — with a boy before. I'd had crushes; all through junior high school and high school, I pined after handsome boys to whom I would never have dreamed of revealing my feelings, adoring them from a distance, half feeling sorry for my plight, half revelling in it, telling myself that if my dreams ever came true, the boy would disappoint me. That he couldn't be the perfect boy I envisioned — that no one was perfect except for someone you create in your own mind. And I'd had intense sexual yearnings, and erotic fantasies, hundreds of them, about the boys in my school, about my teachers, about professional football players, beautiful actors, and even faceless strangers.

But what I felt for Scott was nothing like any of that. I knew he wasn't perfect. I saw all his flaws, and I liked him because of his flaws rather than despite them. In many ways he wasn't the boy of my dreams at all; what struck me about him wasn't his physical beauty but his intellectual honesty. He had a high forehead which made me suspect he would bald young, but I didn't care if he did go bald, as long as he remained the same Scott.

These feelings had crept upon me so stealthily that I hadn't recognized them for the longest time. And the only thing I could do now was to keep it secret from him. He must never know. Otherwise, our friendship would be destroyed. For in my happiness I almost forgot the fact that it was impossible for me to ever have my love requited. For he wasn't gay. I knew that. He was a normal, heterosexual boy.

I peered under the bed. There was a neat stack of girly magazines there, much more classy and tasteful than the raunchy stuff Jonesy had kept there. I flipped through one, noting the big-breasted beauties with their blow-dried hair and perfect, air-brushed skin, glowing and healthy-looking. When I'd first seen these magazines under Scott's bed, I'd felt a little relieved, glad that he was 'normal'. My pristine image of him needed to remain intact. I might have even been a little disappointed if I'd come across a copy of a muscle magazine.

I glanced into the wastepaper basket beside the night table. At the bottom there was a crumpled-up Kleenex like a pale green butterfly which had died there. The sight of it was a raw reminder that Scott, too, had to satisfy the itch of sexual desire.

Unlike most of the others in the dorm, he didn't talk very much about girls. There were those who — even though I knew they weren't getting laid — talked about 'pussy' all the time, as if they were constantly getting it... and then there was Kruk, who obviously avoided a topic he was uncomfortable with. I knew Scott well enough now to realize he was a romantic heterosexual of the old-fashioned school.

Sometimes I would think of Christine's belief in reincarnation and wish to become a girl in my next life so I could openly express my love for him. He would remain the same Scott, of course — nothing would ever change that. But I would be a beautiful young girl who could kiss him on the lips before the whole world...

But that wasn't exactly what I wanted, either. I wanted to love him as a boy loves another boy. The forbidden nature of my love made it that much more precious, more sacred. What I felt for him was what only a boy could feel for another boy, and which could only be satisfied by masculine responses. Against all the censure of the world I wanted to cherish him.

On the other hand, if he were gay, my feelings for him might not have been so intense. There were plenty of obvious gays on campus but I'd never felt for them what I felt for Scott. They were just like me; and they attracted me in a purely sexual way — the kind of sex that might be satisfied in an anonymous encounter in Nightworld. It was because Scott was different from me that I adored him. He was what I longed to be, he was the ideal me.

So I was caught between two feelings; one part of me wished he was gay, but the other part wished just as fervently for the opposite. I desired him sexually, yet I also wanted him to remain pristinely heterosexual. That precarious balance was the equation of my love. If I satisfied my desire for him, I might also shatter my love by the same act.

It was torture, yet I loved my torture. Let it go on forever, just this side of unbearable. Oh, to be young and gay and in love.

I got up and went back into the bathroom. A hint of dampness hung in the air, from the shower he'd taken this morning. His bath towel was on the towel rack, alive with the odor of his sweat mingled with the aromas of his soap and after-shave. I held it up and plunged my nose into it, rooting for the essence of Scottness in its folds. All the articles of toiletry he used for his morning shower had the magical ability to preserve his essence like faithful messengers. Perhaps because we used different brands of everything, the smells his things left behind had a powerful way of evoking him for me.

The bathroom was alive with Scott.

Some mornings I could hear him from my bed urinating in here, and the hollow-sounding gurgle of his piss as it hit the water at the bottom of the toilet bowl was like a secret message from his dick.

In the shower stall, separate metal soap dishes were fixed in the tiled wall. On Scott's light green cake of soap, I would sometimes find a single curly black pubic hair embedded there.

If I heard the shower on when I got back from class, I would come in here and pretend to be busy at the sink, just so I could see the flesh-colored shape of Scott beyond the translucent frosted-glass shower door. We conversed with each other, shouting over the sound of the jetting water. Sometimes I knocked on the shower door and opened it, stuck my head in. He would turn around to face me, the jets of warm water dashing off his back, into my face, the steam all but hiding him. The easy camaraderie of dormitory room-mates did away with any sense of prudery.

When he came out of the shower, I always made sure I was looking at him straight in the face. He would be wiping himself off, toweling his hair dry, wrapping the towel around his middle, his chest and shoulders steaming, the air alive with the smell of his toothpaste, after-shave, and deodorant. But every time I had a chance to glimpse what I most wanted to see, a meddlesome hand 'just happened' to be eclipsing the longed-for sight.

Beneath the bathroom sink was the covered wicker basket we used as a clothes hamper. Scott and I used to wash our clothes together down in the basement laundromat until we decided it was a waste of time for both of us to go. So we elected to share wash-day; once a week, one of us would take both of our loads down and wash them together.

This was my week to do the laundry and I wondered whether

to use the unexpected gift of this free time this morning to do the chore.

I always enjoyed watching the promiscuous mix of his clothes with mine in the dryer, his briefs and t-shirts tumbling about in loving play with my own. And touching his most intimate things as I folded them up afterwards in our room was an act of love for me.

I lifted the top off the hamper basket; a musky smell came up to my nose. I knelt down and fished around in the pile of clothes. On top were some shirts and jeans, and beneath them were our underwear.

He wore size 30 briefs, the same size as me. But his taste in underwear was conservative — standard white cotton BVDs; he said he was too embarrassed to wear the slim bikini styles I preferred. Whenever I handled his briefs, I always looked closely for stains in them, because the faint after-image of urine or semen excited me. Even the traces of brown 'skid marks', far from disgusting me, only made him that much more lovable.

I picked up what I thought at first was a pair of briefs. When I realized what it was I almost had to catch at my breath.

It was a jock strap. Scott's. I knew he took PE, but he'd always put his gym bag away in his bottom drawer, and I'd never seen his jock strap before.

My stomach felt queasy.

I replaced it in the hamper and tip-toed out to the hallway door and listened carefully. All was silent in the dorm. It was still too early for most of the guys to have come back from their morning classes. And anyone who didn't have a class was probably sleeping in. Not even the sound of the TV in the lounge came to my ears. I locked the door and returned to the bathroom.

I pulled the jock strap out again and made my way back to my bed. There, I sat down and examined my find. I flipped the pouch inside out and held it up to get a better look. There was a barely-noticeable yellow stain in the very middle. I brought it up to my nose and caught the briny scent of urine... and of something else: a faint whiff of semen.

I felt faint. The image of the pouch firmly cupping Scott's genitals came to me, and I felt my own dick stir. Feeling the keenest shame, I closed my eyes and licked at the cloth where Scott's dick and balls had nestled.

The ignoble nature of what I was doing shamed me, yet I felt impelled to it. For this was a token of my love — a love for which I had assigned the purest motives. If Scott could see me now, what would he think? I knew all too well.

With a feeling of hopeless despair, I realized that this was as close to him as I could ever get. Unable to caress his flesh, I would caress that which had touched his flesh. This emissary of his body would have to do. Love was selfish, love was blind — and lust was an insane madman screaming for release. I wanted Scott's body, I wanted it now.

With trembling, impatient fingers I undid my belt and fly, and kicked myself free from my jeans. Then I slid my briefs down to my ankles and flipped them away into the corner. My dick was up hard and straining, its flesh stretched taut to bursting point, the glans shiny and pulsing.

I lay back on my bed and brought the jock strap up to my dick. With pounding heart, I buried the head of my dick in the pouch, then wrapped the leg strap and waist band around the rest of my shaft.

I began pumping.

I thought of Scott naked atop his bed, masturbating to his girly magazines. It was a beautiful picture. I imagined him shooting off within seconds, with vigorous young spurts, all the way up to his chin, leaving sudden quivering drops of pure white pearls dotted all across his chest and belly.

A strap had come loose, and was playing rhythmically against my balls. Oh, how I wished I could be this jock strap, encasing Scott's dick and balls so intimately, hugging his hips and buttocks in a firm clamp, feeling his body, hot and restless and hard, boy-clean and innocent, heterosexual. Not queer like me...

I was beyond all shame now. I didn't care about anything, only about that hard rod of muscle I was stroking, into which the whole universe had become compressed, tight in my fist, and nothing else mattered, nothing. Not even if the whole world were to barge in now and see me.

For I was with Scott now, I was one with him. I was encased in his flesh and stroking his dick. I could feel his pleasure brimming up to the rim, to the very lip, where a single drop of lemon juice squeezed out and trickled slowly down the side, and I couldn't hold back any longer, no longer, no more...

I jammed my shoulders back against the mattress and arched my back, made of my body a bow, as the tension drew taut — taut — taut — and then was suddenly, gloriously released as I shot an arrow straight up to heaven, up to the only heaven I knew.

Part Three: Mare Clausum

1

Erewhon, the disco just off campus on University Avenue, was the most popular place to go on Saturday nights. Christine and I liked to go dancing there occasionally, and tonight we had asked Scott to join us, along with a girl named Jill who lived in Christine's apartment building.

Christine (and I, too) had been trying for a while to set up Scott with a girl. We knew he regularly received letters from a girl named Linda, but it was my impression that he didn't care deeply about her. They seemed to be nothing more than friends, though they confided in each other about everything.

Even before tonight, Christine and I had introduced him to a number of girls, usually friends of hers, but nothing had come of them. His shyness was an inhibiting factor. Also, there were very few girls among them who could match him intellectually. Scott himself protested that our solicitous efforts were an embarrassment to him. But Christine reassured him that she thought of him as something like a brother, and wanted to see him romantically happy.

My own motives were a bit more complex. I, too, wanted to see him romantically fulfilled, but even more than that, I wanted him to be sexually active. Though he claimed that he didn't feel deprived in any way, and that he was too busy with his studies to pay much attention to girls, I knew he was a healthy young boy with the normal sexual appetite of a 19-year-old male. To be the instrument of his sexual happiness, even indirectly, would give me the greatest pleasure.

Yet at the same time, another part of me wanted him to remain unattached. I was already jealous of whichever girl would eventually have her hold on him. Maybe that was why every time Christine consulted me about introducing someone to him as a possible girlfriend I always found something wrong with her. I was perfectly happy with the way things were, with the friendship among the three of us.

There was a large crowd of students outside the entrance to Erewhon, some waiting for friends, others (mostly high school girls) hoping for an escort to take them inside. We showed our student IDs at the door and got in at the student discount rate.

Twelve steps led us down into another world, a place very much like Venusberg. For Erewhon was decorated like the inside of a mysterious cave. A red light pulsating from just beyond some realistic-looking rocky crags gave a hellish atmosphere to the place. The music was loud and made my head feel stuffed-up.

"Let's find a table," I yelled, above the sound of the music.

The dance floor was packed, as it usually was just after midterms and finals. A sexual ambience pervaded the whole place, inundated as it was by the nakedness of sexual desire. The beat of the music was sexual, and the bodies dancing to it all around us were writhing in passionate abandon. Boys in tight jeans were sweating from the exertion of thrusting their hips in a gyrating motion. Brushing against them on the dance floor as I led the way to an open table, I could feel that some of them wore no underwear. The girls they were dancing with seemed oblivious to the fact that their breasts were rubbing provocatively against me. There was a dizzying atmosphere of orgiastic promiscuity in here.

The tables on the far side of the crowded dance floor were all but obscured behind some pillars designed to look like stalactites and stalagmites. As soon as we found a table, a waiter dressed as a red demon came over to take our orders for drinks. When he went away to bring them, we headed back out to the dance floor and began dancing.

Whenever I danced, I felt a wonderful sense of freedom, as if I were being unleashed, a comet spinning through black space. The disco beat sent a primal message to my nerves; I felt I was back in the jungle again, back at my roots, in communication with the deepest part of my psyche. The rhythm sparked a genetic memory of my ancestors dancing wildly after a kill, or performing a ritual courtship dance. At times I felt I wasn't dancing with Christine so much as with my ancient blood relatives.

Christine was quite a good dancer. For her, though, dancing was more of a practical physical exercise, a way to work off the accumulated stresses of study.

I looked beyond her to where Scott and Jill were. Scott looked like he was having a good time. He was dancing and laughing with Jill. I noticed her large breasts bouncing, bra-less, against her tight ribbed sweater.

Jill was one of those girls who had a reputation for being easy, and Christine had vehemently protested my choice of Scott's partner. We'd almost had a fight about it earlier. She saw me looking over at Jill now.

"That girl's a pig," she said. "Her room-mate tells me she sleeps with a different guy every week."

"So? If unattached men can have multiple sex partners, why can't women?"

"She isn't for Scott. She'd eat him alive."

"Maybe he'd enjoy that."

"Guy."

When I'd first set eyes on Jill this evening, I'd been a little disappointed that her looks hadn't matched her reputation. I had been expecting a sleazy-looking tramp or a bewitching vamp, but the girl who'd met us at the dorm with Christine was of average looks, a trifle vapid-looking but otherwise nondescript. The skill of her make-up left something to be desired, and she used a little too much perfume. There was only one thing which gave a subtle hint of her promiscuity: her body seemed as if it didn't belong to her. She gave the impression she was only borrowing it for the occasion, as she would wear someone else's dress to create an enticing allure, a sexy gown designed for a woman much older than herself.

I caught Scott's eye and we smiled at each other. At that moment, I felt as if I were dancing with him. He moved toward me, and for a while we danced facing each other, trying to talk over the loud music. I moved against him, and he leaned toward me, pressing his mouth against my ear, but I couldn't hear a word he said.

When we got back to the table, I learned that he'd only been asking for directions to the men's room. I got up. "I have to go, too."

The restroom was in the far corner, hidden behind some hellish-looking 'flames' — actually strands of orange, yellow and red vinyl being blown upwards by a small electric fan.

Inside the restroom, standing at adjacent urinals, I asked him,

"What do you think of Jill?"

"She's all right. A little bit on the wild side, though."

I wondered if he'd heard the rumors about her. For me, Jill's reputation wore itself around her like a cloak, wreathing her in an aura of magic, the magic of the many whispered stories about her. Such girls had always fascinated me; the knowledge that she'd been to bed with so many different boys gave her a semi-divine status in my eyes. I tried to envision all the male virility spent into her, all the boy-skin she'd touched. Some atavistic longing had made me go after such girls in high school. Maybe I'd felt a primal need to connect vicariously with all the boys they'd been with. I knew many boys — straight boys — who shared this subconscious longing to bond sexually with other males, but in a way which left their precious sense of masculinity intact. For them, too, the idea of possessing the girl a friend has once had, and passing her around in a ritual sharing, was a sexual stimulant.

I smiled at Scott. "I think she likes you, Scott. This is going to be your lucky night. I just know it."

He looked uncertain.

"Don't worry," I assured him, misinterpreting his look, "she's supposed to be... you know... friendly. You're almost sure to score."

For a moment I thought I saw a trapped look in his eyes and regretted my subterfuges. My man-to-man assurances seemed only to trouble him. For me, however, the thought that Scott would soon be having sex with Jill gave me a giddy sense of power... and a nervous feeling of anxiety. I felt like a playwright about to see his own work performed on stage for the first time.

We returned to the table where Jill was eagerly waiting to pull Scott back out onto the dance floor. Christine and I followed them. We danced the next several numbers, then returned together to the table, sweaty and tired. Scott and Jill seemed to be enjoying themselves thoroughly. We all sat listening to the music for a while, and talking.

I found myself ordering more and more beers by the pitcher. After a while, it must have seemed to outsiders that we were intent on getting drunk. Christine's words were beginning to slur, and Jill's laughter had turned loud and strident. Scott, too, looked quite drunk, drunker than I'd ever seen him. As I thought of the night ahead, my own intoxication became edged with panic; the scenario I'd sketched so blithely earlier was now fading away in places, leaving sinister blank spots.

"Let's get back to the dorm before we get too drunk to walk," I said.

Jill looked at me with, I thought, a flash of understanding. Had we somehow turned into secret accomplices?

Outside, I put my arm around Christine, and Scott and Jill were walking just behind us, locked arm in arm. My plan was for all of us to go back to the dorm where we would relax in our room. If the atmosphere and timing were right, I could make some excuse to walk Christine home, leaving Scott and Jill alone in the room. But if everybody seemed willing, I could just pull the partition closed, separating the two sides of the room, and both couples could make love right there in the same room. With luck, there might not even be a need for the partition. As I envisioned being able to see Scott and Jill naked in each other's arms, I felt my steps begin to hurry. This would be a night to remember.

Back at the dorm, there seemed to be a party in progress in the lounge, but we sneaked past its door and headed straight for our room without looking in. Only after we'd closed our door behind us did we all burst out laughing.

Jill drunkenly pulled Scott to herself and began kissing him, clumsily guiding him down onto his sofa-bed as she did so. I suspected she was acting drunker than she really was. I looked at Christine; she gave me a wry smile. But when I signalled for her to come to me, she just shook her head.

"Well, you two lovebirds," I said, "Chrissie wants me to see her to her room, so if you'll excuse us..."

As I began guiding Christine toward the door, Scott's passion seemed suddenly to cool. "Wait," he said. "Not before having another drink." The look of uncertainty on his face indicated he wasn't so eager for us to separate just yet.

"Sure." I walked over to the refrigerator where he quickly joined me. As I handed him a couple of cans, he whispered:

"Guy, please. Can we call it off?"

I stared at him. "What? Just when you're about to get laid?"

"I — I think I'd prefer another night. The time's not right."

"It's not?" And then the reason for his reluctance came to me. "Tell me something, Scott. Is this your first time?"

He looked at me ruefully. "Yeah." He blushed and I knew he was telling the truth. Though I knew he was innocent, I'd never quite thought of him as a virgin, perhaps taking for granted that he'd slept at least once with his high school girlfriend.

"There's nothing to be afraid of," I said. "It'll all come naturally."

"Yeah, but — "

"You do like girls, don't you?" I felt like a hypocrite for saying it, but a part of me was suddenly eager to hear his answer — perhaps I still had a faint hope that he was gay. And another part of me wondered if I hadn't planned the whole evening with just this in mind — to prove one way or the other whether he was or not.

"Of course I like girls," he said. "It's not that, but — "

A sudden sense of shame came over me. Why should he have to go through with it just to satisfy a longing in me?

"All right," I said, "I'll make some kind of excuse."

"Thanks."

I went back to the girls. "Hey, listen. Scott says he feels a little sick from drinking too much."

They looked toward him. Sheepishly, he said, "I guess I'm not much of a partyer."

Jill looked a little disappointed. "Are you all right, Scott?"

"Yeah. But I think I should hit the sack."

I said: "Chrissie, could you see Jill home? I think I'd better make Scott some hot coffee."

"Sure."

After the girls had gone, I filled the electric coffee-maker with water and plugged it in. As we sat waiting for the water to boil, I thought about the turn the evening had taken. Though I was disappointed that it hadn't come off as I'd planned, I was happy to have gotten Scott's confession of his virginity. Such a confession isn't lightly given by any boy, and was another link bringing us closer together. I felt a new tenderness toward him.

"It's all right, Scott. My first time was really scary for me, too."

"It's not that," he said. He gave a nervous little laugh. "I've never talked about this with anybody because it's a little embarrassing. I mean, it might sound so trivial to you, but for me it isn't. You see, I'm not like other boys."

I stared at him, my heart almost stopping. "Go on."

"Guy, I have a confession to make. I've never undressed in front of a girl before. And the reason for that is... I'm ashamed of my own body."

"Why?"

"I'm uncircumcised."

I didn't know what to say. My first impulse was to laugh at something so trifling, but the look on his face was serious. "Is there something wrong with being uncircumcised?" I asked.

"Well, it makes me feel different. I know most guys are circumcised, so I guess I have a complex about it."

"You shouldn't. I mean, it seems so foolish to let something like that — " I was thinking: so that's why he always hid himself when he came out of the shower.

"You don't know what it's like. You're circumcised, aren't you, Guy?"

"Yes." When had he seen me?

"So you're in the majority. You have no way of knowing the feelings of inferiority and envy that an uncircumcised boy lives with, seeing the cleaner-looking penises of his friends. For the longest time I felt like a freak and an outsider. Circumcised penises were normal, uncircumcised ones were not. To me, my dick looked sickly and unhealthy compared to my friends'."

"Did anyone ever tell you that?"

"No. But it's something I've felt ever since the first time I saw my friends' dicks. That was when we were about ten years old, undressing in my room to change into swim trunks. It was a real shock to me to see I was different from them. And later, in junior high school PE class, when we undressed for the showers, I saw that almost every kid in class was circumcised."

"Well, at that age, everyone feels like a freak."

"Guy, what did you think of guys who were uncircumcised?"

I shrugged. In junior high school, I, too, was curious — for different reasons — about other boys' dicks. There'd been one boy whose dick was capped with a brown-skinned prepuce. The hood-like foreskin had completely covered the glans, coming to a puckered tip in front. Another boy had a dick which was half-covered; I recalled thinking the glans looked like a turtle's head peeping out of its shell. In truth, the dicks which I'd found most sexy were those with a clean, round, pink glans exposed. But the idea that Scott was uncut — 'blemished' — somehow gave him a slight flaw that made him even more endearing in my eyes. If only he knew how little it mattered!

101

"Nothing," I said. "It's just a minor difference. Like some guys have straight red hair, others have curly black hair. What does it matter?"

"For you, maybe. But try being the guy who's different. It's something you can brood about your whole life."

I could understand, though. Most of the things which bother us so much about ourselves usually mean nothing to a stranger. Still, it was hard to believe that he would be caused so much anguish by a piece of skin covering his glans.

"Come to think of it," I said, "why do we get circumcised, anyway? It's something I've never thought about."

"It's been around so long — more than 4,000 years — that it's become tradition in many cultures all over the world. For certain people — the Muslims and the Jews, for instance — circumcision was a religious injunction; for others, it was a rite of passage, marking adulthood. And in the US — "

"But why did it start in the first place? I mean, there had to be a reason for it."

"That's right. It probably originated from sanitary reasons. You see, because the skin covers the head, sometimes dirt and gunk can get trapped inside. And there's a secretion called smegma which is secreted by the inside of the foreskin as a natural lubricant. Some forms of bacteria feed on the smegma. Back in the days when people didn't take regular baths, I imagine these things sometimes led to infections. So ancient people started cutting off the foreskin, making it easier to clean. It might have been crucial to survival back then, but with today's sanitary conditions, many doctors feel there's no real need for circumcision."

"Then why is it done? I don't remember asking to be circumcised."

"It's a standard procedure here in the US now. When little boys are born, most parents sign a routine consent form as part of the whole birth process, giving the doctor permission to perform the operation."

"The baby boy has no say in the matter, really."

"Right. Some doctors feel that circumcision at birth causes trauma in the child. After all, it is a painful operation — and anesthetics aren't used for newborn babies, as it's too risky."

"But they keep performing it because — that's the way it's always been done."

"Sometimes there are medical reasons for it, though, to prevent infection and so on. And sometimes it's even necessary for grown men to have the operation."

"Why?"

"Apparently, with some men, the glans remains covered even when they're fully erect. Ejaculation is painful, and conception is difficult. So they cut off the excess skin so they can ejaculate normally."

"How about you?" I asked, feeling as if I were stepping to the edge of a cliff. "Do you have trouble ejaculating?"

He didn't seem bothered by the question. "No. As I get hard, the foreskin slips off, leaving the glans completely uncovered. When I was a kid, I didn't know I had a normal glans like the others. It wasn't until I was about 16 that the foreskin could retract all the way, and I discovered I had a normal glans under there. It was a gradual process: at first it didn't slip off all the way, and was painful to move. But when I finally managed to slip it all the way back, you can imagine how happy I was."

A vivid picture of his erection flashed into my mind. "So what's the problem?"

"I still feel that girls will think an uncircumcised cock is ugly. They're used to seeing something different, after all. And that's why I'm so inhibited, I guess."

I laughed. "You're creating your own barrier, Scott. Don't worry. If a girl likes you, she won't care one way or the other whether you're circumcised or not."

"I don't know..."

"You have to get over that feeling of shame about your body, because until that changes, nothing will."

He sat thinking for a while. Then he looked up. "Guy, you seem so confident around girls. I suppose with your looks, you don't have to worry very much about the possibility of rejection, do you?"

"Looks have nothing to do with it. I had to work on my confidence just like everyone else. And anyway," I went on, seeing his expression of disbelief, "what makes you think you're not attractive, Scott?"

"Come on..."

"No, I'm serious. In fact, if you want me to be really blunt about it, you're quite a good-looking guy. I happen to know that girls find you attractive."

"Get out of here," he said with an embarrassed laugh.

"No, seriously."

"Like who, for instance?"

"Well... Christine, for one."

"Did she really say that?"

"Sure. If she wasn't going with me, she'd be after you."

"No way."

"Of course she would. If I was her, I would be, too."

"Come on..."

"I'm serious."

He shook his head with such a comical look of despondency that I had to laugh. Then I said, only half-jokingly: "If Christine had a twin sister, we'd be all set up."

"Right." He ran his fingers through his hair and looked thoughtful for a moment. "How did you meet her, anyway?"

"At a friend's party. We hit it off right away — I think, because she was so different from most other girls I'd met. That's probably why I like her so much. A normal girl wouldn't interest me at all."

"Did you have many girlfriends before her?"

"A lot. Too many, maybe. I think, in a way, it's deadened my feeling for girls. I tend to look down on a lot of them."

"It must be nice to have that problem."

"But I'm serious. When they're so easily accessible, you really start not caring so much for them; you even come to despise them. Sometimes I think it might be better if it was all more difficult."

"I suppose it must be true, then, that the more out of reach something is, the more you desire it."

I looked at him in some surprise. "Exactly. That's exactly what I'm talking about."

He seemed a little alarmed at the intensity of my reaction, and at the serious turn our discussion had taken. I decided to ease up a bit.

"We're starting to sound like a couple of philosophy students at an all-night bull session."

He smiled weakly. "I've never been this drunk before in my life."

A loud burst of laughter from down the hall was followed

by what sounded like the bookshelves crashing down.

"Sounds like those guys are even drunker."

2

It was late at night and I was on my way home to the dorm. I'd been studying at the library together with Scott, but when he'd told me he intended to stay until closing time, I decided to go home first ahead of him. My route took me by the arts building, then up the bicycle path along the football field. As I crossed over the tiny bridge leading to the bicycle path, a lone jogger passed me from behind, then turned off into the woods. I gazed after him thinking of my excursion into Nightworld a couple of weeks ago. I hadn't been back there since then.

I felt a sudden excitement thrill through my nerves at the memory of the secret I'd uncovered then. My steps slowed and I found myself looking around. There was no one else about. Probably because it was just before the finals, a silence pervaded the campus. There was no moon out.

I told myself I should head straight back to the dorm without giving it any further thought. Nightworld was not for me; merely to know it was out here should be enough to satisfy me. There was no need to involve myself in its existence. If I were to go there again tonight, it would be like stepping irreversibly into that netherworld. Did I want to be like those hungry nocturnal shadows homing in like shameless predators upon coyly waiting game? It wasn't worth the risk.

Yet even as I told myself all this, I knew I would be unable to resist its seductive pull; to know it was out there in the night was more than I could stand. Just to go there, to reconfirm its existence, what was wrong with that? After all, I would only be watching it all as an interested observer, as a scientist observes the mating habits of a lower species.

I turned my steps toward the darkness.

As before, I headed toward the restroom just behind the grandstand. The way was now familiar to me; I'd come here several times during the day to enjoy the contrast it provided with what I knew went on at night. As I approached the restroom now, I peered cautiously about, surveying the whole surrounding area, the shadows under the trees. There seemed to be no one out here tonight. In the darkness of the bushes behind the restroom, I noticed the bench was empty. I walked over to it and casually sat down.

My heart was thudding in my chest. I told myself there was nothing suspicious in my sitting here on this bench at this time of night. In fact, I willed myself into believing that I was an innocent student who had studied a little too hard and had just stepped out for a breath of fresh air before going back to his books. Who was to say that I had the faintest idea that this place was a homosexual cruising ground at night? After all, so very few people did.

I wished I had something to do with my hands, a cigarette, perhaps. But it appeared I was all alone here tonight. I began to relax.

More time passed and the quiet nighttime sounds all around me came to seem less sinister. Indeed, there was something rather comforting about the dark. Perhaps this was my natural element. Ever since boyhood, it had always been the dark that I'd been drawn to, the sinister, the criminal and the forbidden. I'd longed to be a creature of the night — able to see where others are unable — and to have a secret power over others.

When I was about seven, there was a weekly adventure series on television called the Black Avenger. For reasons which I forget, the hero, who had another identity during the day — an ordinary banker or something — transformed himself at night into a sort of one-man vigilante, clothing himself all in black from head to foot and going about seeking evil-doers to punish. What gave his situation an unbearable pathos for me was the fact that society in general, and the newspapers and police in particular, were under the mistaken assumption that he was the main criminal responsible for a number of evil deeds. Indeed, all the evidence did seem to point that way. It was only us, the sympathetic audience, who were onto the real nature of the Black Avenger. It gave me such a feeling of helpless anger — and a feeling of superiority over the bumbling, blind authorities — to watch as the Avenger just managed to foil some criminal's attempted crime, only to be discovered by a reporter or someone with the incriminating evidence in his hands — the jewels which he'd just snatched from the hands of the thief, and was about to return to the safe.

The Black Avenger had never been very popular among my friends, but I'd always worshipped him with a secret feeling of collusion. Like him, and like all those creatures which only come out at night, and for whom night is the natural habitat, I knew I was a fundamentally different being. Perhaps the Black Avenger was still the secret idol of my heart, and continued to influence me in subtle ways. For it was darkness which had cloaked his true identity, and which had nurtured his heroic apartness.

I gave a start. Someone had come up from behind me so suddenly that for a second I thought I'd been ambushed. But he just sat down next to me on the bench. It was the jogger I'd seen earlier.

I was too scared to say a word, and for a long time just sat there in silence, gazing straight ahead. I was too nervous to look at him. I couldn't tell if he was looking at me.

From the corner of my eye I could see he was wearing a dark-colored sweat shirt and running shorts. His feet were clad in white sneakers. His proximity was making me nervous and I was thinking of walking away.

Then, without a word, he dropped his hand gently onto my crotch. So sudden had it been that I just sat there. I tried to act calm, peering into the darkness all around, everywhere but at him. I wondered if I should reciprocate. It felt silly just sitting there with his hand on me, as if I were a junior high school girl too scared to react when her boyfriend first puts his hand on her breast.

As casually as I could, I shifted my hand onto his crotch. He was wearing nothing underneath his running shorts, and I could clearly feel his erection straining upward. He had a big dick, perhaps eight or nine inches long.

For the first time I turned my head to look at him. I couldn't see his face clearly in the dark, and had no idea how old he was, but he was well built, probably an athlete. His hair was cropped short and he wore glasses.

I began stroking his dick over his shorts as his hand dropped away from mine. My nervousness had seemed to magically evaporate with my first touch of his dick, as if I'd been energized by the contact. Indeed, I became quite aggressive; my hand felt a need which my mind tried vainly to deny.

Suddenly he got up. I wondered if he was going away. He stepped a few paces away and stopped, looked back at me. Was this an invitation to follow him? Looking around and confirming that we were all alone, I got up and took a couple of steps in his direction. He began walking away.

Again, I wondered if he was leaving. As I continued to watch him, he stopped about twenty feet away and looked back at me. I took several more steps in his direction, and when I came close to him, he again moved off. We continued this stop and go ritual as he led me farther and farther away from the bench.

Finally when we were in the darkest part of the woods he let me catch up with him. Looking around, he leaned back against a tree. I moved next to him and reached my hand down to stroke him. For a few minutes I revelled in the feel of the hardness beneath his shorts. But my partner didn't seem to be relaxed enough to enjoy it; he kept peering around in the darkness.

Abruptly he moved away and I followed.

We were moving into the area south of the football field. I saw that there was a wire fence surrounding the field at this point and just alongside it, a hedge. On the other side of the hedge was a building which I believed was a shower room, or an athletic equipment storage place. The football field was brightly lit, and the contrast between the lights on the field and the darkness of the encircling hedge threw the narrow space between fence and hedge into the utmost blackness.

My partner stood for a moment at the entrance to this narrow space and looked back at me. It was clear that he had led me here on purpose — no doubt this was familiar territory to him.

He stepped between the fence and hedge and disappeared into the darkness there. I slipped in after him. After cautiously feeling my way in the darkness, I came upon him leaning back against the hedge. Here, no one could see us; we were completely shielded from the eyes of the world.

I went up to him and dropped my hand onto his crotch. His dick was still poking straight up, bigger than ever, almost comically distending his shorts. I stroked it, as before, over the shorts, but then, unable to stand it anymore, pulled away the elastic waistband so I could touch actual flesh, feel its warmth.

He grunted softly at the contact. I could smell his sweat in the dark and something else — a strong whiff of semen.

All this time he never looked me in the face but was constantly peering around, jerking his head this way and that. I wished he would relax more, while feeling the wildest excitement myself. I slipped my other hand up under his sweatshirt and rubbed his chest. The muscle tone was firm and elastic. I liked what I felt. He was definitely an athlete, perhaps had played on the very football field so clearly visible just beyond the wire fence. Beneath my fingers I felt his heart pounding.

It seemed as if we were all alone in the world. This complete stranger and I were accomplices in an act of uttermost intimacy, right here in the middle of the campus. Until a few minutes ago, we had had no idea of each other's existence. I felt a surge of power, a giddy drunkenness which made my head swim. In this dark, I was freed for the first time from the burden of being looked at and admired, from the pressure of having to be the beautiful one. Here, I was just another shadow in the night, another boy looking for surreptitious thrills. I was almost overwhelmed by this strange new freedom. Anything goes, I thought. Anything. And no one knows anything about this. What's to stop me?

I pulled his shorts down to his thighs, freeing his dick, and immediately the sexy fragrance of sweat and semen became even more pungent. I stroked him with greater freedom, occasionally strumming his balls lightly with my fingers. I knew he was feeling good, he had to be feeling good. He'd thrown back his head and his eyes were closed. He was no longer concerned about being seen; he had given himself up completely to receiving his pleasure.

I dropped to my knees, and though it was almost too dark to see it, his dick came alive with a pungent immediacy. I could feel its moist heat inches from my face. Kneeling there on the soft earth, I could smell the moldy odor of his tennis shoes, and the sweet perfume of the crushed blades of grass beneath me. I ran my palms up and down his thighs, feeling the wiry hairs there as I lowered my face to his crotch. With trembling fingers I pulled the upright shaft of his dick a little away from its tight cling to his stomach and parted my lips. The moist, meaty warmth of the glans slid into my mouth and I was in a dream.

This can't be happening to me, I told myself. This isn't happening.

I played my tongue up and down the length of the shaft and paused to squeeze the glans softly between my lips. It seemed to swell up inside my mouth like a hot plum as I ran my tongue around it. I pulled my face away and returned to tickle with the pointed tip of my tongue the underside of the glans where it is most sensitive. The whole dick twitched with each contact, straining up harder against the stomach, reaching for the stars. And each twitch of the dick brought a soft cry of pleasure from my partner.

I kissed the crown of the glans and let its blunt moist warmth play along my cheek, sliding it along my upper lip and all around my mouth without putting it in. I wished this could last forever. For the first time in my life I was indulging in one of my most cherished boyhood fantasies. But I could feel my partner was being pushed to the edge of his endurance by my teasing.

I gripped the shaft again and sank it into my mouth as far as it would go, until I almost gagged, then pulled my face back until it was only halfway in. Keeping my head still, I began stroking the lower, exposed part of the dick, leaving the rest buried in my mouth.

Within seconds I heard a stuttered gasp and my mouth instantly filled with warmth, almost gagging me by its suddenness. For the briefest moment, I felt a twinge of panic at what I'd done. And then I concentrated on enjoying the sensation of what was in my mouth, savoring the salty metal taste of it, its gluey texture, before swallowing it down. The essence of come seemed to permeate my mouth, my entire being. It was a taste I knew well from boyhood, having often naughtily tried the flavor of my own ejaculate. But having it warm and fresh from another boy gave it an added deliciousness. I continued sucking him as if urging on a further effusion. His dick in my mouth continued to twitch, even as its rock-like rigidity began softening into flesh. It was still twitching a little as he withdrew it from my mouth, from my universe.

Then I felt him gently push my head away. As soon as I was disengaged he slipped his shorts back up.

I got to my feet and ran my hands over his hard buttocks.

I tried to look him in the face but he was once again peering furtively around into the darkness. He wouldn't say a word.

Still peering around, he began walking away, back the way we'd come. I followed. When he reached the entrance to the narrow space we were in, he stepped out into the open and did three or four squats. Then, without a word or a backward look, he continued his interrupted jog. I watched him running down the bicycle path, his silhouette fading, fading, then blending with the greater shadow of Nightworld.

He never turned around.

3

The air in the room was filled with hazy smoke and Christine and I were lying side by side on my bed. It was near sundown, and in my mirror I could see the reflection of the skies above the women's dorm.

"Have you ever noticed," I said languidly, "that if, instead of looking directly at the sunset, you look at its reflection in the mirror, for example, it looks so much more beautiful?"

"Oh?" Christine blinked at me with heavy-lidded gravity. She accepted the joint I handed her.

"It's true," I continued. "In the reflection it looks like some marvelous, magical landscape with a fairy-tale castle and a golden forest. Like an illustration in a children's book I used to read as a kid. Maybe something philosophical can be read into that: how much more potent illusions are than the real thing."

"Pot profundity," she said, taking another hit of her joint and passing it back to me. "All those lovely thoughts of yours are like so much smoke." She blew out the smoke she'd been holding in. "It only seems deep now. Wait till tomorrow morning."

"You're probably right," I laughed.

Just then we heard a door down the hallway open, then close. We knew Scott was still in the library studying, and wouldn't be coming back for a while. Recently he spent most of his evenings there working on his term paper. Christine had just finished hers — that was what we were celebrating now. We'd invited Scott to celebrate with us but he had declined. He had a strong aversion to drugs of any kind, though he didn't oppose our using it.

"Do you think he'll join us when he's done?" asked Christine.

"No, I don't think so. He knows you're here, and he wants to give us our privacy so we can, you know... Being the gentleman he is."

"I feel badly about that. It's the one thing he can't join us in. I mean, besides smoking marijuana."

"Yeah."

"If only he had a girlfriend..."

"Not that again. He told me he isn't interested in looking for a girlfriend right now."

She shook her head. "Jill was definitely a mistake. She prob-

111

ably scared him off women. Scott wasn't as drunk as he said he was that night. I know."

"He's shy around girls."

"Not around me."

"Well, you're different. How many other girls are there around here who can discuss Dostoevski with him? How many girls actually enjoy watching the movies of Bergman and Kurosawa?" She and Scott sometimes went out to the movies together at my request, though Christine had been a little reluctant at first. I'd told her she didn't need my 'permission' to go out with a mutual friend.

"If he weren't so shy, he might find plenty of girls who share his interests. In his creative writing classes, for instance."

"Those literary girls can be really neurotic. I've met a few of them."

She seemed to be musing on something before she replied. "But you say he's not looking for a girlfriend right now. Do you think he might be gay?"

"Of course not!" I was almost offended. "There's nothing wrong with Scott. He's as straight as they come."

"Then you would think he'd like to find someone to have sex with — if he's anywhere near as horny as you."

I snorted, then turned serious. "Christine, I know the reason why Scott is so shy around girls."

"Why is he?"

"Believe it or not, he's a virgin. That's why he got cold feet that night."

"Really?" Her look of incredulity gave way to wonder as she said softly, "In a way I guess I knew it all along. He's a real rarity in this day and age. It somehow makes him seem pure. Not many boys are these days."

"But I don't think he's happy about it, either. I'm sure if he had a choice, he'd be screwing away like the rest of us. Who wants to be celibate?"

"There's a lot worse things than being pure."

"Not for a guy. You don't know how important it is for a guy to sleep with a girl — to know he can handle it. Until he does, he lives with the fear of possible failure."

"Masculine ego."

"I know. But that's the way we're made. Our sense of self-esteem is directly linked to our sexual performance. With girls it's probably different, but I'm speaking from a guy's point of view."

"If sex is all he wants, there's plenty of girls who are looking for the same thing. Check out Erewhon on any Saturday night. If he's not too picky, he can easily substantiate his precious masculine identity."

I paused. "Maybe I shouldn't be saying this — "

"Come on, he's my friend just as much as yours."

"Well, he told me with a serious look on his face that he had this terrible secret."

"Yes?"

"And when I asked him what it was, he said he's uncircumcised, and he has a terrible complex about it."

"Is that all? That seems to be a silly thing to be bothered about."

"I know. That's what I told him. But that's how he is."

"Hmm. If only he knew how little it means to a girl."

"Yeah." A bold thought had entered my head; I debated whether or not I should say it, then went ahead and did so: "I guess the best way for him to find out would be for you to sleep with him, right?"

"Idiot."

"If only you weren't going with me, you'd be the perfect one for him," I said. "He really likes you, you know."

"Hm." She turned onto her side, facing away from me, and I slipped up against her. I knew this talk was getting her aroused. I'd switched the direction of our talk onto familiar ground — she knew of the excitement we both felt at the way other guys were attracted to her, and of my so-called jealousy of them. At the root of this shared fantasy was the ever-present possibility that she would someday 'betray' me with one of them. Now she probably thought my fantasy had been triggered by my jealousy. I stroked her hips, my mind lazy and unfocussed. The thought that she was thinking about Scott had aroused me, and I let her know of it by pushing my groin up against her buttocks. By now it had gotten dark, but I wondered if my two watchers across the way could see us now, if they were straining their eyes to see...

"You know," I said, "many guys have this sexual fantasy... about their girlfriends sleeping with other guys."

"Don't I know it." I could tell by her reply that she was also quite high. "But Scott isn't the type to do anything with his best friend's girl. He's too much of an old-fashioned gentleman to ever betray you, even if he didn't have his silly inhibitions about being uncircumcised."

"Too bad. What if we broke up? I mean faked a break-up? Then you would be 'free'. You could go crying to him for consolation, and in the process of consoling you, the two of you would almost naturally end up in bed."

"True. That often happens. But in Scott's case, I don't think he would. I mean, even if it was a real break-up. He would still feel loyal to you. He's that kind of guy."

"Then we'll never have him sleeping with you."

"If he didn't think it was me, it might be a different story," she said seductively, in the tone she used whenever we spun out our sexual fantasies.

"What do you mean?"

"What if he thought I was my own identical twin?"

"What? But you don't have one."

"We make one up, silly."

"What's her name?" I asked, eagerly joining in her game.

"Justine. Ever since reading that book by the Marquis de Sade, I've had these delicious fantasies about a depraved alter ego of mine named Justine. The name even sounds like my own."

"Maybe there is a part of you deep down which really is depraved." I knew now she was just as aroused as I was by our talk. I felt an excitement in her like an electric charge. The absurdity, or the illicitness of the idea, had captivated her. There were feelings involved here which I had no way of gauging. I knew somewhere at the core of her being was a desire to betray me, or to be 'shared' between two boys. We'd talked about such topics, in a casual manner, admittedly, but I had sensed that Christine was intrigued by the idea. She wasn't a prude. Not by a long shot.

She was stretching her chin upward, like a cat begging to be stroked.

"I love it when you're like this," I said. "So, we have him believe you have a twin. What next?"

"If he believed I was Justine, he would do it. Or even if he only believed I was supposed to be Justine. That way he won't be going against any of his principles."

"You would pretend you're Justine? But how can you actually get him to believe it?"

She got up off the bed and whisked the curtains shut, then turned on the reading light. Picking up her suede totebag from the floor, she went over to my mirror and began cleaning the make-up off her face with some cold cream. When I'd first met her, she'd used very little make-up, but acquiescing to my desire to make her more attractive in the eyes of other boys, she'd learned the art and magic of cosmetics.

Now she began doing things to her face to subtly alter it. Re-applying the eye-liner in a slightly different way, and using less blusher and a new shade of lipstick, she engineered the creation of a new, more vampy look. She brushed her hair straight back from her forehead, parted it to one side and put some bobby pins into place.

"If only I had a wig."

When she was finished, she turned around to gauge my reaction. She'd done something to her hair which made it look shorter, and made her look different, more confident somehow. She'd changed in some way and become Justine, her nonexistent alter-ego.

She broke into a smile at my reaction. "I'm not Christine anymore. I'm Justine."

And I would have believed it if I hadn't known better. The change seemed to go deeper than mere physical alteration, as if she'd changed her true personality. Just by taking off her usual make-up and redoing her hair, she'd become reborn as another being. It made me realize just how much of a woman was created by her make-up, hairstyle, and clothes. I envied such versatility, such flexibility. I'd never seen Christine like this, the archetypical vamp: a creature of illusion, born to illusion, and master of it.

I was a little afraid of this new woman.

"You even speak a little differently," I said. "You *are* Justine, for all practical purposes. And what happens now?"

She thought for a moment. "I call up your dorm when you're out. Scott answers the phone, and I tell him I'm Justine. I've dropped into town to look up my sister."

"That sounds good," I laughed.

"But 'Christine' is out, of course. We'll have worked that out well in advance. You and I could be on a weekend trip. So I ask him to show me around. Or knowing Scott, he will offer to take me to wherever Guy and Christine are supposed to be — say, a ski lodge up in the mountains. We meet at the cafeteria..."

"How does he react to you?"

"He remarks on the amazing resemblance, and on the little differences. But in my personality, there is much that is similar to Christine's. The Justine I've become is so much like Christine that he feels no shyness at all. In fact, he feels as if he's known me from way back."

"Which he does, of course. But is he completely fooled? Doesn't he suspect anything? Or does he think it's a prank and goes along — collaborating in your play-acting?"

"Let's say he falls for it. Or pretends to. But for whatever reason, he says nothing. At any rate, we get along so well and become so friendly with each other during the course of the evening, that on our way to the mountain lodge, he puts up very little protest when I suggest we go to a motel. I say the hell with meeting Chrissie. I can drop into town some other time."

"Justine is a little bit more forward than Christine. But how about you? The strain of keeping up the pretense, the deception?"

"It would be hard. But once we're in bed, it wouldn't matter. Identities don't matter, illusions don't matter, only the reality of our two bodies against each other. I'll get him over his inhibitions really quick."

I felt a strange welter of emotions in me which I couldn't put a name to. I strongly suspected that Scott was in love with Christine, and here we were, spinning out fantasies about seducing him. I wished I could turn into Justine as easily as Christine could.

"Do you confess to him in the morning?" I ask.

"No, why should I? The next morning, I have to take an early flight back to New York, a little sad that I couldn't see Christine, but happy at my little escapade. We part at the campus plaza, but not before I confess that I have a boyfriend back home, and he must never attempt to contact me in any way. He reluctantly agrees."

"And?"

"And at lunchtime I'm Christine again, and run into him at the cafeteria. He doesn't suspect a thing. But I know what's behind that naughty little smile of his."

Her excitement had been transmitted to me, and I momentarily lived with her triumphant betrayal of me. If in fact it could happen — if Christine ever slept with Scott — I would be linked psychically with him, making love to him in the only way possible for me now.

I fondled Christine's breasts and she curled her body up in response. She purred like a cat, her signal for initiating sex. It was always she who did the initiating nowadays, she who decided whether or not we would have sex.

I thought of Scott. Now, even as I was touching Christine, I was thinking of him. He was between Christine and me, the one who'd excited both of us; and I knew Christine was thinking of him now, too, after I'd prodded her to embroider her fantasy.

I whispered into her ear: "You're beautiful, Justine." A tremor went through her. "Justine." Another tremor.

"Don't, Guy, don't," she whispered.

"Call me Scott," I said.

"Scott..."

My head swam at the sound of his name on her lips. I slipped my hand up under her t-shirt. "You are so depraved, girl, so depraved."

"Yes," she whispered throatily.

"It would be so easy..."

"Hmm?"

"For you to have Scott. Why couldn't you go with both of us?"

"What?"

"Have a three-way relationship. That would be ideal."

She stopped. And then backed away a little so she could look at me. "What are you saying?"

"I was just — "

"Do you realize what you're saying?" She rolled away from me and got up.

"Christine?"

"Guy, that is disgusting. Do you know what an insult that is? Do you?" In her eyes was a flash of tears.

Ashamed at the shock I'd caused, I quickly blamed it on the pot. "It was only a fantasy, Christine. And I'm high. Maybe I don't know what I'm saying. My mind must be skipping a couple of grooves. It's just a sexual turn-on to think of a three-way, that's all."

She gazed distractedly at the wall for a while without speaking.

"Chrissie, I was just embroidering on our fantasy. Scott would never be able to do such a thing anyway. He's too old-fashioned."

"Well, maybe I am, too. A little too old-fashioned for you, it looks like."

"Chrissie."

She said nothing for a while. Then, as if she'd been waiting for the right moment to speak, she said, "Guy, is there someone else?"

"What?" The question caught me by surprise. I looked at her, hoping my shock didn't register on my face. "Someone else? No, of course not. Why do you say that?"

"You wouldn't have said what you just did if you still cared for me."

"You know me. I'm always spinning out crazy scenarios to spice up things."

"It's not only that. I've sensed it for some time. You seem a little distant recently."

It was true. I hadn't been paying as much attention to her lately as I had in the early days. Since my discovery of Nightworld, there were more and more evenings when I told her I was too busy to see her. We still met about two or three times a week, but it was different. Our sex life had undergone a subtle sea-change; it didn't satisfy me as it had before, and she probably sensed it.

"Are you trying to push me off onto Scott? Is that it? You're tired of me and want to break up?"

"No, Christine, no!" This was the first time I'd seen her like this, the first 'scene' we'd had, and it pained me to see her so troubled. And yet, at the same time, it reduced her in my eyes to just another girl mouthing standard phrases. With her suspicious query, she'd lost her special individuality, all that made her uniquely Christine. I was vaguely let down. However, my feelings for her remained tender; and I knew I still needed her. For me, she represented the healthy, accepted daytime world, the necessary counterbalance to that troubled underside represented by Nightworld and my love for Scott. Right now, for my own sanity and well-being, I needed both.

When she spoke next, her voice had gone quite quiet. "If there is someone else, Guy, I'd rather know about it now than find out later on my own."

118

I tried to laugh it off. "Believe me, Christine, there's nothing to worry about. I don't know why you're turning so suspicious all of a sudden, but as far as I'm concerned, everything's still the same between us. There is no one else. Will you trust me on this?"

She stared down at the floor for a long time, then looked up straight into my eyes. "I guess I'll have to, Guy."

"Please. Because it's the truth."

I thought of the way she'd whispered Scott's name and felt a sudden throb of emotion, whether at remorse for mentally betraying her, or for my love of Scott, I couldn't say. I held my arms open and she flowed into them, we melted into each other in the tenderest moment we'd shared since we first started going with each other.

4

The morning was so beautiful, and I felt in such a good mood that I decided to do some jogging. The sky above was the perfect shade of blue, the temperature just the right coolness. In my sweatsuit, I kept up a good pace through the park.

I cut along University Avenue heading toward the bay. There was very little traffic at this hour of the morning, vehicular or pedestrian, and my jogging was going smoothly. At a red light I jogged in place waiting for the green. There was a church facing the intersection on the opposite corner, and apparently the service had just ended; the minister was standing at the door having a few last words with individual members of the congregation as they were leaving.

"Guy, wait up."

I turned around. Someone else in a sweatsuit was jogging up the sidewalk, and as he came up alongside me, I recognized Professor Golden.

"Good morning," he said. He was puffing a little, but seemed to be in very good shape. "Mind if I join you?"

"Not at all. I'd be honored."

The light changed and we continued jogging together. To his credit, the professor didn't look too ridiculous, as so many middle aged joggers do. It was obvious that he was, unlike me, a regular jogger. He kept up quite a good pace, and his form was excellent. I would have to be careful not to show how winded I was.

We reached the bayside park, cut through it and took the path along the water. On our right was the park itself, where people were walking their dogs or strolling. It was peaceful. On our left was the bay, where we could see ships at anchor. Some sailboats glided silently over the choppy waves, the people on them bright splashes of color.

At the end of the path we came to a locked gate. Having no alternative, we turned around and headed back to the park. As we approached it, we slowed down, and Golden suggested we sit down for a little while. I was glad he'd suggested it, as I was secretly getting quite winded.

We found a nice spot beneath some trees from where we could look out over the water.

"How is Christine?" Golden asked, wiping his face and head with the small hand towel he'd had around his neck.

"Fine. She's working this morning. Part-time job at a drug counselling center."

"Lovely girl. Very intelligent. I was quite impressed with her."

"Yes, I remember." I felt vaguely irritated at the way he kept harping on Christine's virtues when I knew he was really interested only in me.

"She seems to be very open-minded about homosexuality. Seemed quite interested in it, actually."

"She's a psych major, so I guess it's in her field."

"Meaning you think homosexuality is a psychological disease?"

"Oh, no. Of course not."

I was beginning to feel uncomfortably warm. I unzipped my sweatshirt. My running had brought out a sweat, and an odor like musky, just-cut grass lingered hotly about my skin. It was a smell I'd always found very sexy — it reminded me of the boys' locker room after football practice. As I pulled my sweatshirt off and laid it on the ground, Golden looked away and pretended to be absorbed in the sight of the sailboats out on the bay. I knew he was feeling self-conscious about my body. I surreptitiously brought my nose down to my armpit and breathed in its enticing tang.

A thin film of sweat encased my arms, causing a faint, glinting sheen to hover about the surface of the skin. My sleeveless t-shirt was drenched and clinging to my torso, and as his glance flicked past my chest I actually felt a tightening sensation in my nipples. The dumb-bells I worked out with every night in front of my mirror had filled out my chest with a solid plate of muscle, making it look as if a pair of smooth shields was thrusting out against my wet cotton t-shirt.

When I looked up I saw his eyes quickly dart away. He'd been eying the tiny spray of golden-brown hairs which peeped from under my armpit. At this moment, I felt we were no longer professor and student. He was merely an older man who was attracted by my youth. Feeling a surge of power flow into my tired muscles, I leaned backwards, resting my weight on my elbows, and closed my eyes. I was in a languorous mood and didn't care what happened. To relieve my muscles I arched my back and stretched, then began rubbing my hand lightly over my stomach, bringing it gradually up to my chest in languid, circular motions. I was well aware that I was putting on a show, provoking the older man. For me, it was a sort of a revenge, to punish him for his pretense of interest in Christine.

He was old enough to be my father, yet I found him strangely attractive. Occasionally, when I thought about him, my feelings for him were distinctly sexual — perhaps inevitable, given his intelligence and strong character. I'd always been drawn to dominant types. Though he was past his prime as far as looks were concerned, his personality almost made physical attractiveness seem unimportant. And there was the seductive thought of his power — he was a full professor while I was just a freshman boy.

He was silent for a minute, and seemed to be thinking about what he was going to say, and then went ahead and said it. "You're not gay, are you?"

"Me? No." My answer was automatic, almost a reflex action. I was taken aback by the bluntness of the question, though I should have expected it.

He laughed. "You needn't look so offended. I was only curious. Do you have a good relationship with Christine?"

"Yes," I said, then hastened to add, "There's no trouble there."

He chuckled. "I didn't mean to imply that there was. Tell me, Guy, may I ask you an even more personal question?"

"Sure." I was afraid I knew what he'd ask, and braced myself for it.

"Have you ever had a sexual experience with another man?"

"Well..."

"Come on, don't be shy. We're both adults here. Nothing you say will be repeated. Trust me."

I knew I could trust him completely. I was only wondering how much I should tell him. I decided that my adventures in Nightworld would be a little too much. I thought of Mark Warren, the boy I'd had an experience with back in high school. I nodded. "Yes. Once. With a friend in high school."

"And what did you think of it?"

"I guess I was a little ashamed of myself. Because I never saw him again."

"Did you enjoy the experience?"

"I really don't know." My answer was purposely vague, as I was still wary of the direction of his talk.

"Well, it's not unusual. Many men have had homosexual experiences, especially in their adolescence. Not all who do so are gay. I'm happy to see you're open-minded about it, and are willing to examine your feelings. Many people deliberately suppress the memory of their homosexual experiences. But apparently yours has left you with a healthy curiosity, I take it."

"Yeah."

He was looking at me as if he expected me to add something more. And the growing silence which fell between us almost begged to be filled with a confession on my part. I was tempted to do so. In my heart, I wanted so much to tell him everything, to unload this secret burden I was carrying, but I didn't feel brave enough yet.

Suddenly he changed the subject himself. "Do you remember the painting Peter Cockle was doing of you?"

"You know Peter?" I was surprised.

"Of course. He was in my art history class as a freshman. We became quite close. Anyway, he finally finished the painting."

"Have you seen it?"

"Oh yes."

"Where is it?"

"In his studio."

I was stunned. "Why did he show it to you when he hasn't even let me see it?"

"He just finished it last Friday and was celebrating in Arabian Nights, a gay bar just off-campus. I happened to run into him there and he told me about it. He was quite drunk. That's probably why he let his guard down. I know he's usually shy about showing his own work. I must be the only one besides himself who's seen his Narcissus, since apparently you haven't seen it yourself. I offered to buy it then and there, but he refuses to part with it. He did offer to loan it to me for a while, though."

"And it's at your house now?"

"No, not yet. I'll give you a call, if you like, when I get my hands on it."

"I appreciate it. He never let me see it, so I have no idea how I look in it."

"Take my word for it, it's a masterpiece. And, if you want to know the truth of it, one of the most erotic pieces of art I've ever encountered."

"Why doesn't he let me see it? He's acting awfully childish about a mere painting. You'd think he was hoarding treasure or something."

"Well, in a way, maybe he is. For him, this Narcissus is more than just a mere painting. I suspect that the real reason he won't show it to anyone — even the boy who inspired it — is jealousy."

"Jealousy? I don't get it."

"Have you ever heard of the Pygmalion legend?"

"I don't think so."

"It's a sort of counterpart to the Narcissus legend, maybe even its complementing opposite. Pygmalion was a sculptor, unmarried, a confirmed bachelor. No, he was not gay. He desired women but was just disgusted with the way the women of his day acted. He felt they were lewd, bold, and unchaste. So, in the loneliness of his studio, he created his own ideal woman, a statue of a beautiful young girl so true to life that it seemed to breathe.

"She represented everything he'd dreamed of in a woman, but had never found in reality. Physically beautiful but at the same time chaste and pure. And because she was a statue, he could gaze at her nudity to his heart's content. Day by day he grew more and more in love with her. She looked so shy in her nakedness that he adorned her with clothes. Not stopping there, he began making up her face with cosmetics. Soon he was buying her little presents. At night he kissed her before going to bed. Before long, he wasn't satisfied with mere kisses — he began caressing her. She, of course, received his tribute in chaste, unresisting silence. So delicate did she look that, though she was made of stone, Pygmalion was afraid the strength of his caresses might bruise her.

"Anyway, his secret love life continued and he was happy. He had the mistress of his dreams in his arms every night; what more could he want? What more? A living woman, of course. So when festival time came — the festival of Venus — he went to the temple of the goddess of love and prayed. He asked Venus to send him a girl just like the one he'd sculpted. In his heart, he'd often prayed for the statue to come to life, but he knew that was too much to ask. However, Venus, seeing that he truly loved the statue, looked favorably upon him. After all, isn't any kind of love, no matter how grotesque, a tribute to Venus? She granted him his desire.

"When he went home that night, he kissed the statue as usual, and lo and behold, her cool marble lips seemed to be responding with a warmth he'd never felt before. He ran his hands down her thighs and felt softness there. Overjoyed, he embraced her. Arms so long frozen into a chaste gesture encircled him, she was getting softer and softer in his arms with each new caress. By the time he had kissed her all over, the statue had turned to flesh, she was alive. And she had loved him all along — pining away in loneliness because she was never able to return his love.

"Well, the story goes on to say they lived happily ever after. She gave birth to a baby girl, and so on. I think it's one of the few Greek myths which has a happy ending."

"Are you saying Peter painted me so he could jerk off to my picture?" I had a vivid mental image of the unattractive artist down on his knees before my painting, caressing himself furiously as he leaned in to kiss it, praying he could be kissing warm flesh instead of dry canvas. Suppressing the real excitement I felt, I mouthed a conventional reply: "That's disgusting. That's the sickest thing I ever heard."

"He's an artist," Golden replied. "What you might see as grotesque is what satisfies him, is what fuels his art. And what's wrong with that? He's happy, in a manner of speaking. As a homosexual, society has always made him feel that his love was unnatural, that his desires are sick. So ever since he learned how to draw, he drew beautiful boys. It was the only way he could get what he wanted. It's easy for you to say it's sick; you don't have to resort to substitutes."

"Well, neither do you." I was thinking of the boy I'd seen him with that day.

"Well, I'm no artist, with an artist's sensibilities." He paused, and appeared to be contemplating something for a moment. "On the other hand, though I have no talent for art, music or literature, I am not completely without artistic abilities."

"Well, as a lecturer, I've found very few others who are as fascinating as you."

"Thank you. But I don't mean that. I'm talking about something else. I *am* an artist, but of another kind. My own art is physical — the physical act of sex. For me, it's an art form just like the others."

"Oh?"

"Why shouldn't sex be considered an art? It requires just as much aesthetic sense as playing music or writing a novel. And with experience, you can become a master at it."

"It *is* like a dance..."

"Yes. Whose choreography I've made my own personal form of artistic expression... for an audience of one. It's a craft I've perfected with time, to the point where I can play a young man's body like a musical instrument. I only wish some of my past performances had been preserved for posterity on film so that others can learn from them, as from a textbook. They were works of art."

Such brazen confidence, far from putting me off, amused me. Did such braggarts exist in real life? Could he possibly live up to his promise? Or was it merely the come-on he used with all boys?

I was laughing at his talk, but his eyes were on me all the time, mercilessly measuring me. "Guy, have you ever thought of repeating that experience you had in high school?" he asked.

I halted in mid-stretch and sat up straight. The suddenness of the question had caught me completely by surprise, and I felt a flush spreading across my face. My nipples felt tight and tense.

"What do you mean?" I asked.

"I mean, of exploring your feelings *vis-à-vis* another man. Specifically yours truly."

I was suddenly brought back face to face with the fact that he was gay and I was gay and he found me intensely desirable. A part of me wanted to accept. I knew that sex with him would be different. I could go to bed with him without feeling the sense of competition that I would inevitably have felt with a younger guy.

And with Golden, I would feel none of the fear or shame which I usually felt about my own sexuality. He was so understanding, and so much more experienced.

But I knew I wasn't ready to think of him in a sexual way. And I still wasn't sure how much I wanted him to know about me. I had never had openly gay sex — it had always been furtive, secret. Perhaps it was this very furtiveness which, for me, was part of the attraction. Would open gay sex have any enticements for me? And with an older man?

The answer was no. For now.

Maybe it was the blunt, straightforward way he'd propositioned me. If he'd been more romantic about it, I might have considered it more seriously. With a sinking feeling I realized that perhaps his previous confession to Christine and me in the student union had been a mere preliminary for this — his proposition. That thought cheapened all that had gone before. Yet I refused to believe he thought of me as an easy pick-up.

But how to refuse? I knew that if I did, he wouldn't press the issue.

Seeing I was troubled, he said lightly:

"That's all right. I don't want you to feel under an obligation."

"I'm flattered by your invitation," I said, "but I really don't think I'm ready for it right now." Even as I said it, I felt foolishly prudish.

"The offer will always remain open. Just give yourself plenty of time to think it over. And if you do decide you want to, just tell me anytime. Because if you're curious about gay sex, you couldn't have a better teacher than me."

"Oh?" I looked for a humorous expression on his face, but saw he was quite serious. "I think I'd better finish the rest of my jogging now." I got up and he did, too.

"I think I've rested enough, myself."

"Unfortunately, though, it seems our routes are different, professor."

"Whatever you say."

I slipped back into my sweatshirt and resumed the interrupted jog. I was glad he couldn't see how short of breath I was, as my heart was pounding furiously.

After class on my way up to my room, I checked my mailbox in the lobby out of habit. The mail usually came at about one o'clock every weekday so it should have arrived by now. Scott subscribed to several magazines of a literary nature, and he was eagerly looking forward to the latest edition of one of them. I checked, but it hadn't come in yet. Instead, there was a postcard for me. It was from Professor Harding, my chemistry professor. I hadn't attended his class for several weeks, intending to drop it, and now he was inquiring about my intentions.

I knew I had to file a petition to drop his class. I'd been putting it off for weeks, and my mid-term grade for the class had been an F. Which wasn't surprising because I hadn't attended a single class since early in the term, when I'd decided to drop it.

Without even bothering to go up to my room, I turned around and went straight to the administration office to get the necessary paperwork. Thinking I'd be able to take care of everything there, I was dismayed when the girl behind the counter told me I still had to go to the professor's office to get his signature. I checked his schedule printed on the postcard. He would be in.

Professor Harding's office was in Makra Hall, the science building. When I knocked on his door, his somewhat high-pitched voice said, "Come in." Heavy-hearted, I entered.

He was one of those dreary scholars for whom the world outside his special field of study was of no interest. On top of that, he had a sarcastic and spiteful nature, and mean-looking eyes. His nose had a pinched look about it, and his forehead was domed, arrogant in its imperturbability.

"Well, Mr. Willard, what have we got here?"

"It's a petition to drop your class, sir."

"Oh?" He accepted the slip of paper and examined it as if he'd never seen one before. "And why, might I ask, are you dropping?" He let the petition drop onto his desk as if he'd lost all interest in it.

"Well, I've discovered that your course is way beyond my level."

"Did you have the necessary prerequisites for the class?"

"Yes. I got a B in high school chemistry."

"And I take it you had something of a rude awakening when you learned that college chemistry was a wee bit more challenging than high school chemistry?"

"Somewhat." A faint spark of anger leapt into my heart.

"You were aware, of course, that you are attending one of the most competitive schools in the state? If you weren't up to the challenge, you shouldn't have come here in the first place." He had a maliciously pleased expression on his face as he saw my reaction. "If you're like most of the freshmen who come here so hopefully in the fall, only to leave so disenchanted before the end of the first term, you're probably more familiar with the inside of a disco than with an open textbook."

"Maybe a disco has more to teach me about life than a chemistry lab." I wanted to smash his self-important face in, but I needed his signature to clear my record.

"Then maybe you should become a professional dancer." He looked at my body. "Or a professional whatever."

"Will you sign the paper. Please."

He looked at me one more time with a smirk, picked up his pen, scrawled on the petition slip and handed it back, then returned to what he was doing as if I'd been dismissed from his thoughts in an instant.

As I stepped out I heard behind me: "Good luck, Mr. Willard. They tell me that life outside the campus can be every bit as tough as the inside."

I took the paper back to the admin office, then went straight to the dorm. I pulled a beer out of the refrigerator and drank it down at a single draft. Despite my anger, I was able to dismiss the smug professor from my thoughts immediately. It was only Scott now who could claim my attention.

He still hadn't come back. He'd told me this morning that he was likely to go straight to the library after his last class of the day. I would have liked to go straight to see him but I knew I would only disturb his studies. Instead, I went down the hall to the lounge hoping to kill some time before Scott came back. Frank was the only one in, and he was sitting alone, watching a cop show. I didn't feel like joining him; from his eyes, he looked stoned.

"Have you seen Scott around?" I asked, as a way of taking my leave as quickly as possible.

"No. Anyway, you wouldn't find him here in the lounge;

that guy's a regular grind."

"Right. Thanks."

He turned his attention back to the TV, watching it blankly, seeing nothing. I went down the hallway to Kruk's room and knocked on his door. He was always in.

He looked surprised to see me when he opened his door.

"Hey, Kruk. What's up?"

"Not much."

"How about heading down to the rec building with me and shooting some pool? I feel restless today."

"Isn't Scott with you?"

"No. He's cramming for a test or something."

"I'm not much of one for shooting pool. Would you like to come in and join me?"

"Sure." I'd never been inside his room before, only talked to him from his doorway. As he closed the door behind me, I spotted a bottle of brandy on his desk. "I didn't know you were a drinker, Kruk. I thought you only liked sucking on sugar cubes."

"I'm not. Today — is different."

"What's up? You finish your term paper?"

"It's my birthday."

"Oh." I felt inexplicably sad at being reminded that people like Kruk, too, had birthdays. The loneliness of the room struck me. Why was Frank, his room-mate, down in the lounge? "Well, let's celebrate. Call the other guys."

"No. If you don't mind. Just us two. I don't want to make a big deal out of it."

"You should have told me beforehand, Kruk." I opened the bottle while he fetched two glasses. It was cherry brandy, and, when I tasted it, was a bit too sweet for me, but I pretended to drink it with gusto. "Happy birthday, Kruk. How does it feel to be of legal age now?"

"No different," he laughed. "Besides, the legal age doesn't seem to matter for anything these days."

"Maybe you're right."

"You look a little bit preoccupied today, Guy. Is something the matter?"

"Me? No. I've just come back from dropping a class I was failing. That should be cause for celebration. I guess."

"What class was that?"

"Chemistry."

"You should have come to me. I would have tutored you, Guy."

"I know. I just seem busy with so many other things these days. Have another drink, Kruk. Let's forget our troubles." I poured for him.

He took a sip of his brandy; he drank it as if he were taking medicine. Indeed, his face became more and more blotched-looking as he drank, with bright red spots appearing on his forehead and cheeks. I would have bet anything that this was the first time he'd gotten drunk. I urged more brandy onto him and he drank it without protest.

"Tell me something, Kruk," I said, as a blissful numbness began to steal over me. "Have you ever been in love?"

He looked at me. "Me?"

"Yes, you."

"Well... of course. Gee, I guess everybody's been in love."

"If you don't mind my prying, who was she?"

After an initial hesitation, he began to tell me of his love life. As I listened, I grew more and more saddened at the unfairness of things. Kruk was a gentle and sensitive soul, just unlucky to be born unattractive. Ever since junior high school and all through high school, he'd nursed a secret crush on the school beauty. In all the time he'd known her, he'd never said a single word to her, though they shared several classes. He had only watched her from afar, content to worship her hopelessly, without the faintest expectation of ever revealing his feelings to her.

"You should have at least tried something, Kruk," I said, knowing all the while that it would have probably been hopeless.

"You don't understand, Guy. She wouldn't have wanted to be seen even talking with me. But that was okay. For me, she was a goddess — literally — and I was happy to worship her in secret. Back home I have a scrapbook — "

He'd cut out pictures of her from the local newspaper, when she made homecoming queen at his high school, when she became the town's Miss Fire Prevention Week, when she received a citation from the mayor for her efforts in charity drives. As he told me of the cult he'd made of idolizing her, I felt embarrassed for him. But I realized it might be good for him to open up about his secret like this. For all I knew, this was the first time he'd ever told anyone about it. I didn't know why he'd decided to tell it to me today, but I suddenly felt a piercing tenderness for his bloated, unsightly body, his pockmarked face, his thick-lensed glasses, his loneliness and sorrow.

"Kruk, believe me, I know what it's like to love someone, and not be able to tell them. I'm going through the same thing now."

"What?" He pushed his glasses up the bridge of his nose and tried to focus his eyes on me. "You? Come on. What about Christine?"

"It's someone else, Kruk. I'm in love with someone else and I don't have the slightest chance in the world of letting that person know."

"I can't believe this," he giggled. "You? If it can happen to you, it can happen to anyone. Now I don't feel so bad."

"Great. Let's drink to that."

"All right." He looked straight at me trying to focus his eyes. "Does this mean you're breaking up with Christine, Guy?"

"I wish it were that easy. It's much more complicated than that. I wish all of life were so much simpler." I picked up my glass and drained the brandy at a gulp. Because of its saccharine flavor it was difficult to swallow, but I did my best. "Here, have another drink." I was in his room, drinking his brandy, and I was acting as the host. But he seemed to want it that way.

"Hear hear." His smile was angelic. He appeared to be listening to bells ringing from high above.

"You know, Kruk, between you and me, you're probably the happier one."

"Oh, I'm happy, all right. Never said I wasn't."

"You should be a philosopher. What's the secret?"

"The secret? There is none. Absolutely none. Once you understand that, you're halfway there."

"We're halfway through this bottle, if that's any progress."

"Oh, it is. It is."

"Drink up. Oh, and did I tell you happy birthday?"

"You did. And did I tell you that it's better to have loved unhappily than not to have loved at all? I'm quoting now."

"Damned philosopher."

"I'm getting drunk, Guy. I can't believe it: I'm getting drunk."

"Empty that glass, Kruk. This is no time to brag."

"There is no time for sorrow."

"Is that a quote, too?"

"Who knows?"

"And who cares, Kruk? Who even cares?"

"Hear hear. Who even cares? No one. Absolutely no one," he cried.

"That's the spirit."

I don't know how long I was in his room. It seemed a short time. When I tried to pour him some more brandy, however, I discovered we'd finished off the bottle. I staggered down the hallway to my own room intending to get some beers from the refrigerator, but by the time I got there, found I'd changed my mind. Scott wasn't back yet. I decided on the spur of the moment to take a nice long shower and go to bed.

I undressed and, leaving my clothes scattered on the floor, walked uncertainly into the shower stall. The blast of cold water felt good. I let it hit my face for a long time before turning the hot water on. The jets of warm water were the most soothing thing in the world.

I thought of Scott's naked body and instantly felt a hard-on blossom, as if it were no part of me, a sudden iron rod poking straight up against my stomach. I hoped he would come back now — burst into the shower stall and see me in this condition. I would stand here just like this. I was drunk and didn't care. I wanted him to see my erection. I was hornier than I'd ever been.

I dried myself off and made my way to Scott's bed. There, I dropped the towel onto the floor and got under his covers. Imagining him in bed with me, I squirmed my hips against the mattress. It felt good. Then I lay still, my head resting on his pillow, my breathing beginning to return to normal.

The room spun slowly around and around and I willed it to stop. I wanted Scott to hurry up and get back, for tonight would solve everything. In my drunkenness I kept muttering: "Who even cares? Who even cares?"

I lay waiting for him, long, long minutes. I pictured him coming though the door. I pictured him seeing me in his bed.

Some time later — I must have dozed off — I heard the door open. My face was turned to the wall, and I heard him bustling about at his desk for a moment before that sound suddenly ceased. He must have seen me in his bed and stopped. I listened all the while, pretending to be asleep but in reality wide awake now, with a hammering heart.

He shook me.

"Guy. What's the matter?"

I mumbled some drunken, incomprehensible protest.

"Darn," he said. He seemed to be thinking for a while. The obvious explanation for my presence in his bed would be that I'd come in drunk and mistaken his for mine. But would it be too far-fetched for him to see through my play-acting, to read my desire, my invitation, my confession? A tiny part of me waxed hopeful on this forlorn possibility; everything depended upon his next move.

"Guy, wake up. You're in the wrong bed."

Still, I thought: Either he really thinks I've come here by mistake, or he thinks he has to play along with my game. So far so good. How could he fail to realize what I really wanted, what I ached for from the very roots of my being?

He shook my shoulder again and I turned over. In the process, I "accidentally" kicked off the cover, exposing my lower half.

For a long moment nothing happened. And then I felt him cover me up again. He went to the closet and pulled out a spare blanket, then went over to my bed. The fool was going to let me sleep in his bed. A true gentleman. Or had he chickened out?

I spent a sleepless night tossing and turning, and he probably did, too.

Early in the morning, at about 5:30, I stumbled out of bed, rubbing my eyes, scratching my head.

"Jesus, what a hangover. What am I doing in your bed?"

He stirred awake. "You must have mistaken it for your own. You were pretty drunk last night."

"Was I? God, I'm sorry. You mean you slept on my bed? You should have kicked me out of yours. I would have."

"No, it's okay. I don't mind."

"Damn!"

"Guy, is something bothering you? I've never seen you that drunk before."

I was touched by his concern, but at the same time chagrined that he hadn't seen through my clumsy ruse. "I dropped chemistry class, and had a few words with the professor. A real asshole."

"You should have come to me. I would have helped you get

133

over it. Gotten drunk with you, anyway."

"Oh, and it was Kruk's birthday yesterday. We finished off a bottle of brandy together."

He whistled. "Kruk, drinking? That must have been a sight worth seeing. I wish I was there with you."

"Yeah? Well, so do I, Scott. So do I."

6

The recreation building was located at the far western end of the campus, and was one of those places which students long ago must have frequented, but which was little used today. An ancient three-story building, it had a rundown, seedy appearance. There was a paperback library and lounge on the first floor, billiards and ping-pong tables on the second, and a long-disused dance floor on the third. The place had obviously seen better days; springs stuck out of the sofa cushions in the lounge, and the green felt of the pool tables was so worn down in spots that it was difficult to shoot a straight ball. On weekday nights you could see a few students there, but during the weekend it was virtually empty. On this Saturday evening, the rec building looked like the last refuge of the bored and lonely.

The type of student who used the place was the straight, rather studious type who — I could tell — had never been popular in high school. These were the kind of people who'd come to this college out of a sort of revenge; a degree from here would ensure them of high-paying jobs which their more popular former classmates could never hope for. To me they all — girls as well as boys — looked rather unattractive, and drably unsexy. Certainly not the type I would have sought for a sex partner.

I went to the paperback library and got a science fiction book, sat down in an armchair and tried to read. But it was impossible for me to lose myself in it. I couldn't get out of my mind the conversation I'd had with Christine a little earlier in the day. I'd told her about the proposition Golden had made to me. To my surprise, she'd been intrigued by it.

"How did you reply?" she'd asked.

"I turned him down, of course."

"You should feel flattered, actually."

"Really?"

"Of course. It's a compliment to your attractiveness. And by reflection, it's also a compliment to my own good taste in men — because gay men have such exquisite tastes in everything."

I laughed, then felt a sudden moment's rashness. "What would you think," I said slyly, "if I'd accepted?"

She smiled. "You like girls too much, Guy." And then she seemed to be musing about something else. "You know, somehow, the thought is very erotic. The picture of two men together is a stimulating one — for me. If I were a man, I wonder if I would do it? Maybe I would... just to see what it was like. Just for the experience. I mean, I would never know unless I tried it."

"You can, you know."

"What?"

"Have the same kind of experience. Just sleep with another woman. It's the same thing. Have you ever thought of trying it?"

"Well, yeah, I guess so. I think all women have at one time or another wondered what it would be like with another woman."

I peered closely at her. "If you were going to sleep with a woman, who would it be with?"

"I don't know..."

"Your old room-mate? Have you ever thought of her in that way?"

"Not really."

"How about that cute Hispanic girl you told me about in your physical education class?" She flushed. No doubt she, too, remembered the time she'd described to me the beauty of a classmate she'd seen in the showers in terms which had been quite explicitly erotic. In spite of the discomfort I sensed in her, I went on: "Well, if you ever feel like trying it, you should. You know you would have my permission. For experience's sake, of course. I know you would view it as a psychological experiment or something."

She laughed, but seemed abstracted.

I felt impelled to add: "Why don't you try it once and see if you like it? For all you know, you might have had such tendencies all along."

She looked at me a little strangely. "Does the idea of my sleeping with a woman excite you so much?"

"Well, yeah. I guess all men have this fantasy of watching

two beautiful women making love. And you've always been one for expanding your horizons. An experience like that could only add to your sexual maturity."

She looked at me challengingly. "Okay, how about this, then? I sleep with a girl... if you sleep with another boy first. How's that?"

I laughed, hoping my agitation didn't show. "That's a good one, Christine. Do you really think I could go through with it?"

"Sure. As horny as you are, there's probably nothing you're incapable of, sexually."

"Why, thank you."

Now it was she who pressed on: "Guy, if you were going to sleep with another guy, who would it be?"

"Come on..."

"No, seriously. If you had to do it. Or, let's say you were offered a million dollars to do it or something."

"I don't know. I never thought of it."

"Would you do it with Scott?"

"Scott?" My voice sounded weak.

"Mm-hmm."

"But he's my best friend. I couldn't."

"Why not? He's attractive... intelligent... sensitive... Nice body, too."

I felt as if I were being interrogated, under threat of torture. Yet her smiling face held no hint of insinuation, nor cruelty. I knew she was only probing me out of idle curiosity, perhaps sensing an untouched area of erotic fantasy.

"I can't. Remember, he's a virgin. If I slept with him, it would be his first sexual experience, and that might mess him up for life. No, it would be better for him to have his first experience with a girl, so that his life won't be made miserable."

"Would it?"

"Of course. No homosexual can be happy."

"How would you know, silly? Maybe they're completely fulfilled."

Impatiently, I changed the subject. "If anyone pops his cherry, it should be you, Chrissie. He would prefer you infinitely more than me. Believe me."

I put my book down. I was beginning to wonder if Christine suspected my true feelings. And yet she wasn't the type to insinuate or hint about something she suspected: she would come right out and ask me. Still, she must have surely been aware that the threeway scene I'd suggested had all the trappings of a homosexual fantasy. And if Scott had told her about my pitiful attempt last night...

Restlessly, I got up from the armchair and put the book away. I hadn't come here tonight to brood; Scott and Christine were at the movies together, and I had the evening all to myself.

I decided to look around a bit before making my move. On the second floor, a boy and girl were playing ping-pong, and another boy was shooting some pool by himself. Others, mostly groups of friends, were playing board games.

There were flights of stairs at each end of the building, with a restroom on each landing, alternately women's and men's rooms. My interest in the rec building tonight was centered upon the men's room at the far end between the second and third floors, the least frequented because of its location. I imagined it must have been used by boys attending the dances once held in the now-deserted ballroom. But my investigations had discovered to me that it was one of the more frequented spots for anonymous homosexual encounters.

However, it was still too early to make my move. Each time I felt the need to urinate, I used the nearer restroom, the one between the first and second floors. It was cleaner, more spacious, and better lit than I'd remembered the other one to be.

By ten-thirty, the rec building was almost empty. I knew it closed at eleven o'clock. Feeling nervous as the time approached for me to make my move, I went up to the second floor to shoot some pool. The girl at the check-out counter kept looking at the clock on the wall behind her. The only people besides me were a pair of girls noisily playing eight-ball.

Finally, at about a quarter to eleven, I returned the balls and put the cue stick back in the rack. I headed up to the restroom as casually as I could. Despite my eagerness to explore it, I was scared. After all, I couldn't rule out the possibility that anti-gay jocks were lying in wait to beat me up if I entered.

The back flight was darker than the other. Some lights had burned out and not been replaced, giving the stairs a forbidding aspect. Still, no one seemed to be around at this hour. And the green-painted door to the men's room looked innocuous enough.

Upon pushing my way in, I immediately sensed something in the air. Some antenna within me made my skin prickle with warning signals. However, the place seemed to be empty. It was just as I'd remembered it from my explorations. There were two sinks, one of which had had its drainpipe kicked off the wall by a vandal.

As soon as I stepped farther in, however, I realized there was someone in the far stall. In the space between stall partition and floor I could see that he was wearing tennis shoes a little the worse for wear. His frayed jeans cuffs were bunched down around his heels.

My heart began to hammer and prickles spread over my skin. I tried to tell myself I had all the reason in the world to be here, that there was nothing suspicious in my actions. For all I knew, he was a straight guy just taking a crap.

Then I heard the bump of a door. He had opened the stall door just a crack, leaving about two inches of dark space between door and jamb. And in the darkness behind that crack floated the glow of an eye like an animal's, peering with an unblinking predatory stare.

A weighty feeling of excitement gripped my stomach. He could see me clearly, I knew. My impulse was to leave the restroom as quickly as possible, but, mastering my fear, I ran some water into the sink, washed my hands, then dried them. I tried to pay no attention to the eye.

I wanted so badly for something to happen, yet didn't want to give the impression that I'd come here seeking it. Everything should happen as if it were a fortuitous, unpremeditated accident.

To cover up my awkwardness, I moved toward the unoccupied stall. As I neared it, the crack slowly opened wider and wider, like a maw, threatening to swallow me. He was the spider in his trap and I the fly inching toward the sticky, sticky web. I felt drawn toward him, sucked in as toward a vortex, against my will, all volition gone.

At the last moment, it seemed, I slipped into the unoccupied stall, closing the door behind me with a bang. My heart pounding, my knees almost buckling under me, I sat shakily down on the toilet lid.

To my left, the toilet paper rack had been torn off the partition between us in what I thought at first was a wanton piece of vandalism, leaving a small hole about six inches in diameter where it had been. Before I could think what to do, a hand suddenly thrust through, the fingers gripping the partition and beginning to drum in a rhythmic, meaningful manner, as if tapping out a message, insistent, demanding. What did he want? Frozen with fear I just sat there. Presently the drumming fingers stopped, and I thought I heard a soft curse, a petulant tisk, and the other's toilet door banged and he was gone. What was that all about? I sat on my toilet seat trying to figure it out.

I looked at the graffiti all around me. Most of it was new, and some previous entries had been crossed out, including the one I'd seen before: *Want to meet a good-looking white guy? Come Friday nite, 11:30. Knock three times.* Anti-gay graffiti was in more evidence — *Kill Fags!* and *I Hate Queers!* Perhaps my earlier hesitation about coming here had been right.

The smell of damp cigarette butts was very strong. A leaking pipe somewhere had left a pool of water on the floor and a whole soggy roll of toilet paper was jammed down into it, moist as a soaked sponge. A dripping sound came from a steam pipe running along the back wall, giving the place a humid, tropical jungle atmosphere.

This was my first foray into this kind of adventure. Hitherto, I'd always avoided this scene; it was much too open for my purposes. Yet I was becoming a little jaded with Nightworld and wanted something a little different from its furtive encounters in the dark. Plus I was beginning to notice the same guys there all the time. It seemed there were about twelve who were regulars (and I even had private nicknames for them,) while most of the others were occasional or even one-time visitors whom I never saw again. This would be something new to add to my secret researches.

For back in my room, in the locked top drawer of my desk was a notebook containing the List of my encounters in Nightworld. From the start of my explorations there, some instinct had made me wish to preserve a record of all my encounters, with entries cryptically describing the men I met: *12+mid. Bleachers. Athlete type with short hair, glasses, jeans, plaid shirt. Sweaty, p: 8, 9 in., big b.*

The number of entries was slowly, secretly growing, for ever since my first time, I'd found myself going back repeatedly. Again and again, my feet took me there as if of their own accord. In fact,

I probably couldn't keep away from Nightworld anymore; I was hooked. The guys in the dorm grew used to seeing me depart at all hours of the evening, and they probably thought I was off to see Christine.

I began to understand the meaning of addiction. The things I did in Nightworld were hateful to me, yet I couldn't fight what drove me to them. Knowing these anonymous, faceless encounters were unwholesome, I still needed them. It was their very anonymity which protected me from my shame at being queer. In the darkest places of the night, virtually feeling my way by touch, I could indulge in my most powerful lusts. And because I couldn't see my partners and they couldn't see me, I could pretend that my desires were still deep within me, secret and unfulfilled.

I fought against the urge constantly. Each time I went I vowed it would be my last — and when I eventually shook off my qualms, I looked forward eagerly to the next time. Especially during periods of stress — during mid-terms, or while working on a particularly difficult research project — I would feel a queasy excitement in my stomach as I thought of the coming darkness. A visit to Nightworld was like a reward for my labors during the day; it was a way to unwind after a hard test.

During the day I was a serious student, asking the professors erudite questions, working hard on my essays. No one had the slightest idea that at night that very same student was down on his knees sucking dick. I couldn't believe it myself at times, so great was the contrast between the two personalities I presented to the world.

The darkness gave Nightworld its glamour; it made me feel like an initiate in a clandestine society about which no one else knew. The daytime world held no sway there; the men cruising Nightworld had their own rituals, their secret signals. They were the sexual outlaws, the subversives who were covertly undermining the foundations of society, the kind of people I'd always identified with.

I was proud of my secret. It made me feel superior to all the people I was fooling. Little did they realize that I had a foot in both worlds, that I enjoyed the love of a very attractive girl, and at the same time, took pleasure in things she could never give me.

I liked to imagine heterosexual desire as something like a burning flame, stoked higher and higher until it became red-hot...

blue-hot... white-hot, but the desire I felt as I prowled Nightworld was like a cold, pale rainbow flickering in a winter sky absolutely devoid of all heat — like the Aurora Borealis snaking silently in the Northern heavens.

Suddenly I heard a sound from outside. Someone else had come in. I sat with my heart pounding, waiting to see what would happen. With a bang, the door of the next stall opened, and someone sat down.

Through the hole, I could see my neighbor — or a part of him. He was sitting on the toilet seat just as I was. But it was only for a moment. He began undoing his jeans and pulling them down, until they were about his knees.

And then I felt my eyeballs grow hot.

Centered in the hole, framed perfectly, was an uninterrupted view of his dick. I couldn't tear my eyes away, I was spellbound. Out in Nightworld, it was usually too dark to be able to see anything with such clarity. This was what I'd always fantasized about: being able to watch another boy's dick to my heart's content.

He brought his left hand up and began playing with it in a way which left my view unimpeded. I watched it swell out, then up.

This was nothing like the cloaking darkness of Nightworld, where every action felt like a dream, where I groped almost blindly to feel a shadowy hardness with my fingertips. Though the lights in here were dim, I could see everything.

I watched as his fist gripped the shaft and made the glans bob up and down as if nodding. Then he began delicately massaging his shaft as if he were signalling me with it. I liked the way he stroked, and felt glad to be able to watch him like this, with nobody to bother me. It was as if he were communicating to me silently, altering the pitch of his strokes, fondling his balls and angling his penis so that I could get a good look at it from all sides. He was stroking himself with teasing motions, luring me, enticing me. I had become the audience in the dark, the spectator in the stands. We were united by his performance. The hole in the partition between us was the only reality.

A violent trembling went through me.

Suddenly I realized what he was waiting for — and what the previous boy had been signalling. Feeling as if my limbs were metal-heavy, I reached my hand up to the hole and put my fingers through,

141

drummed them on the partition on his side.

He stopped stroking and got up from his toilet seat to approach the partition. The next thing I knew, he'd come right up to the hole and pushed his dick through into my side, hard up and big. I reached my hand to grip his shaft. It felt nice and hard — just as hard as mine.

I began stroking him, feeling the warmth of him in my palm. I could feel him twitch in response, straining upward with each stroke. I bent down, bringing my face to his dick. For a moment I savored its nearness, feeling its heat against my cheek, smelling its spermy effluvium. Then I lowered my mouth over it, closing my lips over the throbbing glans, feeling it twitch upward at the contact.

I began sucking.

I sucked like a madman, forgetting everything. This wasn't the hip-sashaying, fluttering, faggoty sort of thing I associated with queers — this was sex in the raw, a brutal transaction which gave me a deliciously perverse thrill. It was unfeeling and impersonal, but that was the beauty of it. Here I was in the shadowy world of piss-smelling couplings, a quick, lurid suck-off in a men's room. I was doing what faggots are supposed to do. At this moment, I felt that all 'feeling' sex was meaningless, was for sissies and girls. What I was doing was the action of a rebel outlaw. I felt one with the criminals and junkies of the old movies, those black and white film characters, tough-talking and brutal. At heart I was an outlaw and this proved it; I wasn't bound by the laws and rules which shackled everyone else.

I had no idea who was on the other side of the partition. It could be anyone: a classmate, a teacher's assistant, a campus worker, or someone who had no connection with the school. His face could be unattractive or he could be a beauty. But for me right now, his dick was Scott's. For it was Scott's dick I always sought whenever I went prowling.

Indeed, it could be said that all my wanderings and explorations ever since I'd first discovered my own sexuality had been but a search for Scott. These caresses with my lips and tongue were what I wanted to do for him alone. And the sad thing was, this hole might be the only gap I would ever find in the gigantic partition which separated us.

With the fingers of my right hand I fondled his balls, and felt the sac tightening, drawing his balls up against the base of the shaft, tiny and tight, ready to explode. With my tongue, I was making his dick dance and twitch. His glans was getting harder and harder in my mouth, swelling bigger and bigger.

I listened to a ticking sound as if it were a clock counting off the seconds before liftoff — it was his belt buckle tapping rhythmically against the partition. My face felt hot but my heart was oddly calm as I awaited his orgasm.

At this moment my pleasure was perfect. Nothing could have increased it or decreased it. The sound of the water dripping from the steampipe behind me was as lovely as an echo in a cave.

Part Four: Ultima Thule

1

It was a clear night and the stars above us were brilliant in their icy splendor. Scott and I had just spent the evening in the undergrad library and were on our way back to the dorm. There were very few other people about and it felt wonderful to be walking like this, just the two of us. The winter term had just ended but the spring term hadn't yet begun. No schoolwork needed to be done. We had just browsed and read the books we wanted to. Scott had been reading a book of interviews with writers, called *Writers at Work*, while I had been poring over a beautiful collection of antique maps which I'd discovered quite by accident.

I've always loved maps, especially old ones which depict worlds which have long since vanished. Even back in elementary school, I used to pore over the maps in my history books which showed the routes the European explorers had taken as they discovered the New World, the dotted lines of their passages hopefully reaching out into the Atlantic, curving timidly away as they approached the unknown. The world must have been so much more forbidding then, so much more exciting. Blank white spaces on maps indicated the Great Unknown. But as explorers gradually conquered the new lands, the unknown grew smaller and smaller, the whiteness giving way to all the colors of the colonizing nations like dye seeping into virgin cloth, pink for England, green for France, yellow for Spain, and blue for Holland.

We'd been walking in silence for some time when Scott abruptly broke my chain of thought.

"Guy, what's been going on between you and Christine?"

Startled out of my reverie, I turned to look at him. "Nothing. Why do you ask?"

"Because it's all so — changed. It isn't like the old days."

"How do you mean?"

"Well... Christine was talking about it with me."

"She was?" I thought I detected an uncomfortable stir. It was obvious that he'd been trying to broach the topic with me for some time. "What did she say?"

"She didn't go into much detail. But I sensed that something isn't right between you two."

I shrugged. "Maybe it isn't."

With a nervous look he said softly, "Christine thinks you're seeing another girl. And she's worried sick. She's been worried for a long time now."

I laughed.

"Guy, this is serious. I've been sort of delegated to — find out the truth. I don't want to be a spy or anything so I'd rather ask you right out: is it true?"

"No. I'm not seeing another girl. No way. You can rest assured on that score."

"Then is it something else?" He looked at me so trustingly that I was tempted to tell him the truth then and there. Seeing my dilemma, he pressed worriedly: "Guy, is something bothering you?"

He had a pained, sympathetic look on his face. I was touched by his concern. "Well, Christine and I are having some troubles."

"A fight?"

"No, not exactly a fight. Just one of those things every couple goes through at one time or another. You'll find out when you get a girlfriend."

"I hope everything turns out okay for you."

"Why are you so worried about what happens between us?"

"Well, you and Christine are so good together. I'd hate to see you break up."

"Nothing is permanent, Scott. If a break-up happens, it happens. If it doesn't, it doesn't. That's all there is to it."

He turned away from me, perhaps a little hurt by the callousness with which I'd replied. But I couldn't help it. Something impelled me to make light of the whole thing.

"It's almost like you wish it'll happen, Guy."

"That's not true, Scott. I wish no such thing."

We were walking along the sidewalk in front of the Arts Building, where normally at this time of night, denizens of Nightworld might be seen lurking in the shadows behind the statues. At the thought of their invisible presence out there, my body began to shiver, to literally tremble like a leaf.

146

"Scott, I feel like getting a hot dog. Do you think Doggie Diner is still open?"

"It should be. They don't close until eleven."

"Come on. Let's grab us a bite to eat."

"Sure."

I knew that from where we were, a short cut to Doggie Diner would take us right through Nightworld. I led the way into the bushes beside the path, down towards the football field. "Come on. This is a short cut."

"I've never been this way before, at this time of night." He seemed anxious, even a little scared.

"It's okay. You're not afraid, are you?"

"No."

Soon we were deep in Nightworld. It was a quiet night, but I detected one or two dark forms flitting among the trees down by the stream. Scott didn't seem to notice a thing. He looked around. "Are you sure it's safe here? I don't want to get mugged or anything."

"Don't worry."

I led the way further into the dark. He followed me, though I could sense he was uneasy. We were approaching the restroom behind the stands. I spotted something going on.

"Hold it." I stopped as if I'd been startled. "Duck down. I think someone's out there."

"Who? A mugger?" He was really scared now.

"Get down and follow me. We haven't been seen. Something funny's going on out here." I led the way to the rise from where I'd first spied on the restroom and all the action which had been my introduction to Nightworld. When we'd attained a good vantage point, I urged him with silent gestures to squat down next to me.

"Look."

There was a boy standing in the doorway of the changing room, leaning back against the wall, all but hidden in the shadows. It was that beautiful youth of the starlit night. I could tell he was peering out into the trees below.

"Who is he?" whispered Scott.

"I don't know. But he seems awfully suspicious just standing there. Let's watch and see what happens."

We waited for perhaps fifteen minutes until we heard some footsteps coming from the direction of the bicycle path. A man was approaching the boy in the doorway. It was that unattractive middle-aged man who had dogged the boy's steps on that first night. I'd seen them occasionally out here, up to their old games. Now they were looking at each other without any sign of recognition, only an alert awareness. The man halted about twenty feet away, his silhouette blending into the shadow of a tree. No words were exchanged. Only silent looks.

And then the man went off under the stands and the boy followed. Since that first time, the boy had obviously relented a little in his coldness.

"What's going on?" asked Scott. "Is it a drug deal or something?"

"Maybe. Let's spy on them." I led him quietly around to the south end of the field, from where we made our stealthy way to the grandstand. There was an announcer's booth in the middle, about halfway up the central aisle. From inside it, by kneeling down and putting our eyes to knotholes in the wooden floorboards, we could clearly see the area below. I'd sometimes hidden myself in this booth just to watch the action that took place beneath the stands, and I prayed we might be able to get a good look tonight.

We did. Though it was quite dark, we could make out the silhouettes of the boy and man against the shadow of a support pylon. It was difficult to see exactly what was happening, but the movements of the shadows clearly implied a sexual exchange. The man was down on his knees and the boy had lowered his pants. By the whiteness of his skin, we could see that he'd bared his lower torso for the delectation of the older man.

"Good God! Do you see what they're doing?" whispered Scott.

"Yeah."

"They're homosexuals!"

"You're right. It sure seems the guy on his knees is blowing the other one."

"Come on, let's get out of here before they see us."

"Don't worry, they won't see us. And what if they do? They won't do a thing. They have a lot more to lose than us." I felt excited by his excitement. As we continued to spy on the couple, I kept glancing at Scott, more interested in his reaction than in what was going on below.

"This is fascinating," he said, his emotion making his words

148

tremble. "I can't believe it's happening right here. I always heard about such things, read about them in books."

Yes, the books I'd lent him. Recently I was much more bold about introducing him to works by gay writers, sandwiching *Naked Lunch* among other more innocuous books. I knew he'd read the 'good parts', but I hadn't yet had the guts to question him about them.

There was a slight commotion below; the boy abruptly pushed away the crouching man and pulled up his shorts. He strode rapidly away while the older man slowly got to his feet and much more slowly slipped away into the greater darkness. Then silence once more — except for the steady throbbing of insect cries which suddenly seemed to get louder.

We waited for a while longer before letting out our breaths and sitting up. We got up from the floor where we'd been kneeling, and sat down on the announcers' benches. From here we had a good view of the whole empty stadium. The brightly-lit field below looked ghostly and haunted, the brilliant green of the playing turf seeming to glow coldly like carved crystal under lamplight.

There was no moon out, and beyond the artificial lighting of the stadium, a velvety blackness seemed to be laid over the whole campus. The lights of the distant houses glinted coldly against the invisible hillside. I could hear, faintly, the music from someone's stereo. Above us, the red and blue lights of a shadow airplane winked in the night sky, travelling slowly from west to east. It was like the beginning of time and we were two cave dwellers looking upon the universe and wondering what it was all about.

"This is amazing, Guy. Do you think it happens a lot?" I noted the excitement in his voice.

"I don't know. It probably goes on a lot more than we think. They didn't seem to be novices."

"There was something cold about it, so mechanical. I wonder how many homosexuals there are in this school."

"Enough, I'm sure. Some of them are really open about it, too."

"Yeah. Sure is different from high school." He seemed a little dismayed.

"Weren't there any boys in your high school who were gay?"

"Well, sure. I mean, there were guys who were effeminate-looking, and everyone called them fags, but I don't know if they were really homosexual or not. I think most of it was just malicious gossip."

"Why? You didn't think it was true?"

"I don't know. Maybe I just didn't *want* to believe homosexuals actually existed."

"Why not?"

"It doesn't seem right that there should be boys so pitiful."

"Pitiful?"

"Yeah. In my school, there were bullies who got a big thrill out of picking on sissies. They were like savage animals acting out the law of the survival of the fittest. Actually, the bullies *wanted* to pick on weaker boys, so they invented any excuse. Homosexuality was a convenient one, that's all."

"Well, I think homosexuality is a topic a lot of boys don't want to think about. Because they're afraid."

"It's a common fear. I mean, a lot of guys are afraid they themselves might be one."

"Sure. Everybody goes through a stage where they have strong feelings for another boy, right?"

"Yeah, I guess so." I was touched by his chaste honesty. He thought for a moment. "Now that you mention it, I had a sort of crush, when I was about eleven, on a guy in the neighborhood who was a great football player. We used to play touch football after school, and he was always the captain of one of the teams. I'd always wish he'd pick me for his side when we chose up. And when he did, I was happy for the rest of the day."

"I had crushes on boys, too. I'll admit that. And if other guys were more open with you, I'm sure they would confess to the same things. It's one of those things that happen when you go through a certain age."

"You're probably right."

"But that doesn't mean you want to sleep with another guy, right?"

"Of course not."

"It's every boy's worst fear — that he might be secretly queer. But tell me the truth, Scott. Have you ever thought about it?"

"Well, yeah. I guess everybody does. At least as an abstract thought. It's natural to flirt with the unknown, with the dangerous and forbidden."

"Do you think you would ever do it?"

150

"I don't know. I wouldn't want to make a habit of it, but — sure, yeah, I'd do it just once, maybe, for the experience." His honesty thrilled me.

"That's what a lot of people would say if they were as honest as you. Voltaire once said: 'Once a philosopher, twice a pervert.' In other words, trying it once is like an experiment — to see what it's like, to satisfy your curiosity. But if you do it just one more time, it means you liked it — and that makes you a homo, a pervert."

"What do the psychologists say, I wonder?"

"They don't consider a person homosexual unless he's had repeated experiences, and actively seeks them out. A lot of boys try it out, especially in their adolescence, but it doesn't change their basic sexual orientation toward girls. Actually, I think everyone is basically bisexual. If there were a meter inside us measuring our sexuality, and one side was homosexual and the other was heterosexual, the needle would point somewhere in between for most people, either closer to the homo or the hetero side."

"You may be right."

I paused and realized a decision had already been made in my heart. My throat felt raw and unused. I cleared it and spoke.

"Listen, Scott. Can you keep a secret? I mean, really keep a secret?"

"You know I can." The expression on his face showed that he guessed the direction of my confession.

"I would never confess this if I didn't trust you completely."

He looked at me, his eyes glowing softly in the darkness. I went on:

"Scott, when I was in high school, I had sex with a guy once."

"Really?"

"Yeah. And you know what? It was my first sexual experience. Even before I screwed my first girl."

"What did you think of it?"

"I don't know. I felt guilty about it afterwards, and disgusted with myself. I never saw the guy again."

He looked somewhat relieved. "So you do like girls, right?"

"Of course I like girls. But — " I looked down at the boards below my feet. "I think that because my first experience was with a guy, I might have been a little messed up for a while. You see, the first sexual experience is so important in forming you. Because my

151

first experience was with a guy, my — I guess you could say I'm sexually ambiguous. If it had been with a girl — "

"What do you mean by that? Do you mean you're gay?" He looked so worried that I decided to soften it. I didn't want to scare him off.

"No. It's true I've often thought, what if — ? But I never acted on it. Scott, listen. When you have your first sexual experience, it should be with someone you love. Because you'll remember it all your life. And you might be tortured by it if it isn't exactly what you want. Yes, I like girls. But maybe not in the way most guys like them. You remember the meter I talked about? For me, the needle veers sometimes, wavering back and forth, first to one side, then the other. But that's only feelings. As far as actual experiences go, I'm still boringly hetero, don't worry."

"But then — " He looked at me, trying to assemble his thoughts. There was an almost desperate look in his eyes, as if he wanted to keep up with me but I was pushing things far beyond what he was comfortable with. "What does Christine mean to you, Guy? What are your feelings for her?"

"She's the most wonderful girl I've ever known. Until I met her, there was no one I could be completely open with. She's the most open-minded person I've ever met. And she profoundly changed my life for the better."

"But — do you... do you love her, though? That's what I'm asking."

I looked at him. It was so dark that I really couldn't see his expression, but I thought I felt the bench under us shiver.

"Yes. I love her. But — " I thought of how I wanted to say it. "I don't think I can love her in the way she deserves — as an all-around normal guy could. There's certain things. Sometimes I think she'd be happier with another guy, a more normal one."

"Is that what's behind your troubles with her recently?"

"No. Well, maybe partly."

He seemed to muse upon this for a while, and I ached to be able to read what was passing through his mind. Suddenly he was struck by a thought. "Does Christine know any of what you told me?"

"Yes." I looked closely at him. "Like I said — she's the only girl I've ever met who I felt I was able to tell. And you're the first guy."

He remained deep in thought. I was worried if I'd made a fatal mistake tonight — whether my instincts had betrayed me. He had fallen strangely silent.

"Scott. Can we still be friends after what you've just learned?"

He looked at me with eyes that looked ready to cry. "Of course, Guy. I understand. As you say, a lot of other guys have probably done the same thing, only they don't like to admit to it. Nothing will change our friendship."

"I'm glad. You don't know how good that makes me feel."

"I feel flattered that you trusted me enough to tell me."

It was starting to get cold sitting on the wooden bench, and I stood up.

"By the way — what you saw out here tonight — it's a secret between me and you, right? Let's not tell the others about it. They might be less understanding and decide to beat up on the fags. You know how most guys are. They're scared of anyone who's different from themselves. We wouldn't want to see that happen, right?"

"Of course not."

"I'll bet there's a lot of material there for your future books."

"You still want to go get those hot dogs?"

"No. I lost my appetite. Let's just go on back to the dorm."

"Sure." Without another word we began walking back towards the dorm.

2

Harry Golden lived in the hilly area north of the campus in an old two-story Victorian house, a ramshackle place with a spacious yard. He had called me at the dorm this afternoon saying he'd managed to borrow Peter's painting of me as Narcissus, and would I be interested in seeing it. My answer had been unequivocal, though it was patently obvious that he was using the painting as bait to lure me.

He was wearing a caftan when he met me at the door. "Take off your shoes and socks, Guy. You won't need them in here. I live in the Oriental style."

My first impression upon entering his home was that I had entered a different world. A vague hint of incense (was it musk? sandalwood?) hung in the air, and there were drapes everywhere, with thick cushions on the floor. It was not so much effete (as I had, perhaps, half-expected) so much as scholarly.

On the walls were cases containing beautiful butterflies of all colors and sizes, and alongside them were exotic prints from Japan, India, China, Korea. Books were everywhere — lying open on the tables, neatly stacked side by side on the fully stocked shelves, piled up on the floor like unsteady towers. There must have been tens of thousands of volumes. Some of them looked like rare and expensive editions, bound in morocco or calfhide, as I would have expected to find in the sort of library I always pictured when I read novels about 'gentlemen of exquisite taste'. But alongside these were worn and tattered paperbacks which looked as if they'd been picked out of a bargain bin or a garage sale.

I got the impression of a man who loved to study and would have been perfectly content to spend the rest of his life researching various arcana. This place was the ideal scholar's retreat from the world, a genuine ivory tower. I had the feeling we were high above the world, among the clouds where none of the world's laws applied; up here we were above it all, free.

The professor went to the kitchen to prepare the coffee while I browsed through the books on the shelves. But as soon as he brought the drinks in on a tray, I was eager to see Narcissus.

"Well? Where is it?" I asked.

"You sure don't wait for the sand to cool under your heels," he laughed. "Right this way." He led me to his bedroom. He switched on the light and I saw a large, bare room with a king-sized quilt mattress on the floor and a covered canvas at its head, leaning against the wall.

He walked over to it and without any ceremony, yanked off the cloth. "Well, what do you think?"

For a brief moment I couldn't believe my eyes. I had the illusion that a window had been opened upon another world. In a secluded grove — lush, overgrown, with vividly real trees and bushes — was a clearing through which could be seen a serene pond, pure and deep. And leaning slightly over the water was a beautiful young boy, about eighteen years old, completely nude.

We never see ourselves as others see us, only faint reflections in glass, in photos. Sometimes when we see our photographs we are surprised; it doesn't look like the face we know in the mirror. And yet other photos verify what we know to be true. That is why

154

there are some pictures we like and others we hate. We only want a confirmation of the picture of ourselves we have in our own minds.

The Narcissus in the painting was the self I sometimes caught in photographs and mirrors, the stranger who bore a faint family resemblance to me. But the more I gazed at him, the more I realized how perfectly Peter had captured me. It was not only a portrait of my body, but of my soul.

I was looking down into the water, and reflected there in the water was my twin. We were gazing into each other's eyes with amazement and wonder, as if just awakened from a dream. And in our eyes was a look of adoration, wonder, and — without any doubt — sexual desire. As if to underline this desire so obvious in our eyes, we both sported full erections, sleekly ripe, an unhideable confirmation of the physical nature of our longing. I had never gone erect before Peter, but with his imagination, he'd filled out the lack. And he'd gotten it beautifully right.

The sight was so erotic I felt dizzy. What made it so unbearably indecent was that the more I looked at Narcissus, the more he began to look like me, in every way. I, too, had gazed into the mirror exactly like this and fallen in love with my twin.

While I'd posed for Peter in his studio, I'd been stripped not only of my clothes, but of all the secrets I'd kept so well hidden from the rest of the world. Peter had seen through everything, to the very essence of me. Anyone could look at this canvas and see that the young boy leaning in to kiss his reflection was sexually excited. And if the "homo" in homosexual means "same" in Greek, the ultimate sameness was surely oneself. A homosexual like me would have to be a narcissist; I am aroused by the sight of a boy's nude body, and the one I can most readily view is the one I see in the mirror.

"My God," I said. "How can he get away with it? Will they exhibit it?"

"Oh," he said, "this isn't the one he's going to exhibit. He's made another copy in which a faint, gauzy piece of cloth covers their privates. *That* will be the public Narcissus. This is the private one, for his own delectation."

I thought of the story of Pygmalion which Golden had told me, and could understand Peter's obsession. I, too, wanted to view this picture at my leisure in private, and to masturbate to it. Did I love myself as much as Peter thought I did? For him, I must have indeed been a Narcissus who was cold and unloving, incapable of loving anyone but myself. Then what of Scott? Perhaps he, too, was nothing more than a reflection in the water, an image of my own self projected onto him. If I were to so much as touch him, he would shiver away and disappear into bits of color and light floating on shimmering ripples.

"It's so vivid," I said, "so alive, so real. I feel I could step right into that world and keep on going. All the trees in the background, the mountains... I've seen them before, in my dreams, in a Greece where I probably lived in previous incarnations."

My portrait was more beautiful, more perfect than me. I should have been flattered, but I wasn't: I was jealous. And what a strange jealousy it was, to know that the painting of me would never change, though I myself would get older, age with the years. But no matter how much time passed, the Narcissus before me would still be as young and beautiful as ever, as I now saw him. Years from now, some boy would fall in love with him, be aroused by him. Even when I was dead and gone, this Narcissus would remain, enticing, seductive, beautiful. Forever.

"You make a wonderful mythical being," said Golden. I turned to look at him, and his eyes were travelling slowly up and down my body; I felt as if I were being licked by them. I was reminded of his boastful words about playing a boy's body like a musical instrument. At this moment it didn't sound quite as ridiculous as it had then.

His eyes came to rest on my groin. He could plainly see that I was sexually aroused by the painting... just as he'd calculated, no doubt. The sight of the painting had left me feeling light-headed and expansive. A trembling started up inside me, but strangely enough, it presaged a recklessness; I felt a boldness creep into me, strengthening my sudden resolve.

"Why make do with a mere painting when you can see the real thing?" I said. Then, with a dream-like calm, I began undoing the buttons of my shirt, took it off, wriggled out of my t-shirt, dropped it to the floor, then pulled down my jeans. The white cotton briefs I was wearing were distended by my erection. Calmly, I slid them down my thighs, stepped out of them and stood before him. He had a stunned look on his face.

"How does the real thing compare to the illusion?" I asked.

The audacity of my own words barely startled me.

I dropped down onto the mattress at my feet, stretching lazily out to await the outcome of my move. Though I'd feigned casualness, my heart was hammering madly now and my palms were wet with sweat. When Golden snapped off the light, I was glad of the darkness.

I shut my eyes and heard the rustle of his caftan being pulled over his head, dropped to the floor. The mattress sighed softly as it received his weight, and I trembled, wondering where the first touch would come. But nothing happened. We just lay there with only the sound of our breathing. Then I heard the click of his glasses being set on the floor, followed by the stealthy rustle of the bedspread. I opened my eyes and saw his face next to mine, so close that his breath was faintly redolent of the cigarettes he smoked. His eyes gleamed in the dark.

"Are you sure you want to go through with this?" he whispered.

I was too nervous to speak, afraid my voice would be a croak.

I felt his hand on my shoulder, then the prickly brush of his beard against my chin, and finally the soft, delicate pressure of his lips on mine. After my initial surprise, I responded to the kiss. I was particularly excited by the strange juxtaposition of the prickly, scratchy beard with the soft, wonderfully mobile lips. I opened my mouth to let his nudging tongue slip in. It was warm, and tasted of tobacco.

I let my hands explore his body, feeling a flabby softness everywhere and, to my dismay, tufts of hard, bristly hairs surrounding the nipples and covering the shoulder blades. It was quite a change from Christine's smooth, resilient flesh.

The kiss pulled away from my mouth only to alight on my cheek. From there it moved slowly toward my ear — alive with scratchy bristles, but with an unbelievably silky softness at its center — leaving a wake of tingly goose-bumps. His lips tugged gently at my earlobe, making his breaths sound loud and close. As his tongue probed my ear, the muffled lapping sounded liquid and underwater. Then I felt a light scrape of teeth against the side of my neck, so gentle that it sent warm flushes all down my back.

He pushed my arm up against my head, exposing the wispy bush in my armpit. I giggled as his tongue began rooting around and searching out the salty nectar deposited there. After a pause,

157

he moved away again, and suddenly when a moist softness closed delicately around my nipple, it was as though I'd been galvanized by pure sensation. The nerve endings there tingled rawly from the touch of his tongue.

Naturally, I'd kissed girls' nipples before, and knew the pleasure it gave, but I had never thought of having it done to me. I arched my back and squirmed to escape the waves of pleasure stirred up by his tongue. I'd never felt this exquisite tickle before; my throat was taut from the effort to keep from crying out; my eyes blurred with tears. His firm hand pressed my shoulder down, pinning me to the mattress as his tongue continued its sweet torture. I finally managed to push his head back with both hands.

I lay gasping, trying to catch my breath, surprised at the intensity of my reaction to this unknown pleasure. When I saw him bend down once again, I tensed up, but he only planted a soft kiss along the inside of my ribcage. Then, in a transition so smooth as to be undetectable, his lips were replaced by the gently brushing tip of his beard — and that, in turn, by the feeblest flicker of eyelashes. The eyelash kiss made its way to my nipple, and so delicate was it caress that this time I could endure it. It felt like the batting of butterfly wings which sent tiny waves of warmth (they could hardly be called pleasure) spreading across my chest. I lay still, absorbing this new delight until it pulled away. After a short moment of rest, his tongue descended again, this time onto my stomach, where it drew tacky arabesques all around my navel before nuzzling into its shallow crater, licking it, kissing it.

I was quite ready for the logical culmination of all this preliminary teasing — and the anticipation was driving me crazy. I felt his beard descend in a tingly dance until it merged and meshed with my own pubic beard. But with the briefest, skirmishing lick at my dick, his mouth moved away again. I felt his tongue line a narrow moistness along the transverse crease of my groin, and this time I couldn't suppress a soft groan. My powers of resistance were rapidly melting away, and I began to give free vent to my feelings.

His mouth moved back toward my genitals, but again bypassed my dick, working its way down to nestle and suckle among my balls. He knew that the short hairs on my balls were like hair triggers of pure pleasure. He tugged and stroked them with his lips, evoking soft cries from me. Then, with the crook of a finger he gently lifted my balls up out of the way to expose my perineum. I felt his warm breath against it, then a delicate lick. His tongue traced a line along the seam of my perineum, then darted in maddening ellipses along the rim of my butthole, making me writhe in response to its provocative dance. There was a brief moment of suspense before — I gasped — I felt it shoot up inside me. As it began to thrust in and out, I lifted my hips off the bed the better to direct the movements of his tongue to my own satisfaction. His hands cupped me under each buttock.

Cocking one ankle, then the other, behind his back, I closed my eyes and let out a long sigh. But just as I was settling down to an exquisite tongue-fuck, his tongue danced coquettishly away again, denying me this pleasure. I felt myself lowered gently to the mattress as he shifted around.

He bent over my thighs and with his mouth began exploring the sensitive hollow down the inside of my thigh. Because I jerked so much in response, he had to hold my leg down. At each kiss, I tried to twist away from the sweet torture.

I felt I was learning about my own body for the first time, from a teacher who used the most exquisite of pointers. These were things Christine could never do for me, for she didn't know my body as intimately as Golden did. Being a man himself, he understood it as no woman ever could. My body was his own, and my pleasures were his; he was in familiar territory. With Christine, no matter how intimate we became, my body would always remain alien; our otherness was biological. We were separated by a river which could never be bridged. Only another man could cherish my body like this and tap its treasures so expertly.

Holding my right leg with both hands, he worked his mouth down its inside: the knee, the shin, the ankle, and out to the toes where he delicately kissed and sucked on each one in turn, ending by lovingly sucking my big toe. I worked my free leg back and forth across the bedspread in response to his rhythmic sucking, agitated more by a mental picture of what it suggested than by any direct stimulus.

Unable to take any more, I reached for his dick. To my surprise, it was still soft. I sat up in order to see it better, and he lay down beside me to allow me.

Because of the darkness, I hadn't yet gotten a good look at his dick. I'd often stolen peeks at his crotch, but knew from experience that it is often difficult to gauge a man's size when he is fully clothed. Now I made the thrilling discovery of his sheer bulk, much larger than any I'd ever fondled. Even flaccid, its heft was heavy in my palm.

At my touches and squeezes, it slowly lumbered up into an even heavier state of excitement. This gradual hardening was something entirely new to me. My own erection (and those of the young guys I met in Nightworld) was almost always instantaneous.

As I stroked it I discovered that even its hardness had a different quality. Unlike the almost inorganic stiffness of my own, Golden's dick seemed to have a softer, more vulnerable quality which invited further caresses. I liked the feel of its heavy weight in my palms and fingers.

Golden was touching my hair, caressing the back of my head with his fingers. I turned to him and whispered:

"Come on, fuck me. Please."

I would never have dared say it to a boy my own age, but the age difference between Golden and me freed me from the need to adopt a tough, masculine facade. Instinctively I knew he wouldn't see my desire as a sign of weakness.

He didn't seem surprised or put off. I heard him sigh, and the floorboards creaked as he got up and walked away.

But he returned shortly and stretched out beside me. There was almost a sadness about the gentle way he now stroked my thighs. Like a patient in the hands of a trusted doctor, I allowed myself to be turned over onto my stomach. I felt my butt cheeks pushed gently apart, then a coolness as ointment was spread in tiny circular motions around and just within my butthole. My stomach muscles tightened in anticipation.

When he was done, he carefully cleaned off his fingers with tissue paper.

I felt myself turned over onto my back and realized that I was going to be fucked face-to-face. The only time I had ever fucked a boy, we had done it doggie style so that (whether from shame or loathing) we didn't have to see each other's faces during the act.

Now, feeling shy, I bent my knees to bring my heels up against my buttocks. When he pushed my thighs gently but firmly apart, I was overwhelmed with a feeling of helplessness. I'd never felt so vulnerable before, so completely at the mercy of another person. Strangely enough, however, the sensation was far from unpleasant. In fact the feeling of surrender, of total passivity, gave me a thrill.

My stomach muscles agitated and went weak. I brought my knees up to my chest, made bold and reckless by my desire.

I closed my eyes.

At the first touch I remembered how big he was. I began to worry about the pain and couldn't help tensing up.

The pressure against my hole grew, and as he began forcing his entry, my sighs turned to a whimpering. I held my breath as I felt him push into me, and very quickly the initial feeling of tightness gave way to sharp arrows of pain. I groaned. He continued relentlessly inward until finally I had to cry aloud. My whole lower back was a scintillating mass of pain.

He stopped. "Are you all right, Guy?"

I gritted my teeth, unable to say a word. Sweat covered my forehead. I felt him withdraw, and because any movement registered as pain, it was just as painful as the entry.

"Is this the first time for you, Guy?"

I said nothing.

"You should have told me — " He brushed my forehead gently with the back of his hand and reached for a tissue to wipe away the sweat.

"I bet you think I'm a real wimp now, don't you?" I said.

"No I don't. You're just a little tense, that's all. It'll go away. Let's take a little rest."

We lay for a while in silence, side by side. I felt embarrassed at my inability to go through with it and wondered how another boy my age would have reacted to my failure.

"Listen, Guy, I'm going to be perfectly honest with you. The first time I saw you, I was head over heels in love with you. You were gorgeous, a faggot's wet dream. But for the longest time I was going crazy because I couldn't figure you out. Usually I can tell right away. With you, I wasn't sure if you were being guilelessly accidental, or whether you were deliberately provoking me." He spoke softly in a pleasant burry tone which was like a tickle in my ear. The darkness magnified it until it was a sensual droning thrum, a hypnotic wash of sound almost void of meaning.

His hand came to rest on my dick. His recital had given me a hard-on. I felt him stir.

"No, wait," I said.

"It's all right."

"Not yet."

"It'll be all right, don't worry."

And again I had the awful feeling of vulnerability as my thighs were pushed apart. But this time I was scared of the pain I knew was coming. There was a slight pinch as he entered me, then the long, slow thrust, deliberate and unhurried, which stretched my tightness. Although there was some pain, it wasn't as great as the first time, and I let out a long sigh as I felt myself gradually filling up. This time he didn't stop until he was all the way in. Then he lowered his body until he lay full-length atop me without moving.

We lay like this for a long time, which gave me a chance to recover from my nervousness. In fact I began to revel in the sluggish, lazy feeling of being filled. The idea that I'd surrendered my defenses and let the enemy in — that my most sacrosanct spot had finally been violated — gave me a perverse and delicious satisfaction. Within the protective clasp of his big strong arms, pressed chest-to-chest in an intimate hug, I felt the stirrings of a tender submission. The secret little girl inside of me came alive and blossomed, gloriously.

With my lips I sought out his; we kissed and held our lips together until I felt faint. His hug tightened, and I curled into it, bringing my legs up until my ankles were crossed loosely above his buttocks.

As if this were the signal to begin, he shifted his weight up off me until he was resting on his elbows. I sighed as the long, slow thrusts began. At first, as I'd feared, there was more pain than anything else. Then gradually — to my dawning surprise — the pain gave way to something else entirely.

The most exquisite waves of pleasure, unlike anything else I'd ever felt before, churned deep within me. Golden's unhurried, deliberate jogging was stirring me up, drawing up from my depths hidden treasures like the oil pumps in the nearby countryside. I hadn't realized it would feel like this; if anything, I'd thought the pleasure was mainly a psychological one, linked with the knowledge of giving someone else his pleasure. But this was so gut-wrenchingly visceral — nothing in the world felt this good — that I could see why it was so zealously, ruthlessly prohibited by society; such deliciousness was positively sinful.

I wished the lovely feeling of being filled... and filled... and filled again would continue into infinity. My body felt so limp and languorous, and the dream-like rocking was making me delirious. I listened to the soft, rhythmic grunts of a boy experiencing pleasure as if they were a stranger's.

My half-open mouth was stopped up with a hot, lingering kiss, and his tongue began to thrust in and out in exact rhythm with the lower thrusting. I wallowed dirtily in the double invasion. The kiss pulled away and I felt a nibbling at my earlobe which made my whole neck flush. My earlobe turned hot and tingly, driving me into higher states of bliss. I was floating in a hazy borderline world from which I could catch tantalizing glimpses of satisfaction... of relief...

Pushed to the limits of my endurance, I reached my hand down and took hold of my dick, stroking myself in rhythm to his thrusting. He knew exactly what I was doing, and purposely matched our rhythms. The double stroking felt like heaven.

I could understand now why some young boys liked older men as lovers. Never before had I enjoyed the luxury of letting go of all my inhibitions, and knowing I didn't have to play a role.

Very quickly, I felt all my psychic forces gather at the root of my shaft and knew I was ready to let go, completely let go for the first time in my life. Golden sensed that I was ready. The slapping of his groin against my buttocks became more furious in rhythm with my own increased pace. We were one smooth machine, perfectly timed, well oiled, lubricated, functioning for the purpose of pure pleasure. I was on my way, well on my way.

"Oh! Oh!"

I felt my sphincter twitch in time to the spasms wrenching me open, pinching Harry's dick in rhythm with my bliss, augmenting it, almost making me scream with ecstacy. Warm, tiny dots of semen peppered my belly, seemingly endlessly.

Golden looked down at the glistening white drops atop my belly and increased the pace of his pumping. The expression on his face was that of one intending violence. With a fearful grimace, he clenched his teeth as his pelvis slammed into me repeatedly. My butthole burned from his furious pumping, but the massage was pleasurable. And then suddenly he stopped, his back arched upward, his face contorted, his body rigid. A look as of pain crossed his face and momentarily he was transported to another realm. And then with a soft whimper he sank down gently atop me. My body shivered beneath his, and I felt the warm paste on my belly glue our bodies together. I could feel his heart beating against my chest. His ragged breathing was like a storm raging about my ears. I closed my eyes and put my arms around him and thought of Scott.

Indeed, at this moment, all I could think of was Scott. Strangely enough, the loss of my virginity was somehow a tribute to him, an affirmation of — even a strengthening of — my love for him. And I'd never felt closer to him than I did at this moment.

3

Just as I was creeping into the silent dorm, the muffled sound of the campanile bells striking four o'clock came to my ears. This was the first time I'd come back this late. I'd fallen asleep in Golden's arms and had only woken up a short time ago, leaving him sleeping on his mattress. Without his glasses he'd looked so helpless and weak.

The hallway was silent. The flicker of the TV screen lit up the darkness of the lounge, but its sound was turned off. Sometimes one of the guys would fall asleep in here but tonight there was no one. I turned off the TV and headed down the hall to my room.

I'd always had a secret fear that once I was fucked in the butt, my walk would change, become the wiggly waggle of the obvious fag. However, there seemed to be no grounds for that fear. My walk was the same as ever. But my butthole was still sore, a visceral token of how profoundly I'd been changed. I'd given up something tonight, but gained a whole lot more, and I felt knowing, superior to my old self. For I'd finally stepped across that forbidden border and violated the sacred taboo; I'd been feminized, had discovered my double boy-girl self, and now wore an invisible gown of glorious sin. I felt exalted.

I opened the door to my room and stepped in, closing it quietly behind me. The first thing I noticed was that the lamp on Scott's desk was on. But he wasn't at his desk, nor was he in bed. I went to the shower room and opened the door but it was dark.

I went back to my bed and sat down.

I couldn't imagine where he would be at this hour. There was no place he could go. All the libraries were closed, and the lounge had been empty. He wasn't the type to go to an all-night diner by himself, though we'd gone together a couple of times. There was only one place he could go, only one place where he would think to go. Christine's.

It was obvious what had happened. He'd become worried about my whereabouts. I usually told him beforehand if I was going to spend the night at Christine's place. And if I felt like going prowling in Nightworld, I would tell him I was going to Chrissie's apartment for a short visit, and he was too tactful to ever contact me there by phone. Tonight, since I thought I was only going to Golden's house for a short while, I hadn't mentioned it to Scott. If I had known what was going to happen, I would have told him something to cover for my absence. However, events had seemed to take a turn of their own.

When it got late, past the time I usually came in, he must have phoned Christine just to make sure I was over at her place. And when he found out I wasn't there, both of them must have begun to worry. So he'd gone over to her place.

He must still be there now.

I decided to head for her place. Better to go than call from the hall phone and wake everyone up at this time of morning.

Outside, the sky had lightened, and the campus had been transformed into a wonderland; I'd never seen it quite like this before. The very air I breathed was fluid, in motion, its damp freshness giving me a clear vision I'd never before possessed. Wisps of fog clung to the ground, giving the illusion that the whole earth was cloaked in a wonderful new garb. Above, the sky was lightening into a murky gray, and over the tops of the trees I could make out the outline of the campanile tower. Only the very tip was clearly visible, thrusting up from the fog like a primitive marker whose meaning no one knew anymore in this white, white world.

All was silent, no one was about. The only sound was the birds twittering. Reality and dream seemed to be mingling, as if remnants of sleep still clung to my eyes. My experience with Golden now seemed all the more wonderful, like a beautiful dream.

I reached Christine's apartment building and went up the steps. But just as I was about to knock on her door, a curious premonition held me back. I leaned down to put my ear to the door, and as I did so, the doorknob turned. I quickly pulled back into the shadows behind the fire extinguisher cabinet and ducked down.

The door opened slowly and Scott stepped out. But instead of closing the door and walking away, he was standing in the doorway, turned back to speak to Christine in her room. They were speaking in whispers, and though I strained my ears, I couldn't make out the gist of it. But the tone of Scott's voice, every nuance of his movements, conveyed an unmistakable tenderness. I felt my body tense up, fearful of discovery, and wished I hadn't decided on the spur of the moment to hide myself. I felt I was peeking at something I shouldn't have seen. An exciting premonition filled me up, almost made me tremble in agitation.

In a moment, Scott had gently closed the door, turned toward the steps and walked down them, out of sight. Slowly I sank to the floor. Was it possible that Christine had betrayed me? The old-fashioned sound of the word 'betray' thrilled me. The scenario I'd spun out in my fantasies had finally come true, the affair I'd engineered so carefully had reached fruition. I felt strangely excited. But mixed with this excitement was a sick, self-pitying emptiness in my stomach, the emptiness I'd felt as a child when I thought I'd been mistreated by my parents.

I got up and went to the door, knocked softly on it. In an instant it was flung open. Christine was standing in the doorway wearing a baggy sweatshirt and pajama bottoms. There was no make-up on her face and her hair looked just washed. Her initial expression of worry changed to relief when she saw it was me. "Guy! Where were you? I was worried sick!"

"You're still up at this hour?"

"Didn't you run into Scott? He just left here a moment ago."

"So Scott was here?"

"Of course. He was here almost all night. He's been going back and forth to the dorm all night to see if you'd returned. Where were you? We kept waiting for you to show up. He's so worried about you. He said you've been depressed lately."

She let me into her room and closed the door behind me. I looked over at her desk and saw a couple of glasses out, and some empty cans of beer. "Damn. If I didn't know any better, I'd have thought you were having a party in here."

"Stop evading the issue, Guy." She looked straight at me. "Where were you tonight? Will you answer me straight? If Scott hadn't called me tonight looking for you, I would have never known that you were out so late. You're fooling around, aren't you? I know it. There's someone else. No, don't lie. I can feel it."

I didn't try to deny it. My own infidelities took place in a world in which she had no existence. So foreign were they to anything she might imagine that they almost didn't count as infidelities. Could she even begin to conceive what I'd been doing last night?

And what about her, and that scene I'd just witnessed at her door? The thought that Scott might have been kissing her just before I'd come, the thought that they might have even slept together, gave me the strength to overcome the feelings of guilt which were playing about the edge of my consciousness.

I sat down on her bed and tried not to wince. "What about you, Christine?"

"What do you mean?"

"You and Scott were acting awfully chummy for a pair who are concerned about a mutual friend. Or is it just an extension of going out to see movies together, to meet for dinner after an evening of study together? You two have so much in common, too..."

"Stop it, Guy. You were the one who asked me to go out with him."

"What's the matter? If you're worried about me, don't be. I'm not the jealous type. And I know I can trust Scott."

She didn't answer. When I looked at her, there were tears in her eyes and I felt a sudden panic.

"What's wrong, Christine?"

She turned away from me. "I wish you wouldn't do this to me."

"Do what?"

"Why don't you come right out and say it?"

I looked at her, flabbergasted. And then I heard her say in a small voice:

"It's all over now, I suppose."

The words I'd secretly longed for, yet dreaded, had finally been uttered. I hadn't expected it to be like this — and surely hadn't expected it at this moment. For a long time, I'd suspected that Christine might have known about my true feelings. But I still didn't want it to break up our relationship. I wanted to make it all work somehow — with her and with Scott. It was as if my need for Scott were bound up inextricably with my relationship with Christine. In some obscure way which I felt unable to unravel, I needed her in order to have Scott.

"Not over, no," I heard myself say. "But I think we should think things over. We've been going together for six months or so now. That's a long time. Maybe we need to step back and look at what we've got. Let's not rush too soon into doing something which we might regret later."

"But you're the one who's making it impossible. Lately you don't seem the same. Guy, you know I don't like lying and hypocrisy, and — I thought our relationship was open. And good."

"It was." I realized too late I'd used the past tense. I felt my heart crushed under a great weight. I continued to look at her, and now she couldn't meet my eyes.

I decided to chance it. "Did something happen tonight, Christine?"

She looked down at her hands. She'd never lied to me before and I knew she couldn't lie now. It just wasn't in her nature — she was constitutionally incapable of lying. The fact was, I myself was afraid to face the truth, but some perversity in me insisted on bringing it out of her now, even as I felt I was punishing her by doing so.

She opened her mouth to speak and something in me wanted to stop her before she confessed — to keep the grubby little secret out of sight for a little while longer so I wouldn't have to face the consequences.

"He was sick with worrying about what might have happened to you. Usually you tell him where you're going. And we couldn't imagine where you'd be at that time of night."

"What did you do?"

"We talked. Had a few drinks. He consoled me. We calmed each other down."

"And? Did anything else happen?"

She whirled on me with a look almost of hatred on her face and I felt sickened. "What do you mean by 'anything else'? I don't like — " And then suddenly she looked very tired. She sighed:

"Yes."

She lowered her eyes and blinked rapidly a few times, then looked up at me with a look which chilled me, and said in the tones of a lifeless zombie:

"For your information, Scott is no longer a virgin. I suppose you're happy now."

I was unable to say a word. I thought of how her face usually looked during sex, and imagined Scott seeing it at firsthand. An atavistic joy filled my soul. Through the channel of Christine's body, Scott and I were now one, linked by the most basic bonds vouchsafed to unrelated strangers. My skin, in nakedness, had touched Christine's, and her skin, in nakedness had touched his. Blood brotherhood was nothing compared to the ritual which had been enacted.

She was speaking so softly that I almost didn't catch her next words.

"I don't know how it happened. One thing led to another. I hadn't intended it at all." She looked so unhappy that I wanted to stop her, but felt unable to. "It was what you wanted, Guy, wasn't it?"

The answer died on my lips.

I thought of the past couple of months, which now seemed like years. It had given me a delicious feeling of power to watch the two people I loved most coming together because of me, in spite of me, in secret from me, but with my blessing. I'd felt as if I were engineering their romance, their infidelity. In this, I was motivated by my devotion to Christine as much as my love for Scott. For if I couldn't have him, then Christine should; for she was the girl he cared most for... cared for in a way I never could. They should be happy together. Their happiness would make mine complete.

She went on tonelessly, as if she were speaking to her innermost self, probably not even caring whether I listened or not, and I felt helpless to do anything but listen.

"I guess our little jealousy games finally came true. We were pushing it to the edge, and this time we went too far to come back. Do you remember that time you jokingly asked about a three-way relationship with Scott — to do him the favor of taking his virginity? In truth, I wasn't ready to go that far. I mean, I know we've been very open to sexual experiences, even to the point of kinkiness. But this was beyond what I wanted. It might have turned you on, but it wasn't for me. I guess I was old-fashioned. But once the suggestion was made, it lodged in my mind and I began thinking about it. It went on and on in my mind and there was nothing I could do after a while to stop it. It got to the point where I didn't want to stop it. It was like I had your tacit permission to — to do what I really, in my heart, wanted. Because I knew that you would never have said such a thing unless deep in your heart you really wished it. It was your way of letting me go, pushing me off onto someone else. And who better than your best friend?"

"No, Christine, no. It wasn't like that."

"It's all right. You see, I'd been so afraid. For the longest time I was unsure about my feelings. I liked Scott as a friend because he was your best friend. But when you asked me to sleep with him, I was scared. Because I was really beginning to feel something for him, even back then, and it was like temptation. You were pushing me where you thought it was still safe, but it was dangerous ground. Very dangerous."

There was a sinking feeling in my stomach.

"And so — it happened. It happened." She raised her hands helplessly and let them drop.

"Happened," I repeated foolishly. The word sounded silly. It had no meaning, it was a ridiculous word which could be applied to anything: matchsticks, curtain rails, toy locomotives. "Was tonight the first time? I mean, has it happened before?"

She looked at me with a helpless expression and raised her hands, shaking her head slightly, which could have meant anything — no, or her helplessness in the face of fate. "When you asked me to do it, you knew in your heart I could never betray you. So I was tortured by your asking me to do it. I didn't think you really wanted it to happen; I was waiting for you to take it back, to apologize, to — I don't know. It bothered me for a long, long time."

"And Scott?" Even as I felt my whole world coming to pieces, I realized I was dying to find out what had happened in her room tonight. To my shame, I wanted to know exactly what had happened, the details. "What was it like for him?"

The look on her face was bitter. "Guy... Scott is in love with me."

"I know."

"I mean, he really loves me. He had tears in his eyes. I felt as if I'd betrayed him, betrayed his love. Because I didn't feel the same way about him as he felt about me."

"How *did* you feel about him?"

"I was killing all my feelings. Can't you understand?"

There was a long silence during which I felt with my skin that I'd done her a wrong, both her and Scott. And yet. She went on:

"No, it's not true that I felt nothing for Scott. But I don't want to go into that."

I knew it was all over. Not just my relationship with Christine, and the happiness I'd felt, but a whole period of my life was ending. I had pushed into territory which should have been left unexplored, and there was no going back now. My whole present, just an instant ago, had turned into the past — a distant past which was receding from me now at the speed of light.

A sob broke from my throat.

"He's a good guy, Christine. Maybe the best I've ever met."

She was silent for a long time. Then: "Guy? You're in love with Scott, aren't you?"

I couldn't say a thing.

"I should have guessed. For the longest time I thought it was just the feeling of friendship between two buddies, the usual male bonding thing which women aren't allowed to understand. I had my suspicions, but kept them down, tried not to look the truth in the face. When you suggested the three-way thing, I knew that was a fantasy often indulged in by men who want to sleep with other men. But I guess I closed my eyes to it. I thought your feelings for me were genuine."

"Oh they were, Christine. I loved you, Christine. I really did. But later I wasn't so sure. I wasn't so sure about a lot of things. But I know you well enough to know that you'd probably understand if I — "

"I still love you, Guy, that's the most pathetic part of it. I love you, knowing you might be in love with Scott. So in a way, my sleeping with Scott was done out of love for you. Can you understand the paradoxical position I was in? Betraying you out of love. But my feelings for Scott are still too confused for me to figure out. The truth is, my feelings for him might be much deeper than I just admitted to you. I've been hiding it from you and that put a lot of pressure on me. I was going crazy from not knowing where I stood, with myself, with you, with Scott. And I was afraid of being found out, too. At least now it's all out in the open. Which might be a good thing, in a way."

"Now that you know how things really stand, do you think the three of us could continue on as we are? But in an open fashion, at least among us? Stranger things have happened."

She shook her head. "There's too much emotion involved. I love you, and I'm jealous of your love for Scott. Scott loves me and would be jealous of my love for you. While you love Scott who can never love you. The ultimate love triangle. Doesn't it form a beautifully perfect, and yet futile mathematical equation?"

"I don't know. I flunked chemistry, and I'm not so hot at math, either." After a long pause, I said softly, "Christine, you want to know where I was all night? I was at Professor Golden's house, getting fucked by him, giving up my virginity to him. Who knows? I might have lost it at about the same time Scott lost his. How's that for poetic justice?"

There was another long pause before she asked in a tired voice: "So what happens now?"

"I don't know." And then it hit me — I really didn't know. Suddenly I wanted to laugh. It seemed so ridiculous that we were discussing everything so calmly, so reasonably. "In the movies, this is the part where someone starts ranting and raving."

"I never saw a movie like this, Guy."

"Neither have I. So I don't know what happens next."

"Will you be all right?"

"Sure. I'll survive. I always do."

"That's good." She looked at me with something like pity in her eyes.

I cleared my throat. "Maybe we should call it a night, huh?"

She nodded, but didn't move.

"Okay, I'm going now."

"Sure."

I got up and left.

4

Outside, the sky had brightened into a clear, unclouded day. The wonderland I'd walked through on my way to Christine's apartment had disappeared. Here and there early morning joggers in brightly colored sweatsuits were gliding among the trees beside the bicycle path. Meeting them as they came onto the path, I felt somewhat like a late reveller confronting early-morning commuters.

In the clear morning air, what had just taken place in Christine's apartment didn't seem real anymore. It was impossible to accept that everything was over. In my heart, I just knew there was still a chance to save everything, to make it all go back to what it had been before. And to do that, I had to see Scott before he saw Christine again.

The dorm was still quiet; most of the guys were fast asleep. When I opened the door to my room, I heard the shower on. Scott was in. I went over to the shower room and opened its door, stepped inside. Beyond the translucent shower partition, I could make out his flesh-colored form. He was leaning his head back, letting the jets of water hit him straight in the face. I pushed open the partition and stuck my head in. As he turned around to face me, jets of warm water glanced off his shoulders, into my face.

"I'm back," I said.

The shower stall was filled with steam and I could barely see a thing. He shut off the water and turned to face me. His hair was dripping wet; he ran his hand through it, pushing it straight back from his forehead. I made sure I was looking him straight in the face, but in my peripheral vision, I noted pearly drops of water quivering in his pubic bush.

"Wait," he said. "I'll be right out."

I went out to his bed and sat down. In a moment he was coming out, wiping himself off, toweling his hair dry. I pretended to be uninterested in the sight of his nude body, and idly flipped through the pages of a literature textbook I'd found lying by his pillow. Wrapping the towel around his middle, he sat down on the bed. His chest and shoulders were dry, but still steaming from the hot shower. The mingled essences of soap, aftershave, and toothpaste came off him.

"Guy, where have you been? I called Christine last night when you still hadn't come back by one. You never stay out that late without telling me first. What happened?"

"It's a long story," I said.

"Oh?" He looked at me hard, and in that look, I sensed that something had come between us. He wasn't the Scott I'd known. He seemed so much more confident than I'd ever known him to be, and I realized it must be the effect of losing his virginity. That experience had profoundly changed him. He was someone else now, someone much stronger, more cunning. I'd changed the thing I'd loved, out of love for it. A part of me felt sadness, a sense of loss. Yet the bigger part of me felt delighted: I'd created this more confident Scott, this healthy, strong heterosexual boy. His new-found adulthood made him that much more desirable in my eyes.

"So what did you do when you found out I wasn't with Christine?" I asked.

"I left a note here and went over to her place. We tried to think where you might be, and I went around to several places — Doggie Diner, Erewhon — but couldn't find you. We couldn't think where else you might be. We could only hope that you would come to her apartment, or back here. I came back here several times to check. Where were you, Guy?"

"I can't tell you right now, Scott."

"I have to tell you she thinks you were with another girl."

"Yeah, I know. We had a little fight over that."

He shook his head. "Guy, I'm worried about you. It's not only last night. Lately you're acting strange. Skipping classes, staying out at all hours. What's the matter?"

I hesitated. My knowledge of what had happened between him and Christine gave me a reckless surge of power. I felt almost giddy at what I knew and he didn't. What added spice to the mixture was his guilt — no matter how hard he tried to hide it, he had to feel some culpability for his betrayal. And I wanted to play upon that guilt. This might be my only chance to save everything.

I let out my breath. "You're right. Something is bothering me. And has been for a long time."

"About what?"

"It's about Christine."

"Christine?" His voice wavered.

"Yeah. Something's eating her. We've had our fights before, and always made up. But this time it's different."

"How? What do you mean?"

I looked at him. "I'll tell you, but you have to keep it a secret. You're the only one I can trust with this."

He looked grave.

I went on, trying to keep my voice steady. "You say she thinks I'm seeing another girl. Well, that's not true at all. If anything, it's the opposite."

"What do you mean?"

"It's me who's suspicious of her."

"Suspicious?"

"Yes. I think she's seeing another guy."

I couldn't see the expression on his face because I hadn't been able to look in his eyes at the crucial moment. But I heard the pain in his voice as he asked weakly:

"What makes you say that?"

I dropped my voice almost to a whisper. "She acts different lately. It isn't anything really noticeable, just little things. And she seems a little distracted about something. Believe me, I can tell something is up."

"Do you have any evidence?"

"Nothing. Yet. But when I'm with her, I can feel another guy there, between us, like his ghost."

I was finally able to look at his face, and what I saw there made everything worthwhile. He was trying to hide his alarm, while at the same time, was obviously wrestling with the possibility of confessing. What stopped him, evidently, was his concern about defending Christine's role in the betrayal. It was thrilling to watch his perplexity. I savored his discomfort, and something mischievous inside me wanted to toy with his feelings some more. My love for him was making me want to hurt him, to see him suffer, as I had suffered. I knew he felt guilty — his guilt was palpable, like something I could almost touch, to caress in my hands and mold, shape in any way I wanted to. I felt god-like.

I went on, "Christine used to be so much fun. She's changed recently. Become secretive. She's not open and free like she was in the old days. And lately she's been saying things like, 'is it possible to love two guys at the same time?'"

His expression was hard to decipher. My head was reeling a little and I was afraid I might reveal everything. I had to tease the confession out of him slowly. To bring everything out into the open too quickly would have destroyed what I was trying so carefully to engineer.

"Scott, do you know anything about it?"

"No."

I felt like an adult seeing through a child's transparent lies. For all I knew, this was his very first lie. It was like witnessing the loss of a virginity — a virginity whose loss was even more delectable than his sexual one.

"Are you sure? She hasn't said or done anything that might give you a clue?"

He looked uneasy. "Uh, I'll try to find out more about it if you want me to."

"Will you do that, Scott?"

He fell silent as if thinking deeply about something. And then I began to get scared — for suddenly I knew what he was thinking about.

"Guy..." He looked at me with eyes that were beginning to fill with tears. "I have something to say."

This was what I'd been waiting for, had been goading him on to, yet a part of me wanted to stop him from speaking. I became afraid that what he was about to say would change my whole life, would forever put him out of my reach. I wanted to interrupt him but my lips wouldn't respond. All I could do was helplessly look on.

"I've done something terrible, Guy."

"What?" My voice responded without volition on my part.

"It's about Christine." He looked down, then away from me as he said, "Ever since I first met her... I've felt very strongly about her. And not just an infatuation, either."

Even though I was expecting it, I was startled. His silence about it had given me my most potent weapon. My open knowledge of it now shattered the hold I'd had over him. To actually hear it from his lips made me feel slightly ill. It was as if in one instant, he'd been removed from me, and was now far, far away.

"I felt so guilty, Guy, because I knew she loved you and you loved her. And you were both my best friends. Even though I kept my feelings to myself, I felt like I was betraying your trust."

"Well," I said slowly, "it's happened before. Guys fall in love with their best friend's girl." It was all I could do to keep from saying: I know, Scott, I know!

"But — it's more than that."

"What do you mean?"

He hung his head. "Guy. I slept with her."

In the long silence which followed, I tried to assess the emotions which were agitating me. Slowly I became aware that it was happiness — a happiness so intense that it threatened to kill me. "You did what?"

His voice was a monotone. "It was just something that happened so naturally. Against my will, almost. I knew I shouldn't have, but it was like it was out of my hands. Guy, can you understand? I love her, and though I knew I was hurting you... I just had to. She means so much to me. She's the only one."

I felt a thrill race through my heart. My love for him had

176

never been stronger than it was at this very moment. His confession was like a drug which was charging me with a strange energy. With it I would be able to crush him, completely, and love it. For in the crazy logic of my ecstasy, I knew that my love could only culminate in his utter destruction.

"So it was you, Scott." I felt drunkenly distant from all that was taking place. I heard myself mouthing the words of a cheap television melodrama: "I never guessed."

He looked crushed. "I don't know what to say."

"It was you she was fucking — my best friend, behind my back."

"Please don't blame Christine for anything. It was me. It's all my fault."

"Yeah, take all the blame like a fucking hero." I turned away and felt his hand on my shoulder.

"Guy, please. Can you forgive me? I know it's abysmally insulting and presumptuous of me to say so, but I convinced myself that Christine was a little in love with me, too. There were all the signs..."

My heart felt full to overflowing. I knew I had already lost him — he was Christine's now.

"I guess you hate me now, Guy. And you have every right to. If you were to punch me, I would understand. Whatever you do, I'll understand."

I felt a crazy singing inside me, my heart spiralling ever upwards, giddily out of control. Nothing but love. "I'm not going to punch you, Scott. I don't want to hurt you. That's the last thing I want to do."

He looked at me, baffled, and his expression changed to alarm when I reached up and took his elbow in my hand. As I pulled him towards me, he made no effort to resist. With my finger I lifted his chin, and before he could say another word, I kissed him on the lips.

His lips were unresponsive, but I didn't care. I was in a dream. Our lips were touching. In the middle of the kiss, as if he'd just realized what was happening, he pulled away. "What are you doing, Guy?"

I had shut my eyes just before kissing him, and now as I opened them, I saw his look of alarm.

"What's going on, Guy?" he repeated.

"I…"

Suddenly he — we both — became acutely aware that he was still naked from the shower, with only the towel wrapped around his middle. He shook himself loose from my light clasp and retreated a few steps.

"I love you, Scott."

"What?"

"I love you. I always have."

He looked at me as if I'd suddenly begun speaking in a foreign language. He wanted it to be a joke and searched my face, his expression veering toward hopeful laughter, and then, when there was no response from me, fright, then questioning. I tried to smile.

He didn't respond. It was as if the life had flowed out of him, leaving his body behind like a husk.

He looked at me closely. "Guy — this seems to be a silly thing to ask at this point, but… you *are* gay, right? I mean, not bisexual, not 'sexually ambiguous', not 'searching for yourself'."

"I'm gay, Scott. And I've always been gay. All my life. I didn't mean to deceive you or anything, but for a long time I didn't know it for sure myself. It's a pretty hard thing to live with, you know."

"You could have told me you were gay. Anytime. You know I would have accepted you."

"I know. But it's not an easy confession to make, even to your best friend. I tried it before and it didn't work."

"Did you try telling Christine?"

"Of course not. No matter how open-minded she is, we were lovers, after all."

"But — can a gay man love a woman? I — I'm confused."

"I know, Scott, I know. I loved Christine as much as I'm able to love any girl. Don't get me wrong — I really did love her, at first. But I've begun to see that for me, she was just a cover-up. Not only for the world, but for me. I didn't suspect the depth of my homosexual feelings until recently. Really, until I met you. Until then, I thought I was just playing around, having little adventures."

"Adventures?"

"That night I showed you that area behind the football field. I knew about it all along."

"I see."

"Don't think I was 'deceiving' Christine in the usual sense. My homosexuality is a part of me which has nothing to do with her, and there was nothing she could do about it."

"So that's why your relationship wasn't working. For the longest time I couldn't understand it. You seemed so perfect for each other. Now I understand."

"It wasn't because of any failing in her. Rather, it was a failing in me. I should have known myself better. Then I wouldn't have had to put her through what I did."

"I supposed it couldn't be helped." His expression went a little blank.

"So. I suppose that changes things a bit, doesn't it? I mean, to know that your best friend is queer."

He focussed his eyes on me. "I don't see why it should. Remember what you said about my being uncircumcised? That it was just another idiosyncrasy, like having red hair? That's the way I feel about homosexuality. Some guys have red hair, some guys desire boys, so what? There's room for everybody in this world. We can be friends, Guy. I always want to be your friend. What exists between us goes beyond all this. And what's more, I'm sure Christine will also accept you as you are."

"Even the fact that I love you?"

He turned away and brought his hand up to his face, covering his eyes. For a moment, he stood in that pose. Then, impatiently, he shook his head and brought his hand down again. There was a look of utter helplessness in his eyes.

"But why did you fall in love with me? I just can't understand it. I mean, I did nothing to encourage it."

"It's nothing you did. It's just for being what you are."

"I feel — I don't know what to feel. Honored? Happy? Flattered?"

"Scott, I know it's something you can't understand. Maybe to you it's grotesque, a cruel joke nature played on me. But for me it's hard reality. And the fact that you are hetero and out of reach doesn't diminish my love for you in any way. In fact it might be what's fuelling my passion. And that's the tragedy of it. I love you as a guy, knowing you're completely heterosexual, knowing you can never share my feelings."

"Surely there are enough gay guys out there looking for friends, for lovers."

"Yes, but none of them are you. There's only one you, and that's just my point. You're the guy I'm in love with... have been in love with ever since I first set eyes on you. You're the only boy I've loved from my heart. It's a feeling I've never had for a girl. Can't you understand? The only time I ever felt it — " Here my voice was in danger of breaking. "Ever since I can remember, I've been looking for someone like you. And now when I finally find him, I can't touch him. Sure, there are gay guys out there — you'd be surprised at how many there are, secret and otherwise. I found out this past year in college. But they're not for me."

He just shook his head helplessly again. But I knew I had moved him by my plight. There was a soft, sympathetic look in his eyes. He wanted to help, and maybe there was still a chance for me to save everything.

"I was afraid you'd hate me forever if I confessed."

"Don't worry, Guy. I can rise above silly prejudices. You know me better."

"I know. But it's been so hard on me not to know for sure how you'd take it. I've been so lonely with my secret, Scott. Sometimes I felt like I was going crazy. Do you think I wanted to be like this? Do you think I enjoy falling in love with guys who'll never return my love?"

He gazed at me in some alarm, his focus shifting anxiously from my right eye to my left eye, and back. "Don't worry, Guy, it'll be all right."

We were looking into each other's eyes with a desperate hope. I felt such a compassionate tenderness in him that I wanted us to stay like that forever, knowing that if I moved, the image would shatter.

"Let me kiss you again, Scott."

"No, Guy. Don't."

"Please, Scott. Just this once. Will you let me?"

Again, he looked so helpless, so guilty, that I almost regretted what I was asking of him. And then he nodded.

5

Before he could change his mind, I moved my face closer to his and kissed him again. At first his lips resisted mine, and his eyes were shut tight. For a while I kept my lips pressed against his, not kissing. Then, when I felt his lips soften, I made my mine more mobile, and his lips responded, tentatively. But his eyes remained determinedly shut tight, as if trying to will away this reality. Undeterred, I began making my kisses more lubricous still, and suddenly his mouth, as if of its own accord, began greedily pushing itself against mine. He had caught fire and his movements became passionate.

His response surprised me a little, coming after his earlier coolness. Perhaps in the emotional turmoil following his confession, then mine, the kiss was even a relief for him, a balm. I felt a little guilty at making him do something so contrary to his nature, at using the emotion-filled moments following the confessions to get my way. On the other hand, he might be merely doing it out of friendship for me, out of pity at my hopeless love. In any case, the kissing was getting me sexually aroused.

My own actions became much more passionate. I pulled away from his mouth and kissed his cheek, then his mouth again, then his eyes. I put my hand up to his chest and felt his heart hammering. Gently, I began caressing his breast with my palm, rubbing in slow circles. As I glanced down, I noted that the towel wrapped around his middle had lifted slightly where his penis had raised its head. His body, at any rate, was responding, if not his mind.

I dropped my hand down onto his erection.

His body stiffened. "No, Guy. Don't."

"Scott, I'm not gonna hurt you. Don't you understand? I need it right now. Don't make me beg for it. Please."

"Guy, I can't. Damn it, you don't know how difficult you're making it. I like you so much. Please don't do anything which will make me change that opinion of you."

"Scott, this is something outside of me, outside my control. I know how I must seem to you, I see it all too clearly. Don't you know how wretched I feel? You of all people should know. Don't make me beg for it."

"No, Guy."

"Scott."

I slipped my hand under the towel and gripped his dick. He caught at his breath. Perhaps he hadn't realized how aroused he'd become.

My boldness was fuelled by a deep despair at my sense of imminent loss. Or was it that I felt this desperate action would save the ideal relationship we'd had for so long, which was soon to dissolve? At any rate, I knew that the guilt he felt about sleeping with Christine had weakened his position with me to the point where he was no longer able to protest even the most insolent assault. This was the proverbial once-in-a-lifetime chance I couldn't pass up. Everything I'd engineered came down to this sweet moment, freighted with the feeling of doom.

For a long time I just kept my hand resting on his dick, allowing him to get used to having it there. I would have to play it very carefully. This was the point toward which my whole life had been leading; after this I could die feeling fulfilled.

His eyes were closed again, and I could hear his breathing come faster. There was an expression of slight apprehension on his face, but apparently his anxiety wasn't enough to quell the basic physical pleasure that my touch had brought him. Keeping my hand on his dick, I kissed him again on the lips. I wanted this precious moment to last forever.

In silence, he awaited my first move in silence, curiously unresisting.

I let go of his dick and reached up to undo the knot at his hips, then slipped the towel off. It slid down to the floor with a slight rustle and Scott was fully exposed.

Dropping my hands to my sides, I gazed in silence. His dick, perhaps because it wasn't fully hard yet, was smaller than I'd expected. It hung, semi-tumescent, angled slightly downwards upon his right thigh. This was my first chance to really examine an uncircumcised dick. Its skin was brownish in color, slightly darker than the skin on the rest of his body. The foreskin covered the entire glans, making the tip look like the mouth of a draw-string purse, with a puckered crease for an opening. The glans was only suggested as a mound under the skin, hidden with the rest of the shaft. The underside of the penis was prickled with individual hairs, as were the balls, which hung loose in their wrinkly sacs.

"Oh, it's beautiful," I whispered. "You're wrong to think it's ugly. It's the sexiest dick I've ever seen."

It rolled a little, as if in response to my words.

"Oh yes," I said. "This is a dream come true. God, I'd love to see you with a sexy hard-on."

Again, it stirred, and began to grow in size, swelling out sideways at first, slowly and lazily, then raising its head upward in clumsy jerks.

"Oh yes."

Unable to resist, I reached up and took it in my hand. It twitched a little at my touch, as if shying away. Gently, I pulled downward, drawing the foreskin off the glans. As the brownish skin slid effortlessly away, the exposed head emerged shiny and pink. It was glistening. With the glans freed, it was just like any circumcised dick, just like my own. I placed my finger gently on the slit and the shaft became even more engorged, and stiffened upward with spasmodic motions.

Scott's eyes remained closed.

"Oh yes!" I whispered.

His dick was up hard, pressing stiffly against his belly. I began touching it more boldly now, running my fingers along it, delighting in its hardness, nudging my thumb against the sensitive underside of the glans, encircling the rest of the shaft with my palm and employing a smooth stroking motion.

It got harder and harder with each stroke, swelling up huge, huger than I'd ever imagined — big, beautiful and hard. The glans was swollen purple, and appeared to be pulsing from within, to the beat of Scott's passion, ready to burst.

My own dick was up hard, had been so ever since I'd first started kissing Scott. All my inhibitions gone now, I snaked out of my shirt and pulled my jeans down. When I pulled the waistband of my shorts off, my dick sprang up and slapped hard against my belly.

I looked at Scott. He was gazing down at my erection.

"Look, Scott, our dicks are the same. Exactly the same."

I moved my body closer to his until our dicks were nuzzling, head to head. I let my glans kiss his, pull away and kiss again, and continued to tease him with these dick kisses until I myself could stand it no longer. I pressed my lower body against his, so that the shafts of our dicks were flat against each other, standing up straight and parallel. Seen like this, we were of a size, the same length, the same thickness, the same color, twins in a mirror, reflected.

Leaning my upper body back a little, I reached down between our bellies and gripped both shafts in one hand and began stroking them together.

For a while there was no response from him, only the sound of his breathing. His eyes were closed again. But in my palm his dick was like an iron rod, and my caresses were making it harder and harder. I watched his balls gradually shrink up into tight, compact nuggets, then retract until they were hugging the base of the shaft in one round lump. The glans was twitching rhythmically, in involuntary response. I looked up at his face.

He had caught fire and was no longer master of his emotions. His expression had become slack and he was responding to my stroking with soft, rhythmic little grunts.

This was what I'd been living for. This was what I wanted: to be able to watch at first hand the face of the boy I loved as he was getting his pleasure. Much as I would have loved to go down on his dick and suck him off, this pleasure was even greater.

At this moment, all my misgivings and doubts had slipped away, all my guilt and anguish about being different from others, all the sordid encounters I'd had in toilet stalls, under the trees, the lying to Christine, to Golden, to the whole world, all the world's condemnation of my queerness... nothing mattered. I was happy because my whole life had led up to this. If I had but this one encounter in my life, it would all have been worthwhile. And I knew this moment would never come again in my whole life.

I watched his face closely, knowing with a sure instinct communicated through my hand that he was moving rapidly toward the point of no return.

I continued my steady stroking, gradually increasing the speed, sometimes stopping to get a better grip. Suddenly he moaned. His whole being yearned only for one thing now — the relief of orgasm. I myself was so aroused that the only thing I wanted was to hold off my own orgasm long enough to be able to enjoy his. Though my instinct was to shut my eyes and give myself up to bliss, I kept them open to record, to remember this sight forever.

The up-and-down motion of my hand was now a blur. The violence of my stroking was making both our bodies jump and jerk.

How much longer could I hold off? It was an endurance contest of the most torturous kind. And then, his head lolled back a little, his mouth slightly open. I watched his lips curl back from his teeth at the moment he crossed the line beyond which all control is relinquished; his body was now on automatic pilot, he could only go along for the ride.

And I was taking him to the end of the ride, the ultimate end.

I felt like kissing him, but his face looked blank, with an

almost death-like pallor. And then, with a soft cry he bit his lower lip hard. From below, I heard a slight rasping sound and felt sudden warmth sprinkle my chest. The first contact of his semen triggered my own orgasm, and I looked down to see my own white fuck jet up in vigorous spurts, all the way up to Scott's chest, then lower down, onto his belly. I thought I would never stop coming. The pleasure accompanying my orgasm was excruciatingly sweet, and only slightly less pleasurable afterwards, as I continued stroking even after I'd stopped ejaculating. I wanted to stay like that forever, with the feel of Scott's warm semen on my skin, the essence of Scott, from deep inside his body. It was all Scott, and I was thankful to be gay, that I might accept this magical distillation which was the most Scott-like part of Scott.

But he had other thoughts. I felt him stir. He made a move to turn away and I said, "Wait." Reaching down carefully, I picked up my jeans and fished in the back pocket for my handkerchief. Tenderly, I wiped my semen off his chest, his belly, his groin. Some had dribbled down into his pubic bush. When I was finished, I wiped myself off. By the time I'd done, he'd gone over to his dresser and gotten out his clothes, had finished putting them on. I carefully folded the handkerchief and began putting my own clothes on. Now that the heat of passion was over, I felt acutely conscious that Scott might have regretted our moment of rashness. What he'd felt couldn't possibly compare to the absolute bliss I'd experienced.

I dropped limply to the floor and sat there for a long while on my knees, stupidly slack. I felt happy, completely happy, maybe for the first time in my life. I could almost ignore that tiny feeling of guilt playing at the edges of my consciousness like some distant lightning not part of my world, but maybe of another one, somewhere over the horizon where people spoke a different language and had different customs.

It seemed like a long while before I looked up at Scott. He was sitting on the bed. Only now did I realize that the door had been unlocked the whole time. Anyone could have opened it and caught us in the act.

"Scott?"

He didn't respond — didn't give any indication that he'd even heard. He looked as if he couldn't believe what had happened.

"Was it... that bad? I mean, you don't seem to want to talk

about it or anything."

Still, he wouldn't say anything.

"Talk to me, Scott. What's your reaction to what just happened?"

When he finally answered, it was in a soft, almost apologetic voice. "Well, it was just something that happened. I don't condemn you for it, if that's what you're worried about. It's finished now. Past, done with. Don't worry about me. I won't hold anything against you."

He was discussing it as if I'd committed a crime, and that made me feel more guilty than ever. I knew that deep down he thought of it as ugly and dirty — something he'd put up with out of friendship or guilt. But I knew that it wasn't sinful and dirty; it was beautiful. I knew it with all my being.

"Scott, what happened just now, for me isn't just a passing thing. I'm still feeling the after-effects of it. The homosexual experiences I've had until now were so unfeeling, with people who meant nothing to me. But with you it was for the first time with someone I truly care about. What happened here just now, it was the most wonderful thing in my whole life. Nothing else even comes close. You don't know how much it means to me. For the first time, I actually felt happy at being homosexual. It was an affirmation, almost a justification of all I ever suffered for being different from the others."

Suddenly, he slammed his fist into the bed mattress, hard. I thought I saw tears in his eyes. "Guy, if you want to know the truth of it... what we just did — I enjoyed it. I mean, physically. And I confess — watching those guys under the bleachers the other night, I got sexually excited. So excited that I almost couldn't sleep all night. I'm worried — I might be gay myself." He turned to me and there was almost terror in his expression. "Do you think I might be gay, maybe, and not know it?"

I felt suddenly very weary. "You're not gay, Scott. You enjoyed it because it was enjoyable. There's no such thing as a maybe gay. You're either gay or you're not, and if you don't know it by now, you're not."

He seemed unconvinced, so I went on:

"Believe me, Scott, if you were homosexual, you'd know. Some homosexuals don't want to face the fact, but deep down, they know there's no denying it. I don't think you are." It felt strange to be trying to convince the boy I loved of his heterosexuality. It could only succeed in pushing him further away from me. At the same time, I needed him to be pure; I loved him for his purity.

"Well, if you say so, then I must not be."

"You love Christine, don't you? That feeling is no lie."

"But you did, too, didn't you? I mean, before."

"But that love was probably different from the love you feel."

"Are you going to tell Christine about what happened?"

"No. In fact, I don't think I'll tell her anything anymore."

"What do you mean?" His face went pale and he looked ready to crumple into tears.

I looked straight into his eyes. "Scott, Christine needs a normal guy, not someone like me."

"Normal? What's 'normal'? I don't think I know anymore."

"*You're* normal, Scott. Perfectly normal. Better than normal, because you're open-minded."

"Open-minded... "

"I know Christine likes you, and you two have a lot more in common with each other than with me."

"Guy..."

"I don't care how you feel about me, but my feelings for you will never change. You're the first person I ever truly loved, Scott. Don't take that away from me. You can think of me as a friend, but from my side, it's love, pure and strong. I love you, Scott. Just accept that. You don't have to return it. Just know that I love you, and don't reject me for it."

"I don't understand. Such a relationship can't exist. There's never been anything like it. Either two people love each other, or they are friends. There's no in-between relationship like that."

"Just let me enjoy the crumbs of your affection, every now and then, like just now. Or I'll go crazy."

"Guy, what I told you earlier — I said it made no difference. But accepting you for what you are doesn't mean I want to join you."

I turned my face away and felt my eyes fill with hot tears. There was silence for a long time as I gazed downward at the floor unable to look up. I felt a heavy weight on my heart, like the weight of centuries of failure, a lifetime of deception, of lost hopes and shattered dreams. All my frustrations were suddenly gathered together into one point and focussed with a white hot clarity upon this moment in time.

I felt his hand on my shoulder.

"Guy, don't take it like that. It can't be helped. There's nothing I can do. You know I'll do anything I can for you as your friend. But there's a certain line I can't cross. Please don't ask me to. What you're asking me to do is something I can't do. If you accept that, there's nothing that will stand in the way of our friendship. You know that."

I said nothing.

"I'll go to the limit for you, Guy. As a friend. That's what friends are for."

Scott suddenly seemed to have become so much stronger than before. In our relationship, I was the weaker one now. He was the conqueror, and I the slave... to my need of him. He knew my secret now — that which constituted my very weakest, most vulnerable point. I almost wished that I hadn't given in to my sexual desire. A moment's rashness had completely altered our relationship. Still, I knew I would do it again, in an instant, if I knew I could hold him in my arms again, kiss him, and touch his dick. What we'd done hadn't diminished my love for him at all. If anything, it had only strengthened it. I still needed him more than ever.

But the vision of the two of them, Scott and Christine, happily heterosexual, content in their relationship, one unbreakable unit, excluding me — forever — seemed to rise up before me. The beautiful picture they made, I wanted to destroy it, utterly.

I felt a thrill race through my heart. My love for Scott had never been stronger than it was at this very moment. It was like a drug which was charging me with a strange energy. With it I would be able to crush him, completely. For the only way I could satisfy my love for Scott now was to destroy him, and his budding happiness with Christine.

In the crazy logic of my ecstasy, I knew that my love could only culminate in his utter destruction. It was all so clear, like a mathematical theorem. If love was need, then love was also selfishness, the ultimate ego gratification.

I wanted to crush him. It would give me a pleasure by comparison with which sex with him was a joke. I knew that my love for him could only climax at the moment of his utter humiliation.

188

Only when he was totally humiliated could I love him completely, to my heart's desire. He had to be dirtied, dragged down to the lowest depths.

I knew, with the certainty vouchsafed only to the gods, that I was perched at the emotional climax of my entire life. My love for Scott had now taken over my human form and was guiding it like an alien intruder.

I faced him calmly — so calmly that my blood ran cold at the mastery I possessed over my emotions, the calculating manner with which I was plotting my own downfall.

"You want to know the truth, Scott? The whole truth?"

"What do you mean?"

His look of concern only goaded me on. I wanted to hurt him — to give him more pain than he'd ever given me. A shadow of concern flitted across his face. I wanted to savor that look of helpless fear. He was afraid of me — of the hurt he'd inflicted on me.

"You want to know something, Scott? Your feelings for Christine... I knew about them all along." Stop, Guy. Don't do it. "I knew you were in love with her."

"What? You mean she — ?"

"No. She didn't say anything. And do you want to know why she slept with you?"

"Guy..."

"Do you think she did it out of love for you? Or because you successfully seduced her? Wrong. I *asked* her to sleep with you."

"What?"

"That's right. I wanted you to lose your virginity. I wanted — "

"Guy! I don't want to hear any more."

"You weren't betraying me, Scott. You had my blessing. It was the way I wanted it. Because that was the only way I could have you — through Christine. Get it?"

"I don't believe it, Guy. I really don't. You're just saying that." Tears flashed in his eyes.

I looked away. "I guess I thought I had a chance of winning your love, even if it was shared with Christine. I don't know what I thought. A threeway scene where we could all be in love with each other. Because I knew Christine is partly in love with you, too. I've known it for a long time, and wanted to see it grow... and mature. I just gave it a little extra push."

He rushed for the door.

"Wait."

The door slammed and he was gone. I jumped to my feet and ran after him, feeling the floor swaying under me. The hallway outside was crazy, reeling and making silence into a long tunnel I had to traverse. I saw Scott at the far end of it rushing down the stairs; one moment he was in my vision, the next moment he was gone.

I leaned against the wall for support, almost knocking the telephone off its cradle. Without thinking, I reached into my pocket and slipped a quarter into the slot, began dialling Christine's number, almost by instinct. I had no idea what I was going to say to her. I just let myself go, watching myself as if I were watching a character in a movie. I knew that Scott was heading for her place. I knew it. There was nowhere else he could go. And maybe I wanted to beat him there, to get to Christine before he could. But when I heard the dial tone sounding, I hung up. There was nothing more I had to say to anyone anymore.

I went back into the room, shut the door behind me.

I went to Scott's bed and sat down. Blankly, I gazed at the wall, at my mirror. From where I was sitting, it was angled to reflect our half-curtained window... and beyond that, the side of the women's dorm across the way. I sat up. I thought I saw a slight rustle of the curtains in the girls' window opposite, and a furtive movement. Was it the wind? Surely it was. It had to be. The curtains were still now. I waited for them to move again. I waited for a long time, but they remained still. Completely still.

6

I heard the *plock plock plock* sound before I saw him. He was hitting a tennis ball against the back wall of the student union. Overweight, wearing a loose gray sweatsuit, he looked ungainly; his weight seemed to flow around him almost gracefully as he ran back and forth.

"Kruk! Take a break."

He turned around, wiped the sweat off his forehead and came

over to me. "Where have you been, Guy?" He took off his glasses and ran the back of his sleeve over his face and replaced his glasses, blinking as if to get his focus back.

"Looks like you're serious about losing some weight," I said, sitting down on a bench nearby.

"Yeah. Besides, I have to get in shape for next term. You need at least three credit hours of phys-ed to graduate from here. I may as well get it over with this year."

As he sat down beside me on the bench, the smell of his sweat wafted over to me, a not unpleasant sensation.

"You're looking better already, Kruk."

"Thanks. You know, it's not supposed to be true, but people do judge you by the way you look. And — I want to look my best, that's all."

"Are you in love, boy?"

"Get out of here." He punched me — hard — on my upper arm. "What have you been up to, Guy? I haven't seen you around the dorm very much lately."

"I know. I've been busy." I'd been with Harry Golden for the past several days, had practically moved into his house. Without knowing the exact nature of my heartbreak, he had consoled me, and I had been glad of his presence. The sanctuary of his home had provided me with much-needed isolation, while our nightly sessions of lovemaking had progressively deepened my understanding of gay sex. And it had all helped me to forget. A little. But after a few days, I knew it was time to move on.

Suddenly Kruk let out a sigh. "Looks like one thief replaced another, eh?"

"What do you mean?"

"Scott stole your girlfriend away from you, didn't he? Anyway, that's what all the guys in the dorm are saying."

"What else do they say?"

"That he's moved in with her."

I felt a pang. "Well, I hope they're happier now."

"It's not fair. It's just not fair."

"I told you once that I was really in love with someone else, didn't I?"

He looked surprised. "You mean you're not upset?"

"Why should I be? I'm happy for them, Kruk. I wish them the best."

191

"Wow. I can't believe how easy you're taking it, Guy. You almost convince me that you wished it'd happen."

"Let's just say I'm only bowing to the inevitable."

"I guess you just don't have any luck with your room-mates, huh?"

"Maybe you're right."

"Speaking of former room-mates, have you heard about Jonesy?"

"No. What about him?" I'd almost forgotten about Jonesy. He seemed like a faint echo now from out of my remote past, in the pre-Scott era, pre-heartbreak.

"Frank saw him in the city. And guess what? He joined up. He's in the Navy now."

"Jonesy in the Navy?" I had a flash of him dressed up in a sailor's suit. Somehow it seemed a perfect picture. I imagined him in a foreign port, in some seedy dive with an exotic-looking woman in bed with him, picked up in a bar. Fist fights, drunken brawls, broken bottles. My image of him had always been haloed with a sinister beauty; now I could all but see him with an unlit cigarette dangling negligently from his scornful lips, one eye blackened, and an anchor tattooed on his chest. It was like looking at a picture postcard found in a musty old trunk. "It's the perfect place for him," I said after a pause.

"He was in a bar with some of his shipmates. His ship is in port for a short stay before they head out across the Pacific."

The free and easy life. Tropical islands. Brown-skinned native boy lying on the sand.

"Listen, Kruk. I have a favor to ask of you. A big favor."

"Sure. What is it?"

"I'm dropping out of school."

"What? But why?"

"I'm just tired of everything. Nothing seems worth it anymore. It's pointless. Maybe I just need a break from school. You know, school is all I've ever known, and I'm beginning to wonder if there's more to life than just school."

He looked a little downcast.

"Don't tell any of the guys," I said quickly. "I'd rather kind of slip out without anyone knowing about it. That's the way it should be."

"What about your classes? The finals?"

"I'm through with all of that."

"So where you going?"

"I don't know. I think I'll just knock around for a while, try to get my head together."

He looked at me with some envy. I couldn't imagine what was going through his head, but from the look in his eyes, he seemed to view me as a romantic hero of some kind.

"Just like that?"

"Yep." I reached into my pocket and pulled out a piece of paper — an old overdue notice from the library — and wrote down my home address on the back. "There's some clothes in my room I'd like you to send home for me. Some stuff I couldn't pack in the suitcase. And some books. Notebooks. It's Sunday today so the post office is closed. And I don't wanna stick around till tomorrow."

"Sure. No problem."

"I appreciate it, Kruk. You're a real pal."

"Will you keep in touch, Guy?"

I looked at him, and suddenly felt all his loneliness flow into me. I saw it all in a flash: the fat ugly boy, unloved, rejected... his whole life reeled in front of me, from the past all the way into his future as a computer technician. I knew that he'd probably tasted miseries I couldn't begin to conceive of, but my own brand of hell was enough for me to bear right now.

"Yeah, Kruk, I'll write. I know your address here."

We shook hands, and I felt unexpected tears well up in my eyes. I turned away quickly to go before he should suspect them. As I walked off, I knew he was looking at my back, trying to impress the memory of this moment into his mind. For several long seconds there was no sound at all. Only after I'd turned the corner and disappeared from his sight did I hear the *plock plock plock* resume, this time more slowly, less vigorous than before.

It was a warm day. All along the campus plaza people were sitting on the benches, eating early lunches or reading. A long-haired boy who, from the looks of his clothes, probably wasn't a student, was playing a guitar and loudly singing a love song, but no one was paying any attention. It was still spring, but for me it felt like the first day of summer vacation.